Praise for Jenny Hale

One of "19 Dreamy Summer Romances to Whisk you Away" in **Oprah Magazine** on *The Summer House*

One of "24 Dreamy Books about Romance" in **Oprah Daily** on *The Summer House*

One of "30 Christmas Novels to Start Reading Now" in **Southern Living Magazine** on *We'll Always Have Christmas*

Included in "Beach Reads Perfect for Summer 2020" in **Southern Living Magazine** on *Summer at Firefly Beach*

"Touching, fun-filled, and redolent with salt air and the fragrance of summer, this seaside tale is a perfect volume for most romance collections."—**Library Journal** on *The Summer House*

"Hale's impeccably executed contemporary romance is the perfect gift for readers who love sweetly romantic love stories imbued with all the warmth and joy of the holiday season."—**Booklist** on *Christmas Wishes and Mistletoe Kisses*

"Authentic characters and a riveting story make it a keeper worth savoring."—**Publisher's Weekly** on *The Summer House*

"This sweet small-town romance will leave readers feeling warm all the way through."—**Publisher's Weekly** on *It Started with Christmas*

"Adorable contemporary romance… a tender treat that can be savored in any season."—**Publisher's Weekly** on *Christmas Wishes and Mistletoe Kisses*

"Jenny Hale writes touching, beautiful stories."—**New York Times** Bestselling Author RaeAnne Thayne

BOOKS BY JENNY HALE

The Memory Keeper
The Beach House
The House on Firefly Beach
Summer at Firefly Beach
The Summer Hideaway
The Summer House
Summer at Oyster Bay
Summer by the Sea
A Barefoot Summer

Christmas at Fireside Cabins
Christmas at Silver Falls
It Started With Christmas
We'll Always Have Christmas
All I Want for Christmas
Christmas Wishes and Mistletoe Kisses
A Christmas to Remember
Coming Home for Christmas
A Lighthouse Christmas

butterfly sisters

JENNY HALE
USA TODAY BESTSELLING AUTHOR

HARPETH ROAD
PRESS®
Nashville

HARPETH ROAD

Published by Harpeth Road Press (USA)
P.O. Box 158184
Nashville, TN 37215

Paperback 978-1-7358458-3-8
eBook 978-1-7358458-2-1

LCCN - 2022931292

BUTTERFLY SISTERS: An unforgettable, heartwarming, love story

This is a work of fiction. Names, characters, places, and incidents
are the product of the author's imagination or were used fictitiously,
and any resemblance to actual persons, living or dead, business
establishments, events, or locales is entirely coincidental.
First printing: February 2022

For Mary
and all the dreamers out there who want to sit
at the Five and Dime and read their books.

Prologue

There was only one what-if in Leigh Henderson's life. She didn't think about it often, because when she let it into her consciousness, it swarmed her: the lost opportunity for a totally different life.

It had been the spring of her senior year in high school. She was hardly old enough to make her own decisions then, let alone to know what was right in front of her. The weather had turned considerably warm that year, the springtime rushing in with summer flare, temperatures in the eighties sending all her friends running for the Gulf Coast beaches of Seaside and Watercolor for spring break, but Leigh had chosen to spend the week at her grandmother's cabin on Old Hickory Lake—her favorite place in the world. She spent *every* summer and holiday at the lake house with her grandmother.

No matter how hard her schoolwork or whatever she might be going through with her sister Meredith (and they were always going through something), her nan could always help her to see a different perspective. That year, Leigh knew she would be saying goodbye to a side of herself that she wasn't sure she was ready to give up, and she'd needed the comfort of Nan and the cabin to soften the blow.

Taking full advantage of the spike in temperature, Leigh's bare feet hung off the edge of the dock, her pink toenails dipping under the cold lapping water below her. She leaned back and turned her freshly bronzed face to the sun, her locks of golden hair puddling on the dock at her back, her fingers spread out on the old wood, taking in the final moments of her youth.

A long, slow whistle caught her ear, sending her reaching for her towel to cover last year's pink bikini that tied at her hips and behind her neck. She twisted around to find Colton Harris walking toward her—no shoes, no shirt, wide smile. She rolled her eyes to stifle the flutter in her stomach that she got whenever he was around. She twisted toward him, taking in the smooth gait of his walk, the olive bare chest, and the square of his jaw, a pang hitting her right in the gut.

"Whatcha doin'?" he asked, plopping down beside her, those dark-brown eyes with gold flecks sparkling as he took her in.

She set the towel back down beside her on the dock.

"It's Sunday. Don't you have to pack to go back home?"

Leigh sighed. "I don't want to," she replied honestly, turning her gaze to the broad lake in front of her. If she looked at Colton too long, she might change her mind about leaving. She swallowed to keep the lump out of her throat, swinging her feet back and forth. The sun reflected off the water, giving it a blue hue with shimmering sparkles that danced across the surface.

His silence finally pulled her attention back to him. That million-dollar smile faded as Colton studied her. He could always read her. "When you coming back?" The question had a hint of desperation in it that only she could notice because she knew him so well. He fiddled with a lock of her hair, his finger grazing her bare shoulder.

"I'm not sure," she answered, paying extra attention to the round of his shoulders and the curve of his face, burning it into her memory and knowing this was it. They were too young; the timing wasn't right. And

while she'd never felt more herself with anyone, she had to keep moving forward. This was what she'd been preparing for her whole young life. "I'm spending this summer in Chicago."

Colton wrinkled his nose. "Chicago? Why?"

"I got into Northwestern University, and I start this fall." The announcement that had prompted cheers and emotional hugs and kisses from her parents withered now on her lips.

He blinked, his hand falling from her shoulder as he looked out at Old Hickory with a frown, digesting this news. Then he forced a smile. She knew it was forced—it was too tight, not his usual laid-back look of amusement. "All them books we've been readin' every summer worked out for ya then," he said.

She nodded, letting him think that it was only the summer books they'd shared over ice cream, stretched out in the grass under the trees—not bothering to tell him that she'd spent every single minute back home in Spring Hill studying, scratching down facts on cards and flashing them to herself each morning as she ran out the door, writing research papers until way past her bedtime, and highlighting notes while holding sandwiches at lunch and rocking babies during her babysitting jobs—work was literally all she did.

"You won't even miss me," she said, trying to make the heaviest of situations seem lighter. "You'll be able to spend every weekend with Teddy and Smash and the guys from baseball you hang out with all the time, and I won't be there to get in the way anymore."

He offered a half-smile, and she knew that her comment hadn't helped. "Maybe I like you gettin' in the way."

Resentment swelled up from the pit of her stomach as she tried to fight the guilt that the look in his eyes caused her. "Colton, I can't hang out with you and your friends forever."

Her point was a stab and the sting showed on his face. "Why not? They not good enough for Miss Smarty Pants?"

"I didn't mean it that way…"

He pursed his lips and looked out at the small peninsula of pine trees jutting out next to the dock.

"We're not wired the same, you and me," she said, still trying to explain, but he was already shaking his head, annoyed.

Colton ran his hand through his sun-streaked brown hair, the golden strands already bright from being outside over the last few days. "What you wanna go to college for?" he asked, teasing her.

"Yeah, what you wanna go to college for?" her younger sister Meredith asked, as she paced down the grassy hill from Nan's cabin to the dock, her wild blonde curls bouncing.

Her sister clamped her blue eyes on Leigh's. If Meredith were choosing sides, it would inevitably be the one opposite Leigh. She was only a year younger than Leigh, but she acted more like an older sister—bossy, independent. Meredith crossed her arms over her T-shirt and grinned in consensus with Colton before staring at Leigh, challenge in her eyes. The few times her sister had actually smiled were all with Colton. He had a way of bringing it out of her when no one else could.

Colton gave Meredith an air high-five and she shot one back to him, holding up the palm of her hand, something they'd started as young kids and never let go.

Even though Colton seemed to have taken an interest in Leigh, he and Meredith had always had a bond. They were like brother and sister, and at times they were so much on the same page that Leigh wondered why he and Meredith hadn't just gotten together. But whenever she let that youthful jealousy get the upper hand and suggested it, Colton always gave her a sideways smile and told her that Leigh was much more his type.

"*Why* wouldn't *I want to go to college?*" Leigh asked, not wanting to admit to Colton or Meredith that she was scared to live away from everyone she knew, terrified to be so far from Nan and the cabin, and heartbroken to leave Colton.

The distress lingering on Colton's face sliced through her. Her skin burning from the heat of the sun, and wanting to get herself out of the conversation, Leigh jumped off the dock, plunging into the frigid water. Her head went under, bubbles floating up from her nose. When she emerged, she put her goose-bumped forearms on the dock and looked up at Colton and her sister.

"You sure you wanna go all the way to Chicago?" he asked, continuing the conversation anyway.

"Yes," she said, completely confident that Northwestern was the best option for her. Until just now, with him right there in front of her. "What do you want to do, Colton?"

"I wanna fish off the side of my boat and watch football out on my porch in the evenings. I wanna go into town and know everybody there."

The idea seemed as comforting to Leigh as a warm hug, but she couldn't let her feelings for Colton hold her back. To break the tension, she splashed him. Getting her back, he stood up and threw himself off the dock in a cannonball, causing a spray that fanned across the wood of the dock. She squealed, pushing away from him, relieved slightly by the lighter moment.

"Y'all are crazy," Meredith said, continuing down the dock on her way somewhere. Meredith never stayed around very long. She'd rather be anywhere but the cabin.

"And what are you going to do for money?" Leigh asked Colton, treading water as she darted out of his range.

"I'll find somethin'," he replied. "Work's just work. Life is what happens after work."

"Not if you do something you enjoy," she countered.

He reached out and grabbed her waist, pulling her in. "I enjoy this. I'm gonna miss you." That day, he leaned in and kissed her, crossing the line, and she knew right then that he understood it was the end for them. She could still feel the soft wetness of his lips, how they fit perfectly on hers, and the ache in her chest that it caused when she thought about leaving him.

He pulled back and looked at her, one hand on the dock, the other around her to keep them steady. "You love hanging out with your nan and living here. Why don't you not worry about all that college stuff and stay here with me?" He swallowed her with his pleading gaze, beads of water on his jaw.

The sting on his face when she'd laughed was burned into her memory. She hadn't meant it to be a jab at him—it had been a nervous reaction, because she couldn't fathom that she'd fit into that kind of life; she hadn't planned for it. And at her age, she didn't even know if she wanted it. Everything she'd done until now was to prepare for the moment when she'd get into a major university and begin building her career in public relations. There was no way she could give up school and move to the lake at the young age of eighteen to fish and watch sports. But Colton definitely wasn't laughing. He let her go and swam away.

"We've got our whole lives ahead of us," she called out to him, trying to backtrack and explain, but he'd already lifted himself out of the water further down the dock. "I have a plan for what I want in life," she continued, sticking to her guns and not letting his gorgeous face sway her.

Those brown eyes bored into hers from the other end of the dock. "So do I," he said, but then his shoulders fell in surrender. "I don't want to argue." He reached down and picked up her towel, peering down at it, his thumb gently rubbing the soft terrycloth, the situation clearly getting the better of him. But he was the best at keeping his composure. He walked the towel over to her. "Let's get you packed."

Academics were what Leigh was built to do. She didn't know how to do anything else.

Until she came to her grandmother's cabin. For those few months every summer and on school holidays like that one, she let her hair down, packed all her favorite novels, and spent time with her family and Colton. That was the only part of her life that he'd seen.

Leigh and Colton had always had an easy chemistry, falling right back into step whenever she'd visit. Every now and again, she'd make the hour drive from her house in Spring Hill on a weekend, and they'd hang out together, but it was when she stayed at Nan's that their little romance would kick into gear. They'd never acted on it, apart from flirtatious moments when one of them would pull away just as the seriousness of their feelings settled between them, which sent an electric pulse through her body whenever it had happened. Leigh wondered if they were both scared that moving past that level would break the spell, and they both loved each other too much to do that. Her mind went back to that day she'd left, pulling up the rest of the memory as clear as the summer water on the lake.

Once she'd gotten to Chicago, she'd tried to call him a few times, but he hadn't picked up. And Nan passed a few months after she'd left, that same year, which had changed everything. Before she knew it, her life had swept her so far away from that moment that she'd stopped calling. But every now and again, she sometimes wondered about Colton. While she piled her brain with the rules of calculus and countless facts about modern Western civilization, and later after she graduated, trying to build a career for herself, moving to New York, she wondered if Colton was back at the lake, rocking on the waves in his boat, hat turned backward, fishing with his buddies just like he'd wanted.

And she wondered if he could've made her happy.

Chapter One

Her phone pressed to her ear, Leigh strained to hear through the buzz of morning commuters who bustled into New York City's Financial District every weekday and gathered at the café on the corner of Wall Street and Pearl, while they waited impatiently for their morning coffee. Her younger sister's voice came through the end of her phone—happy, bouncy. "It's Meredith! You've reached my voicemail, so I'm obviously off doing something incredible. Leave a message."

She wedged the phone against her shoulder while she paid the cashier for her double-shot caramel latte on her way to work. Leigh had resorted to calling after both she and her mother had tried to text Meredith several times with no response, and apparently that wasn't working either.

"Mom wants us to go to the lake house," she said after the beep, feeling strangled when she uttered the words, knowing the resentful look that would show in her sister's eyes when she heard the message. Meredith hadn't given the family or the cabin any thought since she'd left home, something Leigh had never understood. "It's… important. Text me or call me back." She ended the call, guessing she'd have to leave a few messages with something more dramatic for Meredith to actually respond.

Her family had never been that close group of four who went to the movies together or laughed with each other over games of charades or family dinners. It was something Leigh had always longed for, but never seemed to be able to catch hold of.

Her sister hadn't been home for any length of time in the last eight years, other than their father's funeral, which had happened three years after Nan died, when she'd actually stayed a night, before claiming she needed to go. The last time Leigh and Meredith had been in the same place for more than twenty-four hours had been in high school, for Leigh's graduation. When, a few weeks later, everyone had gathered in the driveway to see her off to college, Meredith hadn't appeared with their mother, father, Nan, and their neighbors to wave and cheer as Leigh left home for four years at Northwestern University, her old Ford Escort filled to the brim with all her belongings. Leigh had seethed over it for the first hour of the trip, wondering what she'd ever done to make her sister hate her so much.

Leigh had always been frustrated with Meredith; her behavior put a strain on them. It had seemed as if Meredith would do anything to set herself apart from everyone in their family. And while her sister had appeared as though she'd had no direction her whole life, she had a kind of contempt for them all, as if they were criminals for having their lives together. All her sister had to do was apply herself, but she never did. She took odd jobs and lazily gathered the bare minimum to live on, spending nights on her friends' sofas and living out of her car at times.

But even though her sister was a disaster, Leigh was always a little envious at the way she never had to stay in one place or have anything special to be happy—she'd gotten that from Nan. Meredith could pack a tent and a loaf of bread and leave for a week, coming back looking vibrant and rested. Leigh wished she could have just a little of her free spirit.

Meredith was an artist like Nan, but that and her lack of interest in possessions were about all her sister and their grandmother shared. It had been Leigh who'd spent every free minute with Nan, who'd talked for hours and listened to all her grandmother's stories about traveling across the world, or her latest ideas for a pottery line she wanted to try to make. It had been Leigh who'd stayed at Old Hickory Lake with Nan until her final days, only a few weeks before heading to Northwestern. Leigh hadn't been back to the cabin since Nan had passed away nearly eight years ago—thought had been too much to bear. She'd pushed the heartache down as far as she could, burying it so she could focus on her work, unable to take the time to mourn. She knew that if she *had* taken that time, the grief might have broken her completely.

When her coffee was ready, Leigh weaved through the throngs of people, took her cup from the counter, and headed out into the New York sunshine. Under a bright-blue sky, the winter chill easing slowly as spring took over, Leigh dodged a group of people holding lemonade they'd gotten at the street cart beside them. She paced down the sidewalk downing her latte, her shoulder bag tightly held against the designer suit she'd bought for this morning's meeting with McGregor Consulting's largest potential client.

As a commercial property management consultant, an off-shoot from her years in corporate PR, Leigh was the best. And when one of the partners, Phillip Russo, had given her this account because he'd had too many projects on his plate, he'd told her that there was no one else he'd trust with it. She was "capable," he'd said. Phillip Russo was thin on praise, to say the least, so a term like "capable" spoke volumes.

Leigh firmly believed that he'd trusted her with this because she provided nothing less than excellence. Her work ethic was incredible, and she knew it. It had been that way her whole life. Growing up, while her sister had struggled, spending countless hours with tutors—their parents' attempt to keep her "on track"—Leigh had been a straight-A student. Leigh had spent her Friday nights studying, while Meredith would sneak out after curfew, doing who knows what with her band of rebels. Leigh had been the rule-follower, and it had paid off.

Pacing down the busy sidewalk with forty minutes to spare, she checked her phone to see if she'd missed a call from Meredith. Nothing. She should've known better than to look.

Over the years, Leigh had tried to talk to her sister, but Meredith would cut their calls short, telling her she needed to go. If Leigh knew where Meredith was right now, she would find her, but Meredith was a nomad, traveling across the U.S. on pennies, still taking odd jobs to make ends meet. Last Leigh had heard, she was a waitress somewhere along the West Coast. Even the area code on her cell phone was cryptic—470: Georgia, a state Leigh never knew her sister had even visited, let alone stayed in long enough to register a new cell phone.

Leigh guzzled the last of her coffee, the bitterness burning her stomach. Never stopping long enough for breakfast, she always got a coffee on the way to work, but today, mixed with her nerves over the puzzling call from her mother last night and the presentation this morning, it ate at her insides like battery acid.

"I have something I need to tell you girls," her mother, Katherine, had said last night over the phone while Leigh was preparing for her presentation. "It's important. I can't get Meredith. Think you can wrangle her up and meet me at the cabin?"

"Are you okay, Mama?" she'd asked, worried by the abrupt request that something was wrong. Ever since her father's heart attack and sudden death, her mother's health was the first thing that came to mind whenever she called out of the blue like that.

"Yes. I'm fine."

Years before, when Katherine had finally begun managing her grief enough to face the cabin, she and Leigh's dad had been gearing up to go through Nan's things when her father had had the heart attack. Mama hadn't mentioned going up to the cabin after that. Leigh had wrestled with the idea of returning. In the end, she couldn't do it either. The cabin had been her refuge and the source of her happiness, what her youthful dreams had been made of. If she walked into that house, she would inevitably have to relive the memories of her time with Nan, lying out on the hammock with her grandmother and looking up at the stars, hearing her laugh in that way that sounded like bubbles. It had all been too much to manage.

Leigh tossed the empty coffee cup into the bin just to the right of the oversized glass doors, something she'd done every day for four years. She'd perfected the toss over time, making a shot that would impress any player on the New York Knicks basketball team. She tugged on the heavy door, stepping out of the chill and into the expanse of the lobby, pulling her Manolo Blahniks from her handbag and switching her shoes. Her new pair of heels tapped against the shiny white marble-patterned tiles as she shoved her flats into her bag and made her way to the elevators that would take her to the twenty-fifth floor.

She zipped up to the McGregor offices, waving to her best friend Julie at the front desk, trying not to let the fact that Julie was laughing at something with their newest colleague, Rebecca Mayer, dampen her mood. Rebecca had sashayed in a few weeks ago with a former client list that would fill the entire hallway to Leigh's office if she laid it out end to end. Leigh had considered it fate that she'd been given this account before Rebecca had started at McGregor. But the fact she was chosen meant that Phillip Russo expected she could land this client. And if she didn't—well, she didn't even need to think about it. She would.

Leigh had to focus. Like clockwork, she arrived twenty minutes early to her meeting so she could drink one bottle of water, whiten her teeth, and go over her notes—a ritual she'd found always gave her confidence in these situations. She'd had several big meetings now, nailing every one of them, so her track record was impeccable.

She set her bag against the wall in the conference room, went over to the office fridge—a sleek, stainless-steel box with a glass front, showing off the latest in hip beverages for their clients—and snagged a water. With a twist of the lid, she chased the lingering coffee taste down her throat and pulled the meeting notes from her bag, arranging them neatly at her place at the conference table.

She knew this client backward and forward: Park West Securities, the up-and-coming private investment firm that had risen faster than any of their competitors in the nation. They began with only ten employees, rising steadily and solidly to a staggering two hundred employees in six short years. The boutique investment firm, owned by CEO Mark Shuster, was preferred by celebrities and corporate superstars. This company had their pick of who would handle their expansion. The heavens had opened up and led them to McGregor Consulting, landing right in Leigh's lap. And she was prepared to win them over. She turned on the screen at the end of the office, the company logo coming to life and spinning in a three-dimensional geometric pattern, then set the remote next to her notes and her laptop.

Julie came in with a silver covered tray of the fresh grilled lobster poppers filled with eggs Benedict that Leigh had ordered from Cleo's, the high-end restaurant down the street. She could always count on Julie to pull through for her. They'd met three years ago when Julie had started at McGregor. The only two females in the firm, they'd become fast friends.

Julie set the poppers on the table, along with a stack of white appetizer plates, a pair of serving tongs, and cloth napkins. Leigh had never had a client actually eat the poppers during a meeting, but she'd seen the sparkle in their eyes at the gesture, so she ordered them every time, and she always scheduled her meetings in the morning. As if tailor-made for her, this meeting was perfectly arranged on a Thursday, at 9 a.m. Thursdays were good—clients were in a slightly more relaxed mood with the impending weekend, but they also didn't want to spend too long after nearly finishing a busy work week. It meant a quick yes.

"All ready?" Julie asked like she always did, although Leigh sensed an odd stiffness in her friend's voice.

"As ready as I'll ever be," she replied, trying to place why Julie would be acting edgy. She couldn't be nervous about this client for her. Leigh knew she'd have no idea who was coming in. There was too much going on in the company for her to keep up with who would be where, and they never talked about work on their nights out, so Leigh hadn't mentioned it. She'd speak to her later…

Julie headed for the door. "Good luck."

"Thank you," Leigh said, pulling her whitening strips from her purse and sliding them onto her teeth. She fluffed her hair and applied a thin layer of lip-gloss before poring over her notes in one last run-through. She mentally practiced her opening line, her pitch, and the final moment when she'd say, "And who better than us?" Time to make some magic happen.

With only two minutes to go, she straightened her blazer, removed the whitening strips discreetly with a napkin, balling it all up and dropping it into the trash, and turned the platter just so to make sure the sun coming in through the large glass wall-window shimmered off it perfectly—not a glare, just a bit of shine. Phillip rushed by the room, looking in, and she gave him a confident head nod. She was on her game.

Her phone went off in her bag, and she quickly reached in to turn off the sound, the name on the screen stopping her in her tracks: *Meredith*. Ugh, her sister literally never called her back on the first try. Given her mother's failed attempts at reaching her and not having a clue when Meredith would get to Leigh again, Leigh needed to answer it, but she couldn't. Her heart hammering in her chest, she silenced the call, closed her bag and straightened her suit.

One minute.

The glass conference-room door swung open and she brightened, turning around.

"Oh. Hey," she said to Julie who was standing by herself, wondering why she'd come ahead of the clients instead of just showing them back. She knew Leigh was ready.

"Sorry, Leigh," she said, still holding the door open with one hand while she hovered in the doorway. "Mr. Russo just popped by my desk and asked me to tell you that he moved the time of the meeting."

"Really?" She already worried that the lobster poppers would get cold and she seriously doubted she could call in another order for later, on such short notice. "What time?"

"It was an hour ago," Julie said, distant.

"I missed it?" she breathed, the blood running out of her face, leaving her cheeks ice cold.

Normally, Julie would have swooped in and given her an empathetic smile, promising they'd get a drink right after work and slough the whole timing snafu off. Instead, she dropped her gaze from Leigh. But then she smiled as Rebecca walked by. Not just a friendly smile, but as if they had a mutual understanding of some insider joke. Rebecca pointed her red-nailed, manicured finger at Julie over her shoulder and called back to her, "Last night was not my fault," to which Julie giggled. Had Leigh's best friend hung out with Rebecca Mayer last night?

"You didn't miss it," Julie said, resuming their conversation once Leigh's nemesis had passed, but she was shifty and awkward again. "Don't worry. The clients accepted, Phillip said."

"How, when I wasn't there to close the deal?"

Julie finally met her eyes. "Rebecca met with them."

Her mouth hung open. "*Rebecca.*" It wasn't a question but a statement. Rebecca-with-the-list-of-accomplishments took her client. Correction: was *given* her client. And Phillip didn't even bother to stop just now to let her know personally. Instead, he went all the way down the hallway and told Julie to break the news. Had Julie known? She couldn't have…

"Did he say why he had Rebecca meet with them instead of me?" she asked, trying to make sense of all this, suddenly racking her brain for anything she might have done to change his mind. She'd said something slightly risqué to Phillip about the Macey Group a few days ago, but he'd laughed at her joke… And then there was that one discussion in the hallway over the merits of their new digital real estate software. Had she said something to offend him then? "I could've easily come in earlier."

Julie shrugged helplessly, clearly reading the stress on Leigh's face.

"I'm going to go ask him why he didn't just call me," she said, stacking up the utensils and napkins for the lobster poppers and placing them on top of her things.

"You can't," Julie said. "He's stepped out for an all-day meeting."

"That figures." Her shoulders slumped as she slipped her laptop into her carrying case.

"At least you can have a little time to collect your thoughts?" Julie said with a half-smile.

Was Leigh reading too much into everything? What was going on? Suddenly, her friend's awkwardness made sense. She must have been caught in the middle. Julie would tell her everything. But not here. Leigh could go out with her tonight and find out all the details, and then she could make her plan for how to get back in Phillip's good graces.

"This issue aside, I needed to talk to him anyway to alert him about my leaving this weekend," she said to Julie. "Rather than just putting it into the corporate calendar, I wanted to tell him personally that I'm taking time off next week."

"I haven't known you to ever take a day off."

"It's a family… emergency," she said. Maybe it wasn't an emergency—she wasn't sure—but it had probably better be, given that she was clearly on thin ice with her boss. "Now that I think about it, it might not be the best time to mention that I need a few days, since he's already reassigning my clients." She clicked off the screen and set the remote in the center of the table.

"Maybe just quietly slide it in on the calendar…"

"Yeah," she said, still shell-shocked by Phillip's abrupt change of plans.

Leigh had *never* had anything like this happen to her at work and the disappointment hit her hard. Rebecca was clearly a superstar, but wasn't Leigh as well? Had she reached her peak in the company? Was Rebecca the new-and-improved Leigh? Leigh 2.0? If so, where did that leave her?

She suddenly felt short of breath and lightheaded. She gathered up the rest of her things. "I'm going to step out for a little while, get some air." She handed Julie the lobster poppers. "You can have these."

"Thanks," Julie said. "I'll put them in the lounge."

"All right." Leigh took out her phone and slung her bag over her shoulder. Then, with a wave to Julie, she left the building without a clue as to where she was headed—both figuratively and at this very moment.

Chapter Two

"It's Meredith! You've reached my voicemail, so I'm obviously off doing something incredible. Leave a message."

"Meredith, it's Leigh again," she said, pacing along the sidewalk outside her apartment. She'd wandered there while still trying to process what had happened this morning. "I'm sorry I missed your call. I was in a… meeting. Please call me right back." She hung up and went inside, grabbing the elevator to the eighth floor—home.

Stepping inside her apartment, Leigh kicked off her shoes and dropped her heels and her handbag on the mat, along with the laptop bag that had begun to feel like a boulder with a strap. She set the phone down on the small coffee table that held a brightly colored ceramic bowl Nan had designed for one of her pottery lines, the latest home décor magazines and an unread novel she'd been trying to start but hadn't had a moment for, and flopped onto the sofa, trying not to feel sorry for herself.

Her phone pinged with a text, shooting her back to a sitting position. She grabbed it and peered down at the screen: *Did you get Meredith? I still can't get her.*

It was her mother.

Not yet, she typed back.

Another message floated onto her screen: *Keep trying. She has to be at the cabin for this.*

She responded: *You know I will.*

Her mother's choice of the lake house as a meeting spot was interesting. What did Nan's cabin have to do with whatever it was Mama had to tell them? Going back there would be enough to deal with, without this mystery news.

Leigh's fondest memories of the house on the lake were when she and Meredith were little girls. The waterfront cabin had been in the family since her grandparents had bought it in their sixties. After her grandfather had passed away, it had been just Nan there, and, living alone, she had delighted in seeing her granddaughters every holiday.

Leigh had spent long summers running barefoot down the old trails, the overgrown paths of Willow Swamp Loop being her favorite. In their early years, she and Meredith raced along the bank, and she'd always stop to catch her breath on the boardwalk that crossed the swamp. The humid Tennessee summer air was so thick that it formed droplets of water on her hot skin and doused her blonde hair, causing her sister's to spiral up in wild, frizzy strands. They'd run all the way back home and jump into the lake, the cool water providing instant relief from the relentless summer temperatures.

After dinner, with her skin still warm and pink from spending all day in the sun, while Meredith was off on her own making the latest in braided string jewelry or doodling in one of her millions of notebooks, Leigh would sit on the screened-in porch that stretched across the back of the house and watch the birds with Nan, looking them up in the picture book of bird species they kept at the cabin. There were so many birds along the lake that she could've studied them for hours with the old binoculars that had been in the desk there as long as she could remember.

Leigh brought up Meredith's contact number and hit call but, once again, she got her sister's voicemail. "Meredith, I'm going to fill your inbox until you return my call." She hung up the phone.

She dropped the phone onto the sofa cushion, resolve over returning to the cabin swimming through her. It was time to go back. Living without it was as hard as knowing what Leigh faced returning to it. She didn't know what it would be like to walk through it and not have Nan shuffle up to her, wiping her hands on her apron, and handing her a fresh glass of lemonade and a tomato sandwich she'd made from the tomatoes in her garden. The house would be void of her smile, her gentle way of making everything seem okay.

Leigh leaned back on the sofa, but she felt restless. Perhaps it was compounded by the coffee or the unease of getting all geared up for work today. As she lay there, waiting for her sister to call her back, old feelings of hurt over how things had gone with Meredith welled up, giving her a headache. She should be able to talk to her sister when she needed to. Leigh had worked so hard her whole life to ensure that everything she did was a success. But, no matter how hard she tried, she couldn't figure out her relationship with her sister.

Leigh closed her eyes to rest them, hoping to ease the pounding in her temples, eventually drifting off. In her semi-consciousness, she was back at the cabin in her nan's art studio, a small room with wide windows letting in tons of light, on the side of the house with a view of the woods. Easels flanked every wall, holding large canvases with oil-painted scenes of the lake or her grandmother's favorite European cities.

"Everyone has art inside them," she said to Leigh, but it still hadn't made sense to her. For Leigh, painting was some sort of foreign code that she couldn't crack. It was just the two of them that day. Meredith had run off to find her friends, but Leigh had stayed at the cabin like she always did. "It's just buried deeper in some than others."

"I don't think so," Leigh countered. "I can't even draw a stick man well."

With a knowing chuckle, Nan set down her paintbrush, wiped her hands on the canvas pocket-apron tied around her wide waist, and opened one of the windows, the wisps around her bun blowing in the breeze that was coming off the lake. "Close your eyes," she said.

Standing in the middle of the room, Leigh complied.

"What do you notice that wasn't there before I opened the window?"

With her eyes shut, Leigh honed in on the earthy aroma of the woods. "I smell the trees," she said.

"What else?" her grandmother asked, the delight in her voice clear.

"The cicadas." Their loud, electric buzzing filled her ears. "And the breeze." She opened her eyes to find Nan smiling from ear to ear.

"That's art, darling. It's simply noticing what's around you and then expressing it. Your unique way of bringing it to life is your talent, your art…"

Leigh wasn't sure if it had been ten minutes or an hour when her phone rang. She rolled off the sofa onto the floor of her apartment with a thump, trying to reach it quickly the moment Meredith's name came into focus.

"Hello?" she said, rubbing her eyes.

"Hey." Meredith's voice sailed through the phone calm and unbothered, as if they'd just spoken a week ago, rather than it being two years since they'd uttered a word to each other.

Leigh took in a deep breath to steady herself. "Can you come to the lake house?"

"Why? What's up?"

When their mother had said she was making the trip from Leigh's childhood home in Spring Hill to Nan's cabin and asked Leigh to go, Leigh had immediately put it down in her calendar, telling her she'd be there. Did Meredith really need an explanation to show up?

"Mom has something important to tell us that she needs to say in person."

The line went silent for a tick, and just when Leigh's frustration with her sister was beginning to mount, Meredith finally asked, "When does she want us to come?"

"It took some rearranging of my schedule, but I'm planning to leave midday tomorrow if I can finish up my work, and stay for a week or so, depending on what she has to say."

"You want me to go next week?" Meredith asked, as if the request was completely unreasonable.

Leigh rolled her eyes and sucked in a breath to calm her already frayed nerves. If Leigh could manage to take off work at such short notice, at a company like McGregor, shuffling clients and in-house meetings, squeezing them in during her lunches and coming in early the weeks after, certainly her drifter of a sister could find someone to cover her boardwalk jewelry stand, or whatever it was she was doing these days.

"Yes, next week," she said, trying to remain composed.

More silence.

Another call beeped in through Leigh's phone, and she pulled it from her ear to view the caller: Phillip Russo. While she needed to get that, there was no way she was getting off the phone with Meredith until she had an answer.

She pinched the bridge of her nose, the headache surfacing again. "Will you come?"

"I guess."

Leigh's shoulders were tightening already at the thought of the tension that would be in that cabin with all three of them under one roof. "Thank you," she said, trying to be the bigger person. "What day do you plan to be there?"

"I'm not sure. I have to tie up some loose ends."

"Well, just let one of us know."

"Okay. Hey, I've gotta go."

"Yeah, me too." After all, Leigh was napping on her sofa when she should be at work, and while her boss had called and not reached her. She definitely needed to go.

"See ya," Meredith said.

Leigh hung up the phone and immediately pulled up Phillip's number. She'd probably totally misread things and he'd most likely called to apologize personally for having moved the meeting. She'd tell him that he could always call her out of hours and she'd happily get there early, stay late—whatever it took. No need to ask anyone else. Like Rebecca. Leigh would have it all under control at any hour.

He answered on the first ring, and she felt instant relief. Time to set this little misunderstanding straight.

"Leigh," he said directly.

"Hi, Phillip," she said, squaring her shoulders, as if he were in the room with her.

"I'm sorry…" he began.

A smile spread across her face and she opened her mouth to tell him there was no need to apologize, when something entirely different came through her phone.

"We're tightening up our talent and moving in a different direction," he said. "I've been talking with senior management, and we're reorganizing departments. Rebecca will be our new lead."

Her mouth fell open. Was she now working *under* Rebecca?

He cleared his throat. "We're dissolving the current team."

What did he mean? "Am I going to assume a new role under Rebecca?" she asked outright, her stomach turning.

"No… We're letting you go."

"What?" The word fell out like a slack bag of heavy rocks. She'd given McGregor Consulting every waking minute of her time since she'd been hired. He'd said she was "capable."

"We feel Rebecca will be a real go-getter. She's a star."

His last sentence hit her like a wrecking ball. While she'd always thought Phillip Russo was light on praise, had he only been light on praise for *her*? Her hands trembled as she held the phone, unable to utter a single word. All this time, she'd thought she was doing a stellar job, when her boss clearly had a different opinion. It instantly made her question her abilities and even her relevancy in her chosen career.

"You'll have a severance package," he said. "And any further questions, feel free to email me directly."

"All right," she said, feeling like she was under water, the words coming out in almost a whisper.

He ended the call, and she sat there in the silence of her apartment, unable to move, the phone still clutched in her grip. With shaky hands, unsure of what to do but wanting to talk to someone who'd understand, she called Julie's cell. It rang four times before her friend picked up and she told her what had just happened.

"Sorry, Leigh," she said, as if she were preoccupied with something else. She *was* at work, after all.

"I can't believe it," Leigh continued. "But I can tell you're busy. Want to get a drink tonight and we can talk then?"

"I..." Julie trailed off. When the silence had stretched a little too long for Leigh's comfort, her friend finally spoke. "I'm sorry, Leigh. I can't."

"On a Thursday night? What's up?" she asked, trying to sound like someone who wasn't on the verge of a total mental breakdown.

"Rebecca and I are going out tonight."

"Oh," she said, trying to ignore the betrayal. "Maybe we can catch up after?"

"I don't know... I'm kind of busy."

And just like that, her best friend had fired her as well. "Okay," she said, trying not fall into sobbing tears. "I'll... see ya."

"See ya."

The line went dead.

She waited for the terrified inhale, the gasp of breath as she awoke from this horrific nightmare, but it never came.

Chapter Three

Three hours. That was all it had taken to board a plane this morning and land in Nashville, Tennessee, a whole different world from the one she'd been living in the last four years.

Leigh had left her new suit hanging in the closet back in her apartment, changed her airline departure time online to an earlier one, and now she found herself with the windows down in the Honda she'd rented, the breeze blowing in and the skyline of Music City in her rearview mirror, as she made the drive twenty-five miles upstream, paralleling the Cumberland River toward Old Hickory Lake.

She clicked through the radio stations, the country twang she'd grown up listening to taking her back to the days of her youth. It had been too long since she'd been to this place, and it felt as if her surroundings were peering in on her, wondering where she'd been. Every sight was familiar and with each passing building, she was one step closer to facing the cabin, her broken family, and everything she'd left behind. She kept her eyes on the road, focusing on the traffic instead of her thoughts.

Springtime in Nashville had arrived like a lion, the sun ablaze as if the warmth had trampled winter's door and burst in. The early-afternoon sunshine was already scorching, coming through the windshield at a slant, heating up Leigh's bare legs, her shorts unable to protect them.

She turned up the air conditioning, but it faded into the balmy, humid wind coming in through the open windows. Although it was really too warm to keep the windows open, she didn't want to shut them. Her hair tossing around gave her a sense of freedom that she hadn't felt in a long time. She needed all the peace she could get, considering what she'd just been through and what she was facing.

As a very little girl, Leigh's idea of happiness had been simple: she'd wanted to be a mom—that was it. She'd carried around her baby dolls, tending to them, telling them stories, and making sure they had their plastic bottles at mealtimes. But as she grew, an invisible force pulled her from this idea of family and wedged something in front of it: ambition. Her ability to make good grades and please the other academics around her perpetuated the idea, and before she knew it, those baby dolls were but a child's dream. She'd gotten just where she'd wanted to be professionally, but there was always that whisper deep in her belly that she was missing something. She wanted to have that perfect family where she could run to Meredith and her mother and tell them all her secrets. She wanted big Christmases together, with lots of kids, long talks over glasses of wine, girls' nights in front of the fire. But her little family was different.

Whenever they'd tried to do things as a family, like dinners, Leigh and Meredith would inevitably disagree about something, and they'd sit silent and uncomfortable until they couldn't stand it anymore, when Meredith would excuse herself and run off to who knew where. Their father would draw into himself, hiding behind his newspaper, baffled as to how to bring his family together. And Leigh and her mother would go off to different places in the house and do their own thing.

It wasn't easy to communicate with Meredith. Leigh prayed this trip wouldn't end up with her and her mother on one side and Meredith on the other, which was usually how any discussion between the three of them played out.

As Leigh drove, she steered her mind away from yesterday and the sense of failure that had overtaken her at losing her job to Rebecca. She'd spent most of last night mentally recounting her career and comparing it to what she knew of her new colleague's, but she just couldn't figure out why Phillip had seen her as disposable. And she kept thinking that if she couldn't see why, maybe that in itself was the problem. Even her best friend wasn't standing up for her. There was only one conclusion: Leigh was clueless about her own faults. She'd built herself up in her head as this uber successful person when really, was she? If she wasn't a success, she didn't know who she was.

With Leigh spending all her time at work, Julie had become her confidante, the one person who could understand, but now she wondered if that was even true. At the first instance of someone else coming in, her friend had upped and left her. She suddenly wondered about what she'd missed in all that time she'd spent working.

Nan would've been able to tell her who she was. Her eyes would crinkle at the corners, and then she'd drop one line that would make everything seem easy—that was how Nan was.

"Life is about the whole journey," she'd say. "Not the stops along the way. They're just designed to get you there."

Without Nan's gentle guidance, how would Leigh ever get her life back on track? And, more immediately, how would she manage being without her at the cabin? If only Nan could be there for her right now when she needed her most… But while Leigh felt an incredible trepidation about returning to the lake, there was also something pulling her there, as if getting back to the place she loved could smooth out all the wrinkles in her life. Waking up in the iron-framed double bed under her grandmother's handmade quilts, the window open, letting in the sounds of the birds and the tinkling of the windchimes on the cabin's back porch, Leigh had felt as if she were untouchable by the outside world.

Nestled against the water, down a slew of winding dirt lanes, the lake house was hidden from the public and secluded among the trees. It was the perfect place to get away from it all. And that's what Leigh was hoping it would do for her this week. No matter what her mother had to tell her, she prayed the cabin and Nan's memory could get her through it. She needed to feel close to her grandmother right now, and there was no better place to do that than the cabin.

The city landscape gave way to smaller roads, meandering through the hilly countryside toward the lake. The winding paths were shaded by the trees, the sun offering a sparkle through the leaves as they rustled in the breeze. Leigh slowed way down to the twenty-mile-per-hour limit and passed the old farmhouse, where she used to stop to get fresh peaches on the way to Nan's. Its owner, Bob Hynes, was sitting on a rocking chair on the front porch behind the wooden produce stand, wearing his usual faded bibbed overalls. The man recognized her in the car, raised a weathered hand, and waved as if he'd been waiting for her to drive by. She waved back, allowing the joy of seeing him to settle upon her.

As she followed alongside the cotton fields, a lone, free-standing weather vane on the edge of the meadow turned in the wind and an old tire swing swayed on the branch of an oak tree nearby. These snapshots of southern life outside the city were the fabric of her childhood. And what she hadn't let herself think about until now was that holding all the threads of her memories together was Colton Harris. Was he still there?

She slowed to a stop at an intersection to allow a tractor to cross. As she sat in the idling rental car, she clicked through the channels on the radio, stopping at a country song she hadn't heard before and letting it play. The scent of earth and wild grape blossoms filled the air around her. Suddenly, a Monarch butterfly with a gorgeous array of white-and-black texture overlapping its bright-orange wings flew in through her window and landed on her steering wheel.

"Oh! Hello," she said to it. Its enormous wings fluttered back and forth, as it perched there like it was showing off. "You're beautiful," she whispered, wishing she could show it to Nan.

Her grandmother had a leather-bound sketchbook full of the different butterflies she'd seen. Every time she saw a new one, she drew it and then researched the type, jotting down its name and her feelings about it underneath in pencil. She'd drawn all the different types: Swallowtails, a Mourning Cloak, Red-spotted Purples, and Hackberry Emperors… This could've been her Monarch.

The butterfly in front of Leigh was so mesmerizing that she hadn't even noticed the tractor had gone and she was still sitting at the stop. The insect flapped its thin wings. Then, as quickly as it came, it flew away. She watched it until it disappeared into the woods.

A car came up behind Leigh and tapped its horn, startling her and forcing her to move on from the moment, but as she drove, she couldn't help thinking about the creature. The rolling hills sliding past her window, the silence all around her, the static of the wind, and the warm glow of sunlight all worked together to calm her. It was as if she'd just figured out how to breathe.

As she carried on along the winding roads, she looked down at the map on her phone, only to realize the screen had turned black. She picked it up, tapping it. *Great.* The phone was dead.

She tossed it onto the passenger seat.

She searched the dash of the rental car for a way to plug in but, of course, that model didn't have a port. The last leg of the trip was always tricky, all the roads looking exactly the same and none of them having street signs, but they'd also changed in the eight years since she'd last made the drive. There were fields where there used to be trees, the old maple that sat on the side of the road as a marker now gone. But to her relief, she was nearing Leon's service station, which she remembered was one of the last stops before the lake. She could get directions there.

Leigh pulled into the vintage station, parking next to an old red Ford, complete with *For Farm Use* license plates and a Bluetick hound dog sitting in the passenger seat. The dog watched her through the open truck window as she made her way to the clapboard structure, hobbling across the uneven gravel in her new summer wedge heels. She passed under a covered porch flanked by a pair of weathered rocking chairs, and went inside, the bells on the door jingling when she opened it.

The place hadn't changed a bit since she'd been gone. The pickle jar still sat on the counter with a sign alerting customers that they, too, could have one on their way out, for twenty-five cents. The aisle by the door was stocked with homemade treats from the local baker, just like it had always been. And free firewood was still piled by the door. The unspoken rule was that you could take two logs a day as long as you bought something in the store. Leigh never understood why Leon gave it away, but she didn't argue. It was completely normal to hear Nan call, "Hey, Leigh. I've got a dollar in my purse. Why don't you get yourself a pack of gum and grab two logs at Leon's?"

A long quiet whistle came from Leigh's right, and her heart stopped, the sound pulling her attention over to a man who was eyeing her like he'd never seen a woman before—to her relief, he was unfamiliar.

He winked at her before turning to the refrigerator and pulling out a bottle of lemonade, before he passed her and tossed a few bucks on the counter to pay for his drink. Then he walked out.

"He ain't gonna hurt a fly," Leon said from behind the counter, clearly not recognizing her right away, his attention on the man. He, too, looked the same as he had years ago, with the exception of some gray that had formed at the temples of his brown hair. "Colton'll tell ya, ain't that right, Colton?" He nodded over to the guy two aisles over.

Leigh's breath caught. He *was* there. It had been ages, but her pulse quickened, her heart nearly beating out of her chest. Over the years, he'd become this golden memory that she'd held so dear, and now he was standing right there. Part of her wanted to run over to him and throw her arms around him like she had so many years ago, but she knew their closeness was only a figment of her imagination now. Time had pushed its way between them and, as she looked at him, the young boy she'd known was but a whisper in the past.

A distant memory flashed in her mind of the day she'd met the shirtless young boy, his skin tan from summer at the lake, his light-brown hair laced with golden streaks. He was sitting on the dock with his bare feet hanging off the edge, a fishing pole in his hand.

"Whatcha doing?" a twelve-year-old Leigh asked as she skipped over to him, something he'd end up repeating to her every time he saw her after that. On the dock, he barely looked up at her, almost as if she'd disturbed him. *"My name's Leigh,"* she said, sitting down beside him. She held out her hand the way her parents had taught her to greet someone. *"Nice to meet you."*

He didn't shake it, his grip remaining on his fishing pole. She noticed the dirt under his fingernails.

"Where do you live?" she asked.

He finally looked at her. "You talk a lot," he said, before turning his attention back to the lake and the little bobber that was swaying on the surface.

She swung her feet back and forth over the edge, considering this. She wanted to tell him she didn't think she did talk a lot, but that would be more talking, so she opted to sit silently beside the boy with no name.

The bobber dipped under the water and the boy straightened, winding his reel until a tiny fish emerged. It flipped and flopped on the end of his line. Evidently disappointed, he shook his head, removed the fish and threw it back into the water. Then he rebaited his hook and started again, casting the line out into the swell of the lake.

"You gonna tell me your name?" she asked.

He stared at her, the gold in his dark-brown eyes like fiery diamonds against his tanned skin. No one had ever made her heart beat like that just by looking at her.

"Colton Harris," he finally said, standing up and reeling in his line.

"It's nice to meet you, Colton," she said, getting up and trying again, offering her hand.

He stared at it like he didn't know what to do with it, so she dropped her arm back down by her side. He packed up his sack of things and tossed it over his bare shoulder. "I'll see ya," he said.

Even though he'd been less than friendly when she'd met him that first day, it didn't stop her from writing his name on all her notebooks with a heart and little flowers around it, and she'd known that if she ever got married, she wanted her husband to look just like Colton Harris.

"You live around here?" Leon asked, squinting down his nose at Leigh.

She cleared her throat. "No, I'm just visiting for a few days. I, uh, used to come here to see my grandmother when I was a kid," she said, distracted by Colton, who was now at the back of the store, getting a six-pack of beer out of one of the refrigerated cases. His shoulders were much broader than they'd been when he was a teenager, his body more muscular, but his hairline was the same and his movements were still familiar. "You don't remember me?"

Leon squinted at her before his bushy eyebrows shot up in surprise, his gaze darting between Leigh and Colton before settling back on her. "Leigh Henderson? Well, well, well…" His gaze slid down to her silk shirt and trousers and then back up to her face. "You're all grown up, ain't ya? How you been?"

"Good," she said, her attention back on the empty aisle where Colton had stood.

She jumped when Colton set the beer down on the counter, along with a bag of potato chips, a box of dog bones, and a bottle of water, standing behind her and not saying a word. Did he recognize her? Up close, he was taller than she remembered. His hair was darker, there was a slight stubble of gold on his jaw, and fine lines at the edges of his eyes that worked for him. She caught his appraising glance at her designer bag and wedge heels and the subtle, dismissive shake of his head as the corner of his mouth turned upward when he addressed Leon, mentioning a rainstorm that was on its way in the next few days.

With his attention on Leon, Leigh took in the familiar curve of his face, the natural pout in his lips…

The cash register spat out a receipt for Colton's things and Leon reached around her and grabbed the items, stuffing them into a plastic bag. Even though she had no idea what to say to Colton now, she'd hoped to hear that rasp in his voice directed at her, the "Whatcha doing?". But it never came.

"Did you need something, Miss Leigh?" Leon asked, pulling her out of her head.

"Oh," she said, coming to. "I need directions to Thicket Lane."

Colton grabbed his bag, and she could feel his stare as he stepped away from her, leaving her wondering if he knew which Leigh was standing opposite him. The weight in his silence told her he did.

"That's a mess of turns from here," Leon replied, stroking his chin. "I could tell you, but you'd forget by turn two. Colton, you've gotta go past Thicket, right?"

Colton stopped in the open door, the bag swinging along his side while he held the six-pack at his chest. He had that same look in his eyes as when Leigh had tried to introduce herself all those years ago. And just like when they were kids, he didn't answer on the first question.

"Can you lead her there?" Leon asked.

"The spring game's on. Kickoff's in an hour," he said, his voice like a forgotten melody to her ears.

Leon gave him a loaded look. "Perfect. Thicket's on the way, ain't it?" Leon's easy, friendly way with Colton hit her hard—a stark contrast to the rejection she'd gotten from her superficial friendship with Julie back at work.

Colton turned and eyed the dog that was still resting on the open window of the Ford. The dog raised its head at its master. Then it looked past him into the store as if it understood. Colton shrugged at the hound, who let out a loud sigh and sat up.

"Thank you," Leigh said, allowing her gaze to finally meet Colton's as she joined him at the door, her breathing shallow, taking in those dark-brown eyes.

"For what?" he asked. He set the six-pack of beer on the hood of his truck with a clunk and reached into the bag, opening the box of milk bones and pulling one out. He tossed it through the open window to the hound, the dog catching it in midair.

"For showing me the way."

By the look of fondness with a hint of that sting she'd seen in his eyes that day so long ago, she was absolutely sure right then that he knew exactly who stood in front of him. "Did I say I was?"

She narrowed her eyes. "No, but your dog did," she said.

The dog raised its ears.

"Look at him." She walked over to the truck and reached in through the window. "You wanna take me to Thicket Lane, don't you?" she said to the dog, scratching his head. "What's his name?"

When she said that, it was as if Colton had a hundred things to tell her, but he wouldn't allow himself. He stared at her almost in disbelief. But then he seemed to slide back into the present moment. "You talk a lot," he said, the corner of his mouth twitching upward.

"I only asked his name," she said, trying to deny the flurry of exhilaration that filled her because he'd remembered their first meeting too.

"Elvis," he replied, to which the dog turned toward him.

Leigh nodded, amused. It would be just like Colton to have a dog named Elvis. His whole young life, he'd sworn that Elvis had been the most talented singer of all time, something that had created heated debates with Meredith whenever she tried to argue that the Beatles should hold that title.

"You have a... *new* truck," she said, taking in the faded paint on the Ford.

"Yep," he replied, not elaborating. Colton picked up the bag and his beer and went around to the driver's side of the truck, getting in and starting the engine. Then he leaned across Elvis to address Leigh through the window. "You gonna follow me or just watch me go?"

Her heart ached for more time. She wanted to talk to him properly, tell him that she'd thought about him over the years. But maybe it was better that she didn't try. They were clearly different people now.

He pulled off, leaving her there. Leigh hustled over to her rental car and hopped in.

The old Ford continued down the road in a cloud of dust, as the gravel ground beneath its tires. Leigh put the car in gear and pulled off behind him.

Chapter Four

When they arrived at the lake house, Colton threw a hand up to Leigh out the window, but he didn't stop the truck. She jumped out of her car to say thank you, but having already gone too far down the lane to hear her, the truck continued on and rounded the curve in the road. Leigh watched him go.

She put her hands on her hips and breathed in a deep breath of southern air to steady her pounding heart. Not ready just yet to face the cabin, she closed her eyes and took in another calming breath. The scent of spruce from the nearby pines and the heady aroma of the lake water that lapped onto the shore behind the cabin filled her lungs. The windchime on the porch tinkled in the breeze. Leigh's mother's brown sedan was parked in the drive.

The screen door squeaked open and then clapped shut behind Leigh's mother, Katherine, as she stepped down the three steps to the stone path leading to the driveway. Her bob of gray hair and makeup were both done, and she looked like she'd lost some weight.

"Hey, Mama," Leigh said, wrapping her arms around Katherine, her scent of rose and powder instantly taking Leigh back to her childhood. She wanted to curl up in her mom's lap and tell her everything that had happened to her, but instead she pulled back and gave her a big smile.

Her mother kissed her on the cheek. "How was the trip?" she asked, as she followed Leigh around to the trunk of her car to help her retrieve her suitcases.

Leigh yanked on the handle of the largest bag, pulling it out of the trunk. It landed with a thud in the gravel at her feet. "It was good—a nice, short flight."

"Any word from Meredith?"

"Other than the call where she said she'd come, nope." Leigh got into the passenger seat and grabbed another bag. "I did tell her I was coming today."

"She'll be here then." The look of uncertainty on Mama's face made it pretty clear that she was nervous, too, about whether her younger daughter would come.

No one ever knew if Meredith would actually show up or not. Sometimes she would, but other times she'd call with an hour-long reason why she hadn't been able to make it. Knowing her sister, she was probably saving money by driving from California to Tennessee, so it could be days before they saw her. There was nothing wrong with saving money, and it was good of Meredith to know she needed to. Leigh just hoped she had her own car and wasn't hitchhiking across the country.

"Did you remember how to get all the way here? I almost got lost—it looks so different now. The trees and brush have grown up so much, I could hardly find it," Mama said, carrying two of Leigh's bags up the steps and holding open the screen door for her.

"I had to stop at Leon's and ask directions," Leigh admitted. "Colton showed me how to get back here…"

Mama's eyebrows bounced with that news, making Leigh smile despite herself. "What's he up to?" she asked.

"I have no idea. He was a man of few words. Just showed me the way and took off."

"Sounds like him," she said adoringly. Her mother moved through the porch and opened the door to the kitchen, setting the bags on the old linoleum floor.

Leigh's heart skipped a beat as she took in the striped log walls with white chinking, the gauzy curtains at the windows, and the unique scent of cedar and lavender that instantly reminded her of long nights playing board games around the living-room coffee table with Nan. She fully expected her grandmother to round the corner and throw her arms around them, laughing like she'd just told a joke. But instead, the house was quiet, everything in order instead of covered in things from Nan's day—magazines open on the counter, a candle lid askew from lighting the candle the night before, an empty wine glass on the mantle. Her stomach plummeted, unexpected tears pricking her eyes.

The dark interior walls were just as she remembered them, although the hand drawings she'd made, which Nan had pinned to them, were now gone. She swallowed the lump in her throat as she ran a hand down the cream-colored 1950s Formica table that was covered with the cleaning products her mother had brought. Leigh's fingers came to rest on one of the four mint-green chairs with metal legs where she'd sat so many Saturday mornings, nibbling on homemade strudel that Nan had made especially for her. The old wood floors were still covered in tapestry rugs. Her entire childhood flashed before her like a movie reel, and she had to focus on something else before she broke down.

"Colton has a hound dog named Elvis," Leigh said, clearing her throat and trying to get her mind off of everything.

"He's a hoot." Mama pulled two mugs from the cabinet, rinsed them, and poured them each a cup of coffee from the carafe that was warming on the coffee pot, the weight of this etched on her face as well.

When Nan died, her mom had fallen into a depression. Nan had been *her* rock too—the two of them nearly inseparable. After years of counseling, Leigh's mother had finally been able to manage her grief, but she'd never been able to come back to the cabin.

"I actually ran into him at the market when I got here," Mama said. "He was on his way out and I told him he should stop by. He gave me his cell number."

The idea made Leigh's chest squeeze, after their meeting just now at Leon's. The last thing she needed was Colton Harris sitting on the sofa, neither of them speaking to each other because too much time had obviously passed. She'd rather her memories of him stay perfect as they were.

Mama shuffled over with their two thick, ceramic gray-and-white speckled mugs—the ones they'd had hot cocoa in at Christmastime. She handed Leigh one of the coffees and then settled into a chair across from her and sighed, her gaze floating out the window. "After cleaning everything and going through some of your grandmother's things this week, I finally decided not to drive back home and slept here last night."

"Oh?" Leigh said, all her attention now on her mother. "Were you okay during the night?"

"Despite not having Mom here to tell us all sweet dreams like she used to, and missing her more than I ever have, it was the most peaceful night of sleep I've had in years. It took me a while, though. I had to go through the tears and the hurt first. But about midway through the week, I just decided to embrace the life she left us. I went down the street, catching up with the neighbors and spending time at the market… It doesn't make me miss her less, and I still feel like falling apart when I think of losing her." Her voice broke and she bit her lip.

Leigh nodded. "I miss her, too."

Mama didn't say anything, searching out the window for some imaginary thing, her eyes filling with tears.

Even after all these years, it was still too early to talk about Nan. They both needed more time. "I'm looking forward to a peaceful night, though," Leigh managed.

Mama scooted the cream and sugar toward her. They sat on a little plate with two spoons, making Leigh wonder if they'd need three spoons next week or if two would suffice. Mama was clearly having a difficult time coming back to the cabin. She didn't need anything else to worry about. Leigh prayed her sister wouldn't let them down.

"It's been tough for me lately without your nan," her mother said. "It's too quiet in my little apartment."

When Leigh's father had passed away five years ago, Mama had sold their childhood home, the space entirely too large for one person. Leigh didn't want to think about her mother and the long, silent nights she'd spent by herself. Suddenly, a rush of guilt swarmed Leigh at the thought that her job and her flimsy friendship with Julie had been more important to her than this.

"I'm glad you're here," Mama said.

Leigh nodded.

"Every creak in the house makes me turn, thinking your nan will be there."

"I still feel like she's here, in this house," Leigh admitted, pouring cream into her coffee and stirring the hot liquid, sending a rich aroma into the air. "Like she'll come through the door with a bag of groceries or something."

"I do too," her mother said.

Leigh sipped her coffee, letting the nutty, aromatic taste of it wash over her.

"So, tell me all about your exciting life up in New York City," Mama said, shoveling a spoonful of sugar into her mug and stirring.

"There's not much to tell, really," Leigh replied, yesterday feeling like a blur. There was actually *a lot* to tell, but she just didn't know where to begin or if she even wanted to put her mother through the stress of it all.

"Are you president of the company yet?" Mama lifted her mug to her lips and took a long sip.

"Not quite," Leigh replied, taking a sip of her coffee to avoid crying, the misery of all those years she'd spent working from sun up to sun down, with nothing to show for it, bubbling up.

"Give it time."

If only her mother knew. "I didn't realize I missed this place so much," she said, changing the subject. "Maybe I'll cash it all in and move here instead." She gave her mother a small smile, in an attempt to lighten the mood.

A slight look of uncertainty fluttered across Mama's face just before she took another swig of her coffee.

"You okay?" Leigh asked.

"I'm just so happy you're here."

"You're not getting rid of the cabin, are you?" Leigh asked with an uncomfortable chuckle. "It's staying in the family, right?"

"Of course it is," Mama said. "Nan wouldn't have it any other way."

With a sigh of relief, Leigh allowed her hiked shoulders to settle, and leaned back in her chair. In a strange way, coming back at this moment felt like the perfect thing to do.

While Mama was in the kitchen washing dishes, listening to the latest songs on country-music radio, Leigh walked around the living room. It was still the way Nan had decorated it, with the twin sofas facing each other, bright ocean-blue throw pillows in the corners of them. The wooden coffee table still had tiny droplets of paint from Nan's projects, and a stack of books she'd been reading last. Leigh closed her eyes and imagined her grandmother sitting on the sofa, the book in her lap, beckoning Leigh over.

"Come and sit with your nan before you're so old and busy that you forget to," she'd say.

Leigh sat down on the sofa next to the end where Nan had always sat. "I'll never forget," she whispered. She laid her hand on the empty cushion, tears welling in her eyes, causing her to spring back up before she fell apart.

Pushing her emotion down, she went over to the desk but found herself more emotional as she took in the place where Nan had taught her how to write in cursive. Memories spilled over in her mind like a waterfall, unable to be contained. She pulled out the wooden chair and took a seat. If she tried, she could feel her grandmother's arms around her as she guided her pencil to make the curls of the script.

She fiddled with the handle on the desk drawer that Nan said had always been Leigh's. It was the spot where Leigh had kept all her notes about birds and her colored pencils. It was off limits to Meredith—Nan's rules. Meredith had her own personal spot at Nan's too: the old trunk under the window.

Leigh opened her drawer and peered inside. Her pencils were still there, along with a stack of papers. But an envelope sat on top. She pulled it out to take a look, surprised to find her name on the back in Nan's curly writing. Was it an old birthday card or something?

She looked around to see if she was the only one in the room. When she realized she was, the sink still running in the kitchen, Leigh pulled out the folded paper inside and opened it up, revealing more of Nan's handwriting—line after line of it. The date on it stopped her in her tracks. It was dated two days before she'd gone into the hospital.

"Mom, do you know what this is?" she called, but the water was still running and her mother was singing to the radio, so she hadn't heard her. With another look around to be sure she was actually there and not dreaming, she read the note.

My dearest Leigh,

I know you and your sister are very different people, and sometimes you can't always see eye to eye, but she's family. Remember that. Embrace her. And no matter what, you'll be okay. I'm going to tell your mother to pass on some news to you—it's not something I want to put in writing because you need to hear it as a family. Know that I love you. But I have my reasons. I'm taking a gamble here, and I hope it works out.

All my love,
Nan

Leigh hugged the letter, that all-too-familiar ache that happened when she thought of her grandmother forming in Leigh's chest. She peered over her shoulder at the doorway to the kitchen, wondering if she should tell her mother that she'd found the note, but she decided to keep it to herself. It was as if Nan had offered it to her in the quiet of the living room for a reason. So, Mama's news had something to do with Nan… What could Nan possibly have to say that they didn't already know?

She tucked the letter under the papers in her desk drawer and headed back to her bedroom to unpack, wondering what all this was about. But on the way to her room, she stopped midway. At the end of the hallway, the door to Nan's art room was closed. She stared at it, feeling like Nan was standing behind it. For an instant, she wanted to bust open the door, wishing she could throw her arms around Nan, but she didn't—she couldn't—because the emptiness of the studio would crush her. Instead, she left it shut, and went into her room.

The denim quilt still covered Leigh's bed, the little patches of mismatched fabric Nan had sewn into it still as vibrant as they'd been in her memory. Leigh set her suitcase down on the edge of the iron bed, the soft mattress sinking underneath it, still wondering about the letter Nan had left her. Did Meredith have one, or was it just for her?

Leigh had been the closest with Nan, staying with her every hour of the day when Meredith would run off to hang out with friends on their speedboats or to go to the nightly bonfires. Nan's quiet, pensive nature made her a perfect complement to Leigh, and the two of them were always together whenever Leigh visited. And the cabin had been their hub. Those walls had overseen all the experiences that had made Leigh who she was outside of her academic life. It was in that cabin that she'd learned about love and loss, about true friendships, and the heartache that family could cause each other.

Leigh had gotten everything unpacked and into the drawers in the bedroom when Mama appeared in the doorway. "I was thinkin' maybe we could take the boat out for a ride to get the engine primed for the week."

"It's got gas in it?" She slipped her suitcases into the small closet and closed the folding doors.

"Yeah, I had the marina folks gas it up before I got here yesterday. They brought it over and put it in the water for us." She came in and sat down on the bed. "Wanna go?"

"I'd love to," Leigh replied. "Let me just put my hair up so the wind doesn't wreak havoc with it." She dug around in her toiletries bag for her hair tie as Mama stood by. "I can't remember the last time we rode on the boat, can you?"

Mama followed her into the bathroom and Leigh clicked on the light, drawing her brush through her hair to tie it back.

"It's been ages," Mama replied. "Your nan never liked to take the boat out after your granddad died, remember?"

"Yeah. Meredith used to offer to drive because Nan wouldn't."

Mama smiled, her eyes full of thoughts.

Leigh pulled her hair up and tied it off, raking her fingers along her scalp to straighten out the few lumps, and then grabbed her jacket by the door.

They left Meredith a note in case she came early, even though Leigh knew she probably wouldn't come tonight, and went outside through the back door, passing the old desk with the picture book of birds, through the screened-in porch and down the grassy bank to the dock where the white cruiser was tied up. It bobbed in the water, the small waves splashing against it. Leigh put her hands on her hips and let the visual calm her, melting away everything she'd left back in New York. Tomorrow, she'd sneak in a few job applications and peruse LinkedIn for more possibilities, but today, she was gifting herself this moment.

She helped Mama untie the boat, the two of them working in tandem, the task coming back to her like clockwork. She tossed the rope into the vessel and climbed in as her mother cranked the engine, the old motor whirring to life, the hum of the engine like music to

Leigh's ears. Mama backed it up and then headed out for open water. Leigh's ponytail flew around her, flyaway wisps tickling her face, the cold spring wind rushing against her body, the movement of the boat instantly returning her to the sun-soaked days of her childhood.

The water stretched out in front of them all the way to the tree line, other cabins and cottages dotting the coast. They got to the eastern inlet and Leigh craned her neck to see the house where Colton grew up, wondering if she'd see him there. But he probably didn't live there anymore. She wondered what his place was like. Were his parents still there? She kept her eyes on it until it faded away into the distance. They rounded the bend, and buzzed through the open water until they neared Mariner's Cove, where Meredith used to like to stay out late, her friends' boats bobbing in the water there until the wee hours of the morning.

"Whoa, look at that," Mama called loudly over the roar of the engine, the boat slowing as she reduced the throttle, pointing to the edge of the lake where there used to be trees. However, now there was a strip of shops being built, and decking with boat docks.

Leigh squinted at the sign. "Greystone Properties," she read. "That's a massive strip for this area. It looks like it'll have at least four restaurants. I'll bet it'll be gorgeous when it's done."

"Things just keep moving along, don't they?" Mama said.

She thought about Rebecca at the office. "They sure do."

"You okay?" her mother asked.

"Totally fine," Leigh said, her tone just a little too chipper.

She thought again about Nan's letter and how, no matter what, she'd be okay. She definitely didn't feel like that right now. But as they floated along the water, the ebbs and flows of it gave her hope that this was just a dip and she'd be back up in no time.

Chapter Five

"Let's circle the lake and run through Harvey's Bend before we go home," Mama said from behind the wheel of the boat. "I'm starvin'. Maybe we can grab a burger."

Knowing the silence that awaited them back at the cabin, Leigh agreed, and Mama steered left toward the bend where Harvey's Marina lit up the coast. A band played at the end of the pier, the twanging music sailing toward them long before they'd even seen the crowd gathered under the string lights outside.

They found a clear spot between two other boats and docked along the pier, then made their way to the entrance under the lighted marina sign. The place was buzzing with locals, sounds of laughter coming from the pool tables and the bar that wrapped around two walls before giving way to a wide double door leading to the fishing shop, full of bait and tackle.

Following the sign to seat themselves, Leigh pulled out a chair at an open table for four and Mama sat down across from her. The lively atmosphere did a good job of stripping Leigh of all the things on her mind, and she now understood why Mama had suggested it.

A waitress came over, and Leigh would have recognized those red curls anywhere.

"Shelly?" Leigh asked, remembering the young girl with those pink cheeks and that fiery hair who used to come looking for Meredith.

"Hey!" she said, leaning down and giving Leigh a warm hug before going over and offering Mama the same greeting. "Where's your sister? She here?"

"Not yet," Leigh said, hoping the uncertainty in her answer wouldn't show.

"She'll have to come by when she gets here."

"Definitely," Mama agreed, her eyes moving from the menu to Shelly.

Shelly gave them a big smile and then asked, "What's y'all havin' tonight?" in her thick southern drawl.

Two burger orders later, the waitress leaned in. "Hey, y'all seen Colton yet?" Shelly asked, not skipping a beat. "He's over there, watchin' the game." She pointed around a partition to the widescreen television showing pre-season college football with a group of people gathered around it. Leigh craned her neck to see and found Colton's best friend Smash Hughes first. His face had filled out a little more and he had a beard. She continued through the group until she caught sight of that square jaw and dark hair. Colton had a ball cap on and a bottle of beer at his lips. Then, like a record scratch, he tipped his head down and a blonde leaned in and whispered something in his ear, causing that crooked grin of his to land on his lips, and Leigh tore herself away, glad she and Mama were hidden from their view.

"I saw him earlier," she told Shelly, pressing a smile across her face.

"Oh good," the waitress said, collecting their menus. "I'll be back with your drinks." Shelly gave them a little wave and headed off toward the bar.

"Maybe we should've sat outside, where we could hear the band," Leigh said to her mother, second-guessing their decision to come here.

"It's chilly after the sun starts to go down," Mama said, wrinkling her nose at the idea. "I'd much rather be inside."

Leigh chewed her lip and nodded in agreement, her mind preoccupied.

"You're not upset because Colton's here, are you?"

Her mother's question yanked her out of her thoughts. "Of course not," she said, unsure why she was feeling so defensive. "It's a free country; he can be here too."

Shelly returned with two bubbling glasses of Coke, setting them down on the table, and then addressed another group at a table next to them.

"You two used to be joined at the hip," Mama said, picking up her soda and taking a swig from the straw.

"A lot's changed since we were kids," Leigh said. "We're not the same people we were back then." Her gaze flitted over to him and caught him laughing at something one of the guys had said, sending a little ache through her. She wasn't sure if the ache was from losing the boy she'd left behind or not knowing the man in front of her now.

Just then, he caught sight of her, and they locked eyes across the room. Her stomach flipped when he sent her the faintest hint of that smile of his, before turning back to the television.

After flipping through the channels that evening, and finding nothing to quiet her whirring mind, Leigh clicked off the TV and lay back on the sofa. The static patter of Mama's shower was the only sound in the house. She closed her stinging eyes, conjuring up the smile that lingered behind Colton's pout when she'd caught him looking at her the few times at dinner, his muscular stature, and the masculinity in his hands as he grabbed bottles of beer off the bar. *Things just keep moving along, don't they?*

Even though their reunion was lackluster at best, given the circumstances, it was enough to send her on a million what-ifs. What if she'd gone to Belmont or Vanderbilt and stayed in the area? Would she be a different person now? Would she have ended up here at the lake with Colton? Would they spend their days together out on the porch swing or in twin rocking chairs, watching the sunset every evening?

Leigh shifted on the sofa, reaching around and rubbing the knot that had formed in her shoulder last night and carried on through her travels today. Her eyes burned with the need for sleep, and a pinch of tension swelled in her neck and back. It was as if eight years of not standing still was now collecting in her muscles. This wasn't like her. Leigh relished the race to the top. She was energized by competition and the clawing it took to reach her goals. She hadn't ever tired of it. Not until this moment.

She just needed to get back on track. To get her mind onto something more productive, she got up and pulled out her laptop, browsing jobs back in New York. With a full savings account and her severance package, she had a little time to find something else, but she'd rather not dip into what she'd worked so hard to set aside. She scrolled through a few postings, none of them hitting the mark. With another click, she checked a different site, pausing to read one that looked promising. But it required "a considerable amount of travel," so she wasn't sure if she wanted to commit. She'd bookmark it in case she couldn't find anything else.

Then, suddenly, she stopped cold, her mouth literally hanging open as she read the available position: *McGregor Consulting, Commercial*

Property Management Consultant… That was Leigh's title. They didn't dissolve her position. They dissolved *her*. Squeezing her right out and replacing her with someone new. She stared at it, unable to make sense of what was going on. Phillip had softened the let-down with a severance package, but in the end, it was a straight you-don't-cut-the-mustard firing. She'd done everything right. *Everything*. How could things have gone so wrong?

"Let's roast marshmallows," her mother said, coming into the room in her matching pants and T-shirt pajama set, her hair wet from the shower.

Leigh eyed her, wondering about her behavior. First the boat ride and then dinner out, now marshmallows. The same thing had happened when their father had died. Her mother began fluttering around, putting on a happy face for everyone, not daring to stop moving because if she did, she'd crumble into a million pieces.

"Oh, no you don't," Mama said, scooping up Leigh's laptop, shutting it, and setting it on the desk. "I know you're super important and everyone needs you, but give yourself at least a day before you start working." Her mother padded into the kitchen. "We've got those long skewers in the pantry," she said over her shoulder. "I'll get them."

Nobody needed her. Nobody at all. Rebecca was taking care of everything. Leigh got up, her head beginning to throb, her mother's constant movement making her feel exhausted. Leigh had never seen her like this. Whatever she had to tell them must be huge. She got up and went into the kitchen in a daze.

"I'll get the fire pit started out back," Mama said, whizzing past her with two skewers, an armful of blankets, and a bag of marshmallows.

Leigh pulled down a glass from the cabinet and filled it with water at the tap. Then she rooted around in her handbag until she found her ibuprofen, popping two of them into her mouth and chasing them with the water. She topped her glass off and headed out to the small patio at the bottom of the stairs, below the screened-in porch, where, next to Nan's overgrown flower bed and vegetable garden, they had a stone fire pit with a circle of white-washed wooden Adirondack chairs and a hammock on the tree line. She sunk down into one of the chairs, covering up with a blanket, just as the orange flames licked up at the night sky, sending heat through the chill in the air that always fell over the lake at nightfall in the springtime. Mama sat down beside her, threading a marshmallow onto one of the skewers and handing it to Leigh.

"How long did you take off of work?" Mama asked. She'd loaded up her skewer and had already submerged her marshmallow into the flame.

"I rarely take time off," Leigh said, "so I can have as long as I like… within reason," she added, so it wouldn't be obvious that she had no job at all.

"Oh, that's wonderful! I only got a week off at the bank, but that's fine. I commuted from here for the last two weeks and the drive wasn't too bad." She pulled her marshmallow out of the flame and blew on it. "Besides, I *want* to work. It gives me purpose."

Leigh understood. She wanted to work too. She'd only been there a day and its lulling effects were already messing with her resolve.

"You're quiet," Mama noted. The twinge of fear in her eyes made sense because Leigh felt it too. If she stopped too long, she'd think about Nan's absence.

Leigh shook her head, pushing thoughts of Nan away, her own need to deny the sadness creeping in. "I'm just… unwinding. It's been a busy day."

"Your marshmallow's burning."

Leigh yanked her skewer out of the fire, the charred marshmallow smoking. She let it cool and picked at it, nibbling the inside as the stars came out in the deep-blue sky above them, the soft, swishing movement of the lake soothing her.

"You wanna tell me what's going on?" Mama asked. "I'm not stupid. Something's up with you."

Mama's assessment took Leigh off guard. Was it that obvious? And she was no one to talk. Leigh debated over dropping the bomb that she'd been fired. She wasn't sure she could handle the embarrassment of it. She'd never failed at anything. And she'd failed at this—the biggest part of her life.

"I'll tell you if you tell me your news," Leigh ventured, leaning the skewer against the fire pit.

Mama frowned. "I need to tell you and Meredith at the same time." There was a finality in her eyes that made it clear Leigh didn't need to ask again. Mama wasn't budging. "I'm guessing, though, that whatever it is on *your* chest, you'd probably rather tell only me. Or do you want to wait and tell Meredith too?"

Leigh definitely didn't want to tell Meredith this. Meredith would probably laugh in her face. Her temples began to throb again, despite the ibuprofen. She took a drink of her water. Then, with a deep breath of smoky, earthy air, Leigh spit it out: "I lost my job."

The fire popped and a dog barked in the distance, the crickets beginning their nightly song, as Mama's eyes grew round. "Really? When?"

"Yesterday. They're going 'in a different direction,'" she said with air quotes, the entire ordeal still beyond her comprehension.

The dog barked again, echoing in her aching brain.

"That's the most ridiculous thing they could've done," Mama said with complete bewilderment. "You're a brilliantly smart woman."

Leigh smiled. *Protective mother.*

The bark came once more, this time coming up beside her. In the light of the fire, it looked like… "Elvis?" The hound walked over and sniffed her hand, his long ears lifting in interest as he moved around her legs.

"Hey," Colton said, striding across the grass and setting the six-pack of beer he'd gotten at Leon's on the ground beside him.

"Oh my goodness," Mama said, her face splitting into an enormous smile, the atmosphere immediately lifting with his presence. "Colton, how have you been?"

"Good," he replied. His gaze fluttered over to Leigh, as he dropped down into the seat next to her and picked up a bottle. He popped the top off on the edge of the chair, offering it to her.

"No, thank you," she said, her stomach turning with the admission of losing her job, waving it off politely. Had he overheard? The idea of it made her feel nauseous.

He offered the open bottle to Katherine. Her mother reached across the space between their chairs and took it. His gaze landed back on Leigh as if he were assessing her, making her jittery, her head feeling like she'd been submerged in the lake.

"It's not you. I just have a headache," Leigh attempted to explain to him.

"I can grab you some medicine," Mama said, getting up right away. "We've got some inside…"

"Mama," she said, stopping her mother before she ran back into the house. "I took something before I came out. I'm just tired. It's been a long day."

This was twice now that she hadn't been ready to see Colton. His irritation was clear in his inhalations as he sat by the fire. She wanted to put her arms around him, carefree like they had been when they were young, and look into those dark-brown eyes. She wanted to see him smile at her with that look that was uniquely his. He was the physical representation of the best parts of her childhood. If only she'd been able to tell him that, when she'd seen him for the first time. Not looking at his face, she focused on the muscles in his arms—so different from the lanky limbs that had wrapped around her all those years ago.

Elvis went over near the lake, sniffing around.

Colton reached down and retrieved a beer for himself, popping the top and tipping it up against his lips, swallowing long, deep swigs of it as the crickets got louder. Mama was about to offer him a marshmallow when a light up at the house cut through the darkness.

"Let's get this party started!" Meredith's voice came from the porch. She burst through the screen door, making a beeline straight for Colton, wrapping her thin limbs around him with an excited shriek. Her hair was long, almost to the middle of her back, wild tendrils with bottle-blonde highlights. When she pulled back, her skin was milky and vibrant, as if a day hadn't gone by since they were kids.

"Beer?" he asked, grinning at her.

Meredith got the first real grin. Leigh couldn't even do reunions right.

"Hell yeah," she said, walking over to his six-pack and helping herself. She sat down in the empty chair, her frock dress fanning out over her legs. "Hey," she said to her mother and Leigh, as if she hadn't been gone for two years. "What's up?" Her long fingers enveloped her bottle of beer, three of them wrapped in thin gold rings with different colored stones.

Leigh wanted to get up and run into her bedroom, drop down onto the bed and drift off to anywhere other than the chair where she sat right now. She wasn't ready to deal with all of this just yet. She needed time to process everything before she could be a good hostess to Colton, wait for her mother's news, and handle her sister.

"What?" Meredith asked, dropping the word between them with a heavy clunk, tearing Leigh from her moment of self-pity.

Only then did Leigh realize her eyes had remained on Meredith.

"I came early," Meredith snapped. "You said next week, but I came when *you* did and I *still* get a look." She let out an annoyed laugh.

"Meredith," their mother said calmly, in a clear attempt to defuse the situation.

"Colton doesn't need us to sugarcoat it for him. He knows us all too well." Meredith tipped her beer over to his, toasting the necks of their bottles. "So thankful you're here."

He smiled again. That was two.

"I'm glad you came," Leigh said to Meredith, her words weaker than she'd wanted them to sound. If she let herself, she'd probably fall into tears right then and there, the utter fatigue of the day settling upon her.

Meredith looked at her, the defensive edge in her face melting a little.

Elvis came over and sat next to Leigh's feet as if he knew she needed the support. He sighed and set his head on her knees. Swallowing the lump in her throat, she stroked his soft fur, glad for his company.

"He likes you," Colton noted, his brow furrowing adorably at the idea. "He doesn't warm to people well. He was a rescue, and we don't know what happened to him, but he doesn't trust many people."

Leigh looked into the hound dog's wide dark eyes, the gesture meaning even more now.

"When he does make friends, he's incredibly loyal."

Meredith got up to pet him, and he ducked her hand, letting out a loud, deep bark. In a weird way, it lifted Leigh's spirits having this intangible thing with the dog that Meredith couldn't take from her.

Colton chuckled and Meredith sat back down, stung, and swigged her beer. Leigh patted her knees, telling Elvis it was okay to come back over. The dog kept an eye on Meredith as if waiting for any sudden moves and returned to Leigh, sitting tall and mighty beside her, his chest pushed out, ears on alert as if he would take on anything else that decided to hurt her tonight. At least she had someone on her side.

Chapter Six

Leigh was the first one up the next morning. Still in her flannel pajamas and bathrobe, her glasses on because she couldn't be bothered to put her contacts in yet, she grabbed her mug of coffee and stepped into the crisp spring air on the back porch. Through the sweet malt of her morning cup, she took in the fresh smell of the lake, a soft breeze flowing around her, her shoulders instantly relaxing.

When she was young, she met Nan out there in the mornings, the two of them always up before the sun. They chatted about Nan's tomato plants or they'd bird-watch together. While Nan and Grandpa Joe had settled in the rural area there at Old Hickory, both of them had traveled extensively when Grandpa Joe was in the army. Every now and again, Nan would get to talking about her travels.

"Your Grandpa Joe and I knew we wanted to live by the water after he was stationed at Attersee Lake in Austria. The lake was always so blue, and it stretched out to the most stunning mountains. We sat at cafés with their tables right on the beach—in the sand! And we drank wine and laughed all day long—oh, your grandfather could make me laugh. We'd sit there talking for hours. It was an incredible place," Nan had told her once.

"Why didn't you retire there?" Leigh had asked, pulling her knees up and hugging them as she sat next to Nan on the porch sofa.

"Ah, because it wasn't close to you all. Family's more important." She waved a hand at the lake in front of them. "And we still get a view."

Leigh peered over at that porch sofa, now empty, wondering what Nan would think of the three of them there. Nan had been no stranger to the differences between Leigh and Meredith, but she always had a way of smoothing things over between them while they were staying with her. Nan would bake cookies or suggest a board game, and for a few brief hours, they'd have harmony. Leigh's memories of those times were magical.

Leigh looked through the screen door, out at the lake, her mug steaming in her hand, a source of warmth against the chill. The trees were beginning to bloom again after the cold winter—a vibrant green. The water was calm that early in the morning, with a slight haze of fog rising above it. The stone fire pit was charred inside from last night's fire, the skewers still leaning against it, empty beer bottles sitting on the rim. Leigh set her mug down on the coffee table and stepped out through the door to collect them. The chairs were draped in morning dew, the earth icy cold beneath her bare feet as Leigh gathered up the empty bottles.

Colton hadn't stayed too long last night, and once he was gone, Meredith had said she was beat from the flight. Mama and Leigh had both been flabbergasted that she'd flown there, since flying required actual planning. She went up to the house to go to bed, which Leigh had been relieved about, since she couldn't deal with whatever it was Mama had to tell them. She needed a good night's sleep first.

Leigh held the bottles and danced across the freezing ground until she reached the porch. Balancing them all in one arm, she grabbed her coffee mug and went inside the cabin, the warmth wrapping her in its embrace. With a shiver, she threw the bottles away quietly and went in to the desk in the living room, where her laptop sat, to look for jobs.

As she searched, Leigh pondered what she'd tell someone in an interview as to why she was no longer at McGregor. She didn't want to have to admit she'd been fired. After all the work she'd done for the company, couldn't Phillip at least have given her a heads up so she could've found something before she was let go? She stopped scrolling, halting at a job in Brooklyn that looked promising. It was a property management director position for a small firm. She had all the qualifications… She took a drink from her coffee mug and pulled up the website, finding the application, filling it out, and attaching her résumé.

There was another one in Manhattan that was a bit below her, but she went ahead and filled out the interest survey. Maybe they'd be so blown away by her overqualification that they'd neglect to notice the fact that she hadn't cut it in her previous position.

"Morning," Meredith said, yawning as she came into the room.

Leigh quickly shut her laptop.

Her sister breezed past in nothing but an oversized T-shirt, her toned bare legs and a slight peek at purple lacy underwear visible. She didn't give Leigh a glance before she headed for the kitchen.

Meredith clinked things around in the other room and the coffee pot began to gurgle again. Leigh looked down into the last third of her coffee, and decided to get up and have another cup. She'd need the caffeine to deal with Meredith anyway, she was nearly sure of it.

"Morning," Leigh returned, coming into the kitchen, hoping to start off on the right foot. "You're up unusually early, aren't you?"

Meredith rooted around in the pantry, pulling out a loaf of bread and unbending the twist tie. "I needed to get up," she said, pulling two slices from the bag and popping them into the toaster. "Want some?"

"No, thank you." Leigh tugged the carafe out from under the coffee maker, the sizzle of coffee dripping onto the hotplate causing Meredith to turn.

"You're impatient," Meredith said. "Haven't you already had a cup?"

"Yes," Leigh replied. She wanted to say more, but didn't have the energy to argue her point for having a second cup, so she let it go.

"Do we have any avocados?" Meredith asked, her purple-laced bum front and center as she dug around in the fridge.

"I don't think so," Leigh said, shaking her head as she focused on the creamer she was pouring. "There's some jam in the door."

Meredith grunted and grabbed the jar of strawberry preserve.

The toast popped as Leigh finished fixing her coffee and took it to the table, eyeing Meredith while her sister reluctantly spread the jam and then made herself a cup of coffee.

"So, why did you have to get up?" Leigh asked.

Meredith pinched a piece of the toast by the corner and took a bite, walking over to the kitchen chair and sitting down with her mug of coffee. "Colton and I are going fishing."

"You and Colton?" It wasn't that her sister was going fishing with Colton. But the fact that he'd made plans with Meredith, when he hadn't seemed to care one bit about seeing Leigh, caused disappointment to fall upon her like a summer rainstorm.

"Yeah," she said, the words coming out mumbled through the toast held between her teeth to free her hands to stir her coffee. She set the toast on the bare table, the mug in her hand. "What?"

"Nothing." She was already irritated by Meredith's tone. "You don't even know Colton anymore," she spat before wanting to suck the words back in, but they were out there now.

Meredith zoned in on her with those dagger eyes of hers, their deep blue like lasers. "What do you mean, I don't know him?"

"It's been eight years since we've spoken to him, Meredith."

Her sister leaned on the table and folded her arms. "Maybe since *you've* spoken to him. I text him every now and again and call him on his birthday every year."

Leigh's jaw fell slack. He'd never called her back in college… Fire raged in her veins at the idea that Meredith, who couldn't give a hoot about anything, had stayed in touch with the one person from Leigh's childhood that she'd cared about most.

"What's that face?" Meredith said, leaning into Leigh's view. "What, are you *jealous*? Come on, Leigh. Grow up."

Leigh set her coffee mug down with a clunk. "I'm not jealous." Jealous wasn't the right word at all. But she didn't have the right one, so she just sat there, stewing.

"If Colton and I had anything going on, don't you think it would've already happened? I'm going fishing with my good friend, who I've known for years. Yet somehow, in this house, I get flack for even that." She blew air through her lips and took a bite of her toast.

"What about Mama's news? Don't you think you should stay to hear it?" Leigh asked, switching gears to get the focus off of Colton.

"I won't be gone *that* long. It's just fishing." She popped the last bite of her toast into her mouth, putting her bare foot on the chair and pulling her knee to her chest. "He should be here in a sec to pick me up. We won't be gone more than a few hours."

"Colton will be here in a minute?" Leigh asked in alarm. "Don't you need to put some clothes on?"

Meredith rolled her eyes and got up, flouncing out of the room with her mug, the second slice of toast untouched and still on the counter.

She returned wearing a pair of cut-off Levi's, dragging her curls into a ponytail on top of her head. Her hair barely brushed and with no makeup on, she was still stunning, giving Leigh a little punch to her self-confidence. Leigh took off her glasses and folded them, placing them on the table, and ran her fingers through her hair.

Meredith slid on her old boots and snagged the second piece of toast from the counter, the red Ford pulling up in the driveway. "See ya," she said, opening the door and loping out.

With a sigh, Leigh turned away. But the sound of Elvis's barking pulled her attention back to the door, and she stifled a grin as she looked through the window. Meredith had the passenger door open, but Elvis was on her seat, yapping and growling at her while Colton attempted to quiet him down.

Colton got out of the truck, his dusty boots hitting the gravel. He marched over to Meredith's side. Leigh cracked the door to hear what was going on.

"Let her in, Elvis," Colton said, reaching into the truck to pet him. Elvis dodged his hand, still barking.

Every time she tried to climb in, the dog barked louder. "He doesn't like me."

"Elvis, let her in or you're sleepin' on the sofa tonight."

That got Elvis's attention for a second, until Meredith started to get into the truck and the dog went ballistic again. Leigh laughed from inside, and both Colton and Elvis turned to look at the door. She darted behind it, closing it slowly. Sharpening her hearing, she listened to try to figure out what was happening now and, to her relief, she heard the truck door finally shut and Elvis was quiet. Leigh pulled herself away, staying clear of the windows until they were gone. She grabbed her mug of coffee and took a long, warm drink of it, savoring the nutty flavor to get her mind off the earlier conversation with Meredith.

A knock sent her jumping out of her skin and coughing up the sip. Leigh set the mug down, still coughing, and opened the door to find Colton standing there with Elvis by his side. Meredith was in the truck.

"Hey," he said, an unreadable look on his face.

"Hi," she returned, clearing her throat before another cough surfaced.

"I hate to ask this, but your sister suggested it. Can Elvis stay with you? He won't be in the same vehicle with her."

Leigh looked down at the hound, the dog's deep-set eyes on her, his ears up.

"I thought he'd be okay after meeting Meredith last night, but evidently he's still spooked."

Leigh opened the door wider and addressed the dog. "Want to hang with me today?" she asked, gesturing for him to come inside. The dog peered up at Colton.

"Yeah, it's fine," he told Elvis.

The dog walked through the doorway and sat down next to Leigh.

"Thanks," Colton said, taking a step away from the door. "I'll come back for him in a few hours." He pointed inside the cabin. "You get to stay here," he told Elvis.

Leigh reached down and stroked Elvis's head. "Does he have a leash?"

"Nah. He won't go anywhere."

"Any special instructions?"

The corner of Colton's mouth turned upward. "Nope."

"Okay then. Have… fun."

Colton turned away and threw up his hand as he jogged back to the truck, getting in and starting the engine. Elvis sat next to Leigh, Colton driving away down the dirt road, the dust kicking up behind them.

"Well, I guess it's just us now," she told Elvis. "You're an excellent judge of character, do you know that?"

Elvis's ears went up, his head turning to the side.

"I'd bark at her too."

Elvis turned back to the door, and Leigh could have sworn he knew what she was saying.

Chapter Seven

Mama came into the living room, crisscrossing her yellow terrycloth bathrobe, approaching Elvis with a curious grin. "You woke me up this morning," she told him. "What was all that ruckus?"

The dog followed her with suspicious eyes.

"Colton's dog is staying with us today," Leigh told her. "Meredith went fishing with him this morning."

"What did she eat? I was going to make breakfast."

"Toast."

Mama frowned. "Is she planning to stay out all day?"

"She says she'll be back in a few hours. The only reason I believe that is because Colton's with her and he'll keep time."

Elvis perked up at the mention of his master.

Mama reached out to pet the dog, and he dodged out of the way, nearly jumping into Leigh's lap, making them both laugh.

"All right," she said, holding up her hands in surrender. "I won't bother you. I'm making a cup of coffee so you won't have to worry about me. Want one, Leigh?"

"No, thanks. I had two earlier."

While Mama filled her mug in the kitchen, Leigh grabbed her laptop and opened it, checking her inbox: empty except for sale emails from Neiman Marcus and Target, and one from an online book club she'd joined but never had time for. So, she searched the job listings online to see if anything new had popped up in the last hour, knowing how ridiculous that was. As expected, nothing stood out. Then, out of curiosity, she decided to look into the development they'd seen yesterday.

"What was the company building those new shops we saw from the boat?" she called in to her mother.

Elvis sat up, his ears going crazy. Leigh grinned at him, petting him and settling him back down.

"It was Greystone Properties, wasn't it?" Mama replied, coming in with her coffee. She sat down at the other end of the sofa, crossing her legs and setting the steaming mug on her knee.

Elvis inched closer to Leigh's leg.

"Yeah, that's right," she said, typing the name and location into the search bar. "I wonder what good restaurants are coming." A few articles came up and she clicked on one, scanning for shop and restaurant names that she might recognize. But as she started reading, she slowed down, focusing more on the article. "This says that the development has stalled…"

Mama leaned closer to see the article, the milky sweet scent of her coffee wafting over. "Stalled? Why?"

Leigh twisted the screen toward her. "Look here," she said, tapping the second paragraph. "They're struggling to get a foothold…" she read aloud. "Interest by retail and the food industry has been incredibly low and the developer is at risk of going under."

"That's terrible." Mama leaned back, looking out at the water through the window. "The last thing we need is an abandoned eyesore on the edge of the lake. It looks like a great location to me."

Leigh stroked Elvis's ears. "I know. It shouldn't be vacant. There's no reason that people wouldn't want to be in that location. It's prime real estate. Doesn't Holly Brush Lane go right by the back of it?"

"Yes. That's a straight shot to the main road." Mama pursed her lips, the coffee mug dangling from its handle in her fingers.

"So, it's centrally located. It's got fantastic boat access…" Leigh closed her laptop. "I wonder what retail stores they've contacted."

Mama shrugged. She reached over to pet Elvis again, but he still wouldn't let her.

"You know, this is what I do for a living," Leigh said, considering the issue.

"Build restaurants?"

"No. I secure clients for businesses. I sell the company to them, make the offer seem irresistible."

"Given the struggle it sounds like they've had, there's got to be something wrong with it. I'm not sure you can make an empty development with articles written about how the owner is about to go under seem irresistible to anyone."

"You'd be surprised," she said, an idea prompting her to open her laptop back up. She began searching for statistics about Old Hickory Lake. "It's all in how you spin it. I've had worse than this."

"What are you looking for?" Mama asked, only half listening now as she grabbed her novel and opened it to the page she'd dog-eared.

"Background data," she replied, focused. "Sell them on the potential for customers and the ease with which they'll appeal to those customers, and that's half the battle." She clicked on an article and marked it.

"What kind of background data?" her mother asked, looking up.

"I'm checking for statistics on things like how much seafood is purchased at the local grocery stores, the number of boat charters in the area, how many houses are owned versus rentals. All of this will give me a picture of whom to target for Greystone."

"You could work for *them*!"

Mama's wriggling excitedly caused Elvis to bark at her, simmering her down right away. She laughed, playfully reaching out for him only to receive another bark.

Leigh tapped on her computer. "It's a small company. I doubt they'd have enough properties or income, given their situation, to take on a full-time employee for a position like mine, but what it could do is get me a nice project for my portfolio that might help me land another job somewhere else. I can see the headlines of the articles now: 'Local woman saves retail at Old Hickory Lake; Business is now bustling.'"

"But even if you could make it work for them, you're not staying here for long," Mama said.

"I'd need to be available in person for the meetings with the potential companies, but everything else could be executed remotely." She kept the Greystone website up and typed the number into her phone. "It's worth a call."

"I'd say so." Mama stood up and set the novel back down, having not read a single page. "Want something to eat? I'm starving."

"That sounds wonderful." Leigh looked at Elvis. "Do you like bacon?"

Elvis twisted his head around and eyed her.

"I'll bet you do. Come on, boy. Let's get some breakfast."

Meredith came through the house, laughing at something Colton had said, punching him in the arm, the two of them spilling onto the back porch where Leigh was sitting, still in her pajamas. Leigh's chest tightened, but she hid it with a pleasant greeting.

Elvis dove off the porch sofa from his spot tucked up next to Leigh under their shared blanket and bounced around Colton.

"Where's Mom?" her sister asked.

"She ran to the market." Leigh couldn't help but feel like an outsider around the two of them. She set down the novel she'd brought with her—the one she'd had for four months and never opened back home— and pulled the blanket up to her shoulders. She'd made it to chapter four. "Did you all catch anything?" she asked, trying to be sociable.

Meredith snorted and then fell into laughter, her eyes on Colton, the two of them sharing some sort of insider joke. It made Leigh's skin crawl.

Her sister crossed her arms and shivered dramatically. "It's freezing out here. I've spent enough time outside. Let's go in," she said to Colton.

"I'll be in, in a minute," he replied.

Meredith ran back through the door, shutting Leigh, Colton, and Elvis out on the porch.

"How'd he do?" Colton asked, patting Elvis on the side.

"Fine," she replied, self-consciously tucking her hair behind her ears. She hadn't expected them back so soon.

He pressed his lips together and nodded, his gaze roaming as if he wanted to say more. Then he sat down next to her, his unique scent of spice and cedarwood tickling her senses. She took shallow breaths to avoid it as much as possible, removed her glasses, and set down her novel. Elvis jumped up on the sofa with him and put his head on Colton's leg.

"I've never left him with anyone before," Colton said. "But he seems to really like you."

"He's a sweet boy." She shifted away just slightly, sucking in the clean lake air. "Did you and Meredith have… fun?"

"Yeah, you know how she is. It was all jokes and laughs."

Leigh actually didn't know what he meant at all. Meredith had never been all jokes and laughs with her. Not even once. "Why do you think she's so easygoing with you?" she asked.

"I don't know. I guess it's because I don't ask anything of her."

"We don't ask anything of her," Leigh said.

Colton shrugged. "You'll have to ask *her* then."

They sat there together, the quiet swishing of the lake water filling the silence between them. So much time had passed. They were both so different but it also felt very much the same sitting next to him.

"Colton," she started, feeling as if they'd gotten off on the wrong foot yesterday. "That last summer we had together, when we'd talked about our futures, I didn't mean to laugh…"

"What?"

"It's bothered me my whole adult life."

He batted her comment away. "It's been years… It's fine."

"It might be, but I've held onto the guilt over it. I wasn't laughing at *you*."

"Really. It's okay," he said before clearing his throat, the topic not settling well upon them, only serving to make Leigh's guilt worse because she knew how, at that impressionable age, it would feel to have someone he cared about dismiss him. "We had two very different life paths." He fiddled with something on Elvis's collar. "Looks like things turned out all right for ya." His gaze remained on the dog, unsaid thoughts all over his face.

"You too," she said. "You look happy."

That was when he turned toward her, those dark-brown eyes meeting hers. "Yeah… I'm good."

The door opened and Meredith stuck her head out, which put Elvis on alert. "You coming in?" she asked Colton, ripping through the moment.

"Yep," he said, standing up, clenching his jaw. "I'll see ya later."

Leigh nodded, wishing he'd stay, but not stopping him. She felt as if she needed to get to know him all over again.

"Come on, boy." Colton went into the cabin with Elvis at his heels.

Chapter Eight

"I got us fresh strawberries and blackberries from the Johnsons' farm," Mama said, sinking her hand into the brown-paper bag, "and they had the biggest cucumbers I've ever seen! I got three." She pulled out a jug of milk, a couple of different cheeses, and fresh snap peas before she asked, "Where's Meredith?"

"I don't know," Leigh told her. "I stepped into the shower to get ready for the day, and when I got out, she was gone again."

Mama shook her head, disappointment showing.

"It's like she doesn't even care that you have something to tell us. I feel like she's just here to make an appearance and that's it."

"Let's give her the benefit of the doubt. Maybe she just forgot something on the boat and she's run to Colton's to get it." Mama reached around the container of blackberries to retrieve her phone. "I'll text him to see if she's there."

Leigh put the milk in the fridge and set the cucumbers on the counter. "I called the Greystone company and left a message while you were gone," she said, folding the paper bag and tucking it under the sink where they kept them.

"Oh?" Mama ran the basket of blackberries under the stream of water at the sink.

"I told them I'd heard they were having trouble filling the property on the lake and I thought I could help them."

Mama dumped the blackberries into Nan's strainer to dry, the way Nan always had. "That's great. Maybe something will come of it," she said, pensive, her attention back on her phone. "Colton says he hasn't seen her."

Leigh couldn't help the niggling fear that her sister had just upped and left. It would be just like her to run, chasing something else and leaving them there. "She wouldn't have *gone*, would she?"

Mama's hands stilled and she set down the tomato she was wiping. "Are her things here?"

Leigh and her mother walked into Meredith's room at the back of the cabin. Leigh huffed out a small sigh of relief mixed with frustration when she saw her sister's suitcase. Meredith's strappy sandals were still tucked under the chair in the corner, a pair of cut-offs on the bed, and her bag against the wall.

"Promising," Mama said.

"Yes, but it's selfish of her to just leave without saying anything," she said, as they both returned and headed back to the kitchen. "She doesn't ever think about anybody but herself."

"Maybe she's outside somewhere. Have you checked?"

Her frustration mounting, Leigh went out to the back porch to look. She scanned the tree line, the dock, down by the water, the hammock, the fire pit—all empty. "Meredith?" she called, but all she got in return was the soft whistle of the wind. "She's definitely not here," she said, coming back inside.

Mama met Leigh in the living room.

"How are you ever supposed to tell us this mystery news of yours? Can't you just let me hear it first?"

Mama stared at her as if deciding. "I've been debating whether or not to tell you first," Mama replied, with an uneasy frown. "I kind of think I should, but there's a part of me that wanted to include Meredith in this so she didn't feel like I was choosing sides. She deserves to know when you do, although I think you're going to have a harder time with it."

A cold flash slithered through Leigh at the idea that she'd take whatever it was Nan had so cryptically warned her about harder than her sister, although it wasn't all that surprising, since her sister wasn't the least bit invested in their family.

"If she can't stick around long enough to listen for even a second, she *doesn't* deserve to hear it first."

Mama chewed her bottom lip, clearly deliberating. "We'll give her an hour. If she doesn't come back by then, I'll go ahead and tell you."

Leigh sat on the screened-in porch while her mother bustled around picking up, the fan above them whirring. It was a perfect spring day— the birds chirped in the trees and occasionally a boat would buzz by on the lake. After texting her sister with no response, Leigh had spent the last hour building a quick document for the possible businesses she'd like to reach out to on Greystone's behalf, overpreparing in case she got a phone call. She had descriptions of the businesses, photos of their other locations, and her guesses for how much they would probably pay in rent, based on their other spaces. The ideas flowed like wine in Nan's cabin. She could develop this plan with her eyes closed, and the fact that it was coming so easily to her filled her with a sense of purpose.

The lake was a striking change to the pace she'd been living the last four years, and with everything going on in her life, being there brought her calm. Even without Nan physically there, she had a sense of relief, as if Nan were present in the wind, and on the scent of the pines. She could almost hear her grandmother talking her through it all.

"This is just a bump in the road," she'd say, her gray hair pulled back, her weathered hands on Leigh's knee. "You have everything you need to be successful."

While her studies had prepared her for success, it was her time at the cabin with Nan that had made her who she was. Leigh made herself a promise that, no matter what, she'd come back to the cabin more often. It had been far too long since she'd been there. Maybe she could plan more visits—a few a month. It would be good for her soul to spend time in the place that had built her.

"It's been an hour and a half," Leigh said, looking over at her mom, who'd been sweeping the porch.

Mama leaned the broom against the porch railing. "I know. I'm just trying to give her time, hoping she'll walk through that door."

"I don't understand her," Leigh said, shaking her head as she closed her laptop. "She seems to do things just to get under our skin."

Mama stared at her, and her silence spoke volumes.

"Go ahead and tell me. I doubt Meredith will even care."

"I'm so torn," Mama said. She sat down next to Leigh, wriggling into position to face her. "I want to do this as a family."

"Has Meredith *ever* acted like family?"

Mama looked down at her lap, wringing her hands. "I comb through my life, wondering why she's so different from us... I just can't understand it." Tears welled up in her mother's eyes and Leigh scooted over to comfort her.

"What's going on?" Meredith's voice pierced the moment like a sharp knife as she stepped out onto the porch.

Mama wiped her eyes. "We just wondered where you were," she said, clearing her throat and blinking away her sadness.

Meredith held up a paper cup. "I went to get coffee. I've been dying for a good cappuccino and I had to drive almost into Nashville. Do you know how hard it is to find good coffee in this town?" She plopped down on the sofa, pinning Leigh in the middle.

Leigh turned to her sister, years of irritation scratching at her insides. "You could've told someone," she snapped.

Meredith's wall slid up, her lips a straight line. "I didn't know it would take that long. I thought I'd be back before you were even out of the shower. Mom was gone. There was no one to tell." She set her paper cup on the table and stood back up. "Geez. I'm a grown woman. Can I not step out for a cup of coffee? Mom, did you leave us a note that you were at the market?"

"I told Leigh," their mother replied.

Meredith threw her hands up. "Of course you told Leigh," she spat.

Katherine sat up straight. "You were off fishing with Colton! How could I tell you?"

"You two can sit around pointing fingers at me and being miserable. I miss Nan too—like crazy. But I'm trying to enjoy life the way she did. That's what she would've wanted. You asked me to come down here, but I'm met with misery at every turn." She faced the lake and shook her head. "Just tell me whatever it is and then I'm out of here. You two would rather me leave anyway."

Mama stood. "That's not true."

Meredith seemed to notice Leigh's silence, looking over her shoulder at Leigh and then letting out a frustrated sigh. It wasn't that Leigh wanted her sister to leave. She just wished that they could all enjoy each other, and she didn't think they ever would.

"I don't want to fight," Meredith said, coming down off her rant, her tone softer.

"I don't either," Mama said. "Look, we haven't had a chance to be a family in a long time. Why don't we do something together before we worry about anything else."

As she gazed between her sister and her mother, Leigh thought about Nan's letter: *No matter what, you'll be okay.*

Mama's voice broke into her thoughts. "We need a chance to bond. That's what Nan would've liked to see."

Meredith softened even more at the mention of Nan's wishes, facing Leigh. It was as if she were there, trying to direct them all in silence.

Both Meredith and Leigh stared at each other, neither of them saying a word, the two of them knowing that finding something everyone enjoyed was easier said than done.

"I think you should just say what you need to tell us, Mom," Meredith said.

Mama looked around the ceiling as if it would give her some sort of hidden insight. "I can't tell you yet. The three of us need to be on the same page before I drop this news."

"I don't have *that* long. I'm off to Paris soon," Meredith said, her remark surprising Leigh. She hadn't seen that coming. "Getting us on the same page is gonna take more time than that," Meredith added.

Paris?

Realizing right then that she had no idea who her sister really was, Leigh got up and stood next to Meredith, ignoring her little jab. "How are we supposed to be on the same page when we barely speak? You're my sister and I don't even know what you do for a living or where you live. Or how in the world you've managed to plan a trip to Paris."

Meredith faced her, pursing her lips. "You've never asked about any of it. Neither of you have."

Leigh took a step closer to her. "Well, I'm asking now."

Meredith looked down at the wooden edge of the porch's screen frame, picking at a splinter that was jutting out. Her chest filled with air, and she met Leigh's gaze once more. "I lived in a camper for two years, saving all my money from bartending. I bought a handful of canvases and got to painting, putting them up in different cities, saving my best ones along the way. And I opened a gallery in San Diego. It launched in January."

"That's amazing," Mama said, her face lighting up.

"How's it going?" Leigh asked, completely blown away that her sister would have pulled off something this huge without backing out or changing her plans. "Have you sold any paintings?"

Meredith seemed to stand taller as she answered, evidently taking Leigh's question as if Leigh were skeptical of her success when she'd only asked out of curiosity. "I've sold fifty-two of my paintings since the gallery opened. At $1,000 a painting. My trip to Paris is paid for. It's to do a commissioned painting for the actor David Ferguson. He's decorating his farmhouse outside the city."

Mama gasped. "*The* David Ferguson, the one from all those action movies?"

"Oh my goodness. That's incredible." Leigh suddenly felt terrible for being so flippant about the fact that Meredith had said she'd need to have a little notice to get things tied up before she left for the cabin.

"I'm so proud of you," Mama said, clearly still in awe, blinking as if to internalize what Meredith had said, her eyes glistening with emotion.

But instead of happiness, something flashed across Meredith's face—resentment? "Thank you," her sister said, straight-faced, not basking in their joy.

"You should be happy, Meredith," Leigh pointed out. "We're both so thrilled for you." As she said it, she inwardly cringed, knowing she'd drawn that invisible line with Meredith on one side and Leigh and her mother on the other.

"I don't need your approval to be happy," Meredith said. "I've lived without it this long; I definitely don't need it now."

"I'm not giving you my approval," Leigh said, a bite of pent-up anger in her rebuttal.

Mama beamed through her tears. "This is no reason for a fight," she said, with the same manic happiness she'd had in the days after their father had died. "We should *celebrate*. Let's get a bottle of champagne and have the neighbors over. We can enjoy ourselves without the pressure of having just the three of us."

"It's fine. You don't have to go to all that trouble," Meredith said.

"It's absolutely no trouble. I'm already thinking of people we can invite. We can also call Colton and tell him if you haven't already, see if he can come over, too."

For the first time since she'd stepped onto the porch, Meredith softened at the mention of Colton. "Okay. I'll call him."

Leigh couldn't help the slight envy she felt that Meredith could call up Colton on a whim, yet Leigh had barely even been able to talk to him, and she still had so much to say. She wanted to make sure he knew what a great childhood she'd had because of him. And how she was a better person for having known him. She didn't want him to think for one second that her memories of him were anything less than wonderful. With Meredith there, she wondered if she'd ever get a chance to tell him. But, as Meredith dialed his number on her cell phone, a tiny smile on her lips, Leigh knew it was her sister's moment right now, and she wouldn't let it get the best of her.

"Hey, I'm headed out to find something to paint," Meredith said, with a knock on Leigh's doorway.

Leigh looked up from the last-minute studying she'd been doing on her laptop to prepare for her pitch to Greystone Properties. Her sister had a canvas under her arm and a sack-style bag heavy with art supplies crossing her body, paintbrushes peeking out from the top. "I want to see if I can get a few paintings done before the big party tonight. So, I figured I'd let you know where I was going." She rolled her eyes.

"Thanks." Leigh shifted away from her computer, leaving it behind her on the bed.

"Where are *you* headed?" Meredith asked, noticing Leigh was dressed in her best linen trousers and tank with matching cardigan and flats.

"I have a meeting for work… local company," she said, lying just a little. Greystone had no idea she was coming by, but when she'd gotten no response to her message, she figured it was worth popping in.

"Well, we're both working. I never thought I'd see the day when we were *both* doing the same thing."

Leigh gave her a half-smile. "Can I ask you something that I've been wondering for a long time?"

Meredith waited, her expression expectant.

"Why don't you like to spend time at the cabin? You're always rushing out."

Meredith visibly began to close up, that wall she was so good at raising sliding across her face.

"I'm not judging you," Leigh scrambled. "I don't have any opinion on it at all. I've just always been curious as to why you stay gone so much, and I've never asked."

Meredith blew air through her lips. "Lots of reasons, but mostly because being in new places energizes me. I don't even have a house in San Diego where the gallery is. I'm better off in a hammock in the trees somewhere than trapped inside four walls."

Leigh smiled. "You and I are so different," she noted.

"Yes, we are."

A heavy silence fell between them until Meredith filled it. "Well, I'm headed out. Mama's in plan-mode." She made a face.

"Oh no. Really?"

"I think she's called everyone in town."

"She's just excited." Leigh knew it was more than that. It was Mama's way of remaining on the surface of the water so she didn't go under, because if she did, she might not surface again.

Meredith seemed almost annoyed by Leigh's comment, as if she knew too, and they both paused uneasily. After a moment of what seemed like deliberation, her sister said, "All right. I'm gonna go. See ya." She flew out the bedroom door and left Leigh in her room.

With a sigh, Leigh shut her laptop and got up, staring at her reflection in the mirror above the dresser, still stunned that Meredith's gallery seemed to be a wild success when she'd only taken a few years to plan for it, while Leigh's entire life had led up to the career she was scratching and clawing to keep hold of. It didn't seem fair, but she was happy for her sister. It seemed like Meredith knew exactly who she was while Leigh floundered.

She ran her fingers under her eyes to smooth her makeup—she looked tired. She turned away from her reflection and picked up a framed picture of Nan on the beach, her gray hair blowing in the wind. "Am I on the right path?" she whispered to the smiling face of her grandmother, her chest aching in the silence.

With no answer to her question, she squared her shoulders and walked out of the room.

"You look nice," Mama said from the kitchen table, as she flipped through one of Nan's magazines.

"Thanks. I saw online that Greystone has an office next to the development. I'm going to stop in and see if I can speak to someone. Want to ride over with me on the boat?"

"Oh, I think I'll stay here. I have a few more people to call for Meredith's party tonight and I'd like to run out and get some food for it." Her eyes fell fondly on the magazine in her hands. "But right now, I'm taking it all in. It's nice to just sit in Mom's world for a little while," she said.

Leigh walked over and put a hand on her mother's shoulder. "Nan seemed to make everything okay, you know?"

"I do."

"Remember how she used to string lights outside on the porch and light all the tiki lamps the first night we got here every summer? She had all the candles burning and something cooking in the oven—like a casserole loaded with her homegrown veggies."

"I do," Mama said with a nostalgic smile.

"The whole house smelled of cheese and jasmine from the candles."

"Oh yes," Mama said. "It seems decades ago, not years."

Leigh nodded, lost in the memory. "She'd have some sort of beach music blasting," Leigh continued, indulging in the reminiscences.

"And when we asked her to turn it down, she'd grab our hands and spin us around."

"I used to love to watch her do that with you and Meredith when you two were little girls." Mama's focus fell to the magazine—an old edition of *Southern Style*. "I still can't bear that she's gone," Mama said, her voice breaking.

Without warning, Leigh's eyes pricked with tears.

"It's not the same without her here. It just seems empty."

"I know. I keep waiting for this to feel normal," Leigh said. "But it doesn't. Not at all."

Mama fluttered her hands in the air. "I'm sorry, I didn't mean to bring you down. I know you want to try to get that job…"

"It's okay. I never mind talking about Nan. And even if it doesn't feel normal yet, it's good to be back here. Maybe in time we'll come to terms with it, and the cabin will feel like ours again."

Mama smiled, something indecipherable on her face. But then she cleared it. "Go! Work that magic of yours and win them over at Greystone."

Leigh kissed her mother on the cheek, grabbed her purse, and headed out the door. This could be the start of something great. She had to believe that.

The sun beat down on her as she knocked for the second time on the trailer door outside the development. She could hear a mumble of talking inside, so she'd left some time between knocks in case the project manager was on the phone. There was nothing wrong with taking the initiative, so when no one answered the second time, she took it upon herself to peek in.

"What is it?" an older man barked, slamming his office phone into its cradle. He stared at her, his baseball cap turned around backward, curls of gray hair escaping underneath it, two deep lines between his eyebrows.

"I'm so sorry," she said, unruffled, stepping inside. She never let the attitudes of potential clients get to her. And she'd had some doozies. "I wanted to speak with the project manager of Greystone Properties."

He stared at her as if her presence had ruined his day, the window unit buzzing like an air compressor, spewing an ice-cold draft through the warmth of the little space.

"Is that you?" she pressed, producing her most authentic smile, given the circumstances.

"Who's asking?" he growled, flipping open a binder and jotting down numbers onto a legal pad.

"I left you a message," she said. "I heard you need occupants for your development here. I think I can help with that."

His attention remained on the papers in front of him.

"My name is Leigh Henderson. I'm a commercial property management consultant for a large New York company, and I happen to be here on... vacation. I saw your development and thought I might be just the person to help you out."

"I don't have a budget for that, so you're wasting your time." He shut the binder and spun around in his chair, pulling out a file drawer and thumbing through it.

"I'd do it pro bono," she said.

He turned back around. "Why? What's in it for you?"

"Experience," she replied. "This would be fantastic to add to my résumé."

He shook his head, returning to his files. "You need experience," he mumbled. "All flash and no fire."

She leaned on his desk and addressed the back of his head, the brim of the hat facing her. "There are exactly eight restaurants within a fifteen-mile radius, and of those restaurants there are no—make sure you hear this—*no* pizza restaurants. The number one food in the country is pizza. After a family day on the lake, what will the kids want before they head home? Pizza. Gourmet pizza is what we need occupying the unit at the end of the strip with the circular deck. The outdoor space would make a fantastic outdoor eating area."

He faced her again and folded his hands, a skeptical squint in his eyes.

"Last year, Americans spent over two billion dollars on flip-flops," she continued. "Guess how many summer clothing stores are within a ten-mile drive of Old Hickory Lake."

His squint had faded to a stare.

"I said guess. Do you know?"

He reluctantly shook his head.

"Zero." She leaned in closer, her blonde locks dangling above his faded desk calendar with a coffee ring in the center. "I *know* what you need."

The man didn't flinch. "I wanted to have local businesses and I can't get a single one to commit."

"You're thinking too small with local businesses," she added without a breath. "Plus, the farmer's market has that niche covered. You want a wider range."

"And how are we supposed to get these businesses interested?"

"That's where I come in." She looked him straight in the eye. "We haven't met." She held out her hand. "As I said, my name is Leigh Henderson. And you are?"

"Jimbo Peterson." He didn't shake her hand, the glare returning.

"Jimbo...?" She'd read in one of the articles that the project manager's name was *James* Peterson. Judging by the two-day stubble on his face, he was definitely casual in his business approach, so she safely assumed this was the same man.

"Yeah," he said, his lips now set in a straight line, showing his annoyance at her mere presence. "Look, I don't know who you are or what you really want, but we're hanging by a thread here. I don't have time to mess around. I'm a busy man."

"I understand," she said. "So, Jimbo, let me leave you with my card." She had one ready to go in the pocket of her linen trousers, pulling it out and sliding it across the dirty calendar. "Whenever you're ready, I'd be more than happy to talk about the client list I've already curated for you."

He stared at her, fiddling with it.

She almost had him. She could see it in his eyes.

"Maybe we could get coffee sometime. Oh wait, we can't yet. Not until you let me get the coffee roasters into your development... But that's your call." With a feeling of satisfaction, she turned on her heel and headed out the door.

Chapter Nine

Leigh pulled to a stop outside the cabin, behind Colton's Ford. She grabbed the champagne bottles she'd bought at the market on the way home from seeing Jimbo—another attempt at smoothing things over with Meredith—and got out. Elvis sauntered up to her. "Hey, boy," she said, rubbing the top of his head. "Where's your daddy?"

"Right here," Colton answered from the house, materializing under the porch in the open front door.

When she reached him, he leaned against the frame with his hand in the pocket of his jeans. He was barefoot, wearing a T-shirt that was tattered in all the right places, giving her stomach a flip. She focused on the open doorway to make the feeling stop.

"Your mama called to see if I could help her get the food ready for tonight. She's invited half the town."

"Really?"

Colton took the bottles of champagne from her, bringing them into the house, Elvis by his side. When Leigh entered, she was met with the scent of jasmine, and she had to catch her breath. From the kitchen doorway leading to the back of the house, she could see the twinkle of the string lights outside, a nostalgic buzz swimming through her.

"Where's Meredith?" she asked.

"I think your mom said she's still out painting or something." He pulled the champagne bottles from their bags and slid them into the fridge.

"She'd better come," Leigh said under her breath. "It's *her* party."

"She will," he said, his dark eyes on Leigh. "You never trust her."

Leigh wasn't going to argue with Colton, but he hadn't spent his life listening to Meredith's excuses. "She always shows up for you," she said instead.

He fixed his gaze on her. "It's because I believe that she will, and she knows that."

Leigh considered his point, the idea having not come to her before this. Was it because Leigh never really had faith in whether Meredith would come through for her? Perhaps Meredith could sense it...

"Can I ask you something?" He stepped into her personal space, looking down at her.

The seriousness of his expression, and the intimacy of just the two of them, made it difficult for Leigh to breathe.

She took a step back. "Sure."

"What happened to you to make you so edgy?"

His question took her off guard. "I'm no different from the person I was."

Colton shook his head. "You were always passionate, but never edgy. I could tell the minute you walked into Leon's. Your shoulders are up near your ears somewhere." He put his large hands softly on her upper arms and the tension instantly melted, her shoulders sliding downward. She hadn't even realized they were tense until that moment.

"I was just busy today, that's all." She wasn't sure why she wouldn't admit to Colton what she was going through, but she didn't want him to know. Maybe it was because if she tried to explain herself, she knew she couldn't. She didn't have a clue why she'd lost her job. Or why she hadn't been strong enough to come back to the cabin over the years. Or, worse, why she hadn't come back to see *him*. She'd wanted to be in a better place in her life than she was right now before she ran into Colton again—now definitely wasn't the best time.

"Oh! How'd it go?" Mama asked, coming into the kitchen with a rag and a spray bottle.

Elvis barked at her—one loud woof—his suspicious eyes following Mama as she walked through the kitchen.

Leigh quickly shook her head from behind Colton to quiet her mother's questions. "I got us three bottles of champagne," she said, throwing out any words she could think of to change the subject. She wanted to get this job before she mentioned it to Colton. In some strange way, she was hoping to prove that leaving him had been for the best, so she wanted to get her career back on track before talking about it.

"Great," her mother replied, questions on her face as her gaze darted between the two of them. "We've got about an hour before people start arriving. I've invited everyone we know down this street, Rutledge Way, and Trout Lane." She threw the rag and bottle under the kitchen sink and flicked on the water. "Colton, in about forty minutes, could you preheat the grill for the burgers and hot dogs for us?"

"Yep," he replied, sending a curious look over to Leigh as if he were already in her head.

"Leigh, the salad fixin's are in the fridge. Why don't you throw a big bowl together for us? And do you mind arranging those cookies onto a tray?" Mama fluttered back out of the kitchen, leaving Leigh and Colton together once more.

"Help me peel cucumbers?" she asked, pulling them out of the fridge, along with tomatoes, a bag of lettuce, and a block of cheddar.

"Of course."

She got one of Nan's handmade serving bowls down from the cabinet—a swirl of pink, yellow, and teal meandering round the rim of the cream-colored pottery. She dumped the lettuce into it.

Colton washed his hands at the sink while Elvis flopped down in the corner of the kitchen with a snort. While Leigh ran her own hands under the stream at the faucet and lathered, Colton reached around her to get a paper towel, and she had to hold her breath to keep from inhaling the woodsy fragrance of his aftershave.

"Your mama's been busy," he said, wiping his hands.

"Yes, she has." Leigh grabbed the Swiss peeler and a knife from the drawer and set them on the cutting board. "She's really going all out for Meredith. I've never seen her quite like this before..." she said, picking up a cucumber and peeling it with ease, something she'd done for Nan many times over the years.

Colton nodded, the seriousness in his eyes giving away his ability to sense her worry about Mama. "It's Meredith's time, you know?" he said, clearly sticking to a lighter subject.

"Yeah." She handed over the peeled cucumber.

He took the knife and began slicing, dropping the slices onto the mound of lettuce in Nan's bowl.

"How about you? What are you doing now?" he asked, that earlier curiosity she'd seen in his eyes returning with a vengeance.

"I'm a property management consultant in New York." She hoped he couldn't hear the thinness of her words—the present tense that she knew good and well she'd used. "How about you?" She handed him another cucumber.

He paused just enough to make her question whether he feared that she'd judge him on his line of career. If he only knew there'd been many times when she'd wondered if she'd have liked a slower pace.

"After high school, I worked on Jax Wrigley's cotton farm."

Biggest cotton farm north of Rutherford County. She could still hear the raspy voice of old man Jax, boasting about his fields in town.

"When the old man passed, he left it to me. I've been running it ever since."

"Oh wow… just you?" She didn't want to pry, but she did wonder if he'd met anyone over the years or if he'd only dated casually like she had.

"Yep. That's how I like it," he replied, but his words didn't hold their truth in his eyes.

"You *like* being alone?" she challenged, unsure of why she wanted him to be honest with her when she wasn't being entirely forthright with him.

"It's easier. Not so… complicated." He gave her an appraising once-over, making her feel self-conscious. "Besides, I'm not entirely alone. I've got Elvis."

The dog perked up. Colton grabbed a sugar cookie from the cookie sheet beside him and tossed it through the air, Elvis catching it with skill. The dog smacked his chops, his tail wagging furiously.

"He's a great dog." When she said it, she could almost swear by the way Elvis's eyes met hers that he understood. He moseyed over and nudged her leg. Leigh bent down and gave him a little cuddle.

"He likes you," Colton said. "It's amazing. He hasn't warmed to anyone but me. That's how I knew he was the right dog when I got him at the shelter."

She kept her attention on him and picked up the knife he'd been using to begin chopping tomatoes, dumping them into the salad.

"When we walked along the cages, they said not to bother with the dog at the end. 'He's not friendly to anyone,' they'd said. But he was looking straight at me and I couldn't take my eyes off him. I asked if they'd open the cage and when they did, he came right to me and nuzzled my leg."

She looked down at the dog and smiled. Elvis wagged his tail. "It's like he knew the kind of person you were. He could sense your kindness."

"But your mama's kind. Why can't he sense that?"

She shook her head. "I don't know. Maybe he had some sort of sixth sense that you were his person."

The corner of Colton's mouth turned upward and he reached down to pat Elvis's head. "Maybe." Then Colton's dark eyes found hers. "So, what does he think of *you* then?"

Meredith burst through the door, her canvas hanging from her fingers, sending Elvis into a barking frenzy. "Hey," she said to Leigh and Colton, reaching down to pet the dog. Elvis darted away, barking louder, and Colton shushed him.

Meredith leaned her latest painting against the wall.

"This is incredible," Leigh said, squatting to get a better look.

Meredith had captured the yellow and orange in the sunrise, the sparkles on the lake, and the way the light slanted down through the pines, a small rope swing in the distance. Her technique was soft and gentle, the lines blurred, giving it a uniquely southern farmhouse feel.

"Thanks." Meredith bounced over to Colton and gave him a playful jab in the arm. "Hey there!" she said just to him, as if she'd needed to greet him personally. "Making salad?" She plucked a cucumber slice from the bowl and popped it into her mouth.

Colton grinned at her, and Leigh's stomach tightened at their easy chumminess.

"What in the world?" The words trailed behind her sister as she was suddenly distracted by Mama's decorating outside. As quickly as she came in, she was gone again.

"That painting is... wow." Colton carefully picked it up and held it in front of him. "She's so talented."

"Yes." Leigh peered at it, and for the first time in her life she felt inferiority creep in. The mere idea caused her cheeks to flame with heat. What was going on?

Elvis jumped up and walked over to her, nudging her hand as if he could tell. She bent down and rubbed his neck. Perhaps it was being back at the cabin, or everything else going on, but she felt oddly emotional, as if she could have a breakdown any minute. That was all she needed—to take away from Meredith's moment with a mental collapse. Meredith would never let her hear the end of it.

Colton set the painting against the wall where it had been, and reached over to give Elvis a pat, his chest grazing Leigh's arm and causing her pulse to quicken.

"You and Meredith get along so well," she noted, wondering how he could turn on her sister's warmth the way he did.

He rolled his eyes. "You're not going to start that again, are you?"

"Start what?"

"The insinuation that something's going on between me and Meredith. Come on, Leigh."

"Why haven't you ever thought about it?"

"Her lack of a schedule would make me crazy, she has a terrible temper, and I have nothing in common with her. But she's fun to be around."

Leigh nodded. She wanted to ask what he'd ever seen in *her*, but she stayed quiet. No sense in digging up old emotions. It would only muddle everything. She wasn't staying and he certainly wasn't going anywhere if he had Jax Wrigley's farm to run.

"Are the cookies and salad ready?" Mama asked, peeking her head into the kitchen.

Leigh took in a steadying breath. "Almost." She pulled the platter over.

Once they were alone, Colton turned to her. "It's good to see you," he said.

She'd been waiting for that since the moment she'd run into him at Leon's and just that one sentence lifted her mood. She'd missed him.

"Same," she returned, trying not to let her incredible fondness for him show. Instead, she arranged the cookies in a layered fan round the edges of the plate, working her way to the middle. "It's good to be back."

"Is it?" A soft breath moved through the slack in his lips, as if he had a hundred more things to tell her, but he'd stopped there.

She fought the urge to wrap her arms around him and bury her face in his chest; she needed to break the spell immediately before she burst into tears, everything she'd gone through spilling out of her, right there in the kitchen.

"You know I love this cabin," she replied, knowing he'd expected more in her response. She finished the cookies, picked up the plate, and headed outside without looking his way.

Colton grabbed the bowl of salad and followed her out, with Elvis following along.

The soft spring breeze and the familiar swishing of the lake water relaxed her the minute she stepped outside onto the porch. Coupled with the happy buzz of the few people who had arrived already, her spirits were instantly higher. Thomas and Rosemary Peabody who ran the local market were there. Thomas used to keep a cooler of popsicles for all the kids who were at the market with their parents. Leigh's favorite flavor was cherry, and he'd save one of them just for her.

Meredith was admiring Rosemary's artsy earrings as if they'd spent no time away from each other at all. But that was how people were here: years or days, they still treated each other as if they were family. Rosemary had the first stall at the outdoor market, her tables covered in handmade jewelry and knickknacks. She used to share her booth with Nan whenever she had pottery to sell, and Mama owned a couple of her rings.

Their neighbor, Luella Wilson, who had to be pushing ninety, had come over and was working to sit down on one of the chairs; a new addition, an antique plate piled with scones covered in plastic wrap, sat amidst Mama's spread on the table. Luella lived in a little yellow cottage through the trees, and before she'd got so feeble, she would take morning walks every day, often dropping by with her homemade scones. Leigh hadn't realized how much she'd missed that until now.

Leigh set the platter of cookies onto the table next to Luella's scones. Colton followed suit with the salad bowl before being pulled over to the grill by Mama.

"Hey, Leigh," Meredith called up to her. "Mom says there's champagne in the kitchen. Let's crack it open!"

"All right," she returned, going back inside to put the champagne on ice.

Leigh opened one of the kitchen cabinets and started pulling down the glass flutes, setting them onto the counter to take them out to the table on the porch. Elvis had followed her in, so she filled a bowl of water and set it down for him.

"You sure are sweet, you know that?" she said, stroking his back as he lapped it up. Elvis had been a happy surprise, some sort of divine intervention to provide the serenity that Nan had taken with her. "You have a good daddy too, but I'll bet you know that already."

Colton stepped into the room, the corners of his mouth twitching upward before something occurred to him to wipe his fondness away. "I need to get the pack of hot dogs for the grill." He peered down at Elvis, subtly shaking his head. He retrieved the pack from the refrigerator.

As he shut the door, Meredith came rushing back in.

"Were you ever going to bring us the champagne?" she teased, getting a bottle out of the fridge. She unwrapped the cork and handed it to Colton. "Can you get this?"

Colton blinked as if switching mental gears and untwisted the metal casing from the bottle, working the cork. With a *Pop!* it came loose in his large hand, releasing the carbon dioxide from the inside of the bottle in a white puff.

"Thank you," Meredith said, taking the bottle from him and snatching a glass off the counter. She took hold of his arm. "Come! Make us food. I'm staaaarrving." Whatever he'd been thinking about was now gone as he headed out the door with Meredith.

With a sigh, Leigh gathered up the glasses and took them to the table Mama had set up on the back porch. As she lined them along the center, Colton was down at the grill, laughing at something Meredith had said. Her sister was the picture of happiness in her gauzy sundress with the denim jacket on top, her long curls trailing down her back. Meredith reached down to pet Elvis and he darted away, making Leigh smile.

Suddenly, Leigh's phone buzzed in her pocket, alerting her to a call. The caller unknown, she almost dismissed it, but the local area code prompted her to answer. "Hello?"

"Ms. Henderson?"

"Yes?" She set the last glass in its place and then went back into the kitchen, rooting around in Nan's cabinets for the silver champagne bucket she'd used at Christmastime.

"This is Jimbo Peterson of Greystone Properties."

"Oh, hello." She perked up, pausing at an open cabinet.

"I'm not agreeing to anything," he said, "but I'll hear you out. Meet me down at the building site at four o'clock?"

She looked at her watch. That was in an hour. "Is there any way we could meet tomorrow?"

An audible sigh hit her ear. "I can't. I'll be out of town. I leave tomorrow and come back Thursday morning. It's four or forget it."

This was Meredith's celebration—and while Mama had literally thrown it upon them, Leigh needed to be there. They'd probably notice if she went missing for an hour or two… But with Jimbo out of pocket, who knew if he'd come back to her until well after she'd gone home. She needed to get the ball rolling and start setting up meetings if she wanted to make this happen before it began to significantly impact any interviews she could get in New York.

She chewed on the inside of her lip, deliberating, her gaze on her sister. Meredith had hardly looked for her all night long. The only time she'd called on her was for the champagne. And Mama was too busy trying to hide from her real feelings to want to talk to Leigh. She'd already pulled up a chair next to Luella and had settled in, legs crossed, arms resting on the sides of the chair, laughing politely at something the woman was saying. Maybe Leigh actually could slip out without anyone spotting and then slide right back into the party…

"Meet you there," she said, before ending the call and joining the party to be sure she was seen for the next hour.

"Oh, my stars!" Colton's mother Ruby said as she threw her arms around Mama, right after giving Leigh a big squeeze. "It's been too long!" She reached over and held Leigh's hands out. "You look fantastic! But I always knew you'd grow up to be a stunner." She leaned in and gave her a kiss on the cheek. Ruby adjusted her cotton button-down and fiddled with the rolls on her sleeves, her salt-and-pepper hair tucked behind her ears to show off her matching denim button earrings. She'd clearly dressed up for the day.

Colton's father Paul walked out into the yard. He put his hands on his lower back to stretch and then straightened, his tall frame towering over all of them. Then he produced the same warm smile that he'd offered them when they were all kids. "Good to see y'all," he said with a nod.

"And Meredith!" Ruby continued. "You don't look a day over twenty! You and Leigh are just positively gorgeous young ladies." She threw a hand to her chest adoringly before fluttering off to say hello to the others.

"This is a delightful party," Rose Thompson, their neighbor and the town veterinarian said, standing next to Ruby after coming up to say hello. Her silver bracelets that matched the shine in her gray hair jingled against her wrist as she held up her plate of fruit salad and a cheeseburger. "And the food is delicious, although we know how Colton likes to cook." She broke into a large grin.

"Colton likes to cook?" Leigh asked, the comment distracting her from her attempts to leave the group, her mind entirely now on Colton. How much he'd changed from the young boy who lived on chocolate Moon Pies and Dr. Pepper from Leon's.

"Oh, yes. You didn't know? His dinner parties are incredible."

Leigh had to keep her mouth from hanging open. "Dinner parties?" She waited for the punchline that never came. As she peered across the yard at Colton leaning over the grill, a bottle of beer in one hand, a pair of tongs in the other, that old T-shirt falling just right on his hips, she couldn't imagine him having any sort of formal dinner party.

"Everyone, get your glass," Mama called out to the group of people who'd assembled on the lawn and the screened-in porch. "Let's do a toast to Meredith."

The crowd buzzed around, gathering up their glasses and happily turning their attention to the woman of the day.

Leigh sneaked a peek at her watch. 3:45. She sucked in a breath. She needed to be pulling out of the driveway right now if she wanted to get to the main road, through town, and over the bridge to the other side of the lake by four o'clock. She raised her glass, backing away, but Colton noticed and came over to her.

"I have to go," she whispered. "Distract Meredith until I get back."

His brows pulled together, a look of interest blanketing his face. "Why? Do you have some sort of surprise for her or something?"

"No," she replied, "it's something for work. I couldn't get out of it."

His grin faded, his disappointment showing. "Aren't you on vacation?"

"Sort of. But sort of not." She took another step back, but he followed.

"What in the world could you have to do at the lake? You know there's no internet out here. If you're trying to get a connection somewhere, you're better off attempting to send something from the cabin."

She looked at her watch again: 3:49. "I have to go," she said, her tone apologetic. "Try to keep her from knowing that I'm gone."

His jaw clenched as she tried to leave once more.

The crowed toasted, cheering Meredith.

"Stay," he urged, reaching for her arm.

"I don't have time to discuss it. I won't be gone long, I promise. You'll never miss me."

Colton put up his hands with a frustrated frown. She'd have to try to offer an explanation later. She ran inside, grabbed her laptop, and headed for Greystone Properties, firing off a voice text to Jimbo that she was on her way.

Chapter Ten

On the way to the development, Leigh went over the facts she could remember in her head; not having any time to rehearse for the presentation, the rest she'd have to pull up on her laptop. When she arrived, Jimbo was waiting for her out front.

"This had better be good. You're my last shot," he said, as she got out of the car with her laptop tucked under her arm. "I just got the final note from the bank. I've got about six months to get the first rent payments or I'm closing it all down and putting it up for sale."

"Six months?" she asked, but reined herself in. "Fine. We'll get it done."

They walked over the sandy mound of dirt that hadn't been graded yet and stepped up onto the dock that ran along the length of the property. Jimbo slid the key into the lock on one of the storefronts, the smell of new paint and freshly cut wood hitting her along with the cool of the air conditioning. He put on the lights.

"This is nice," she said, stepping onto the shiny white tile floor and taking in the sleek counter and the drop-lights above it. "This space would be great for Green Hat Coffee Roasters." She set her laptop on the counter and opened it, pulling up their webpage on her hotspot. "It's a coffee company that not only styles each of its shops around local history, but it also donates proceeds to providing food and water to the underprivileged across the world. Coffee and charity—a great combo."

She clicked open the document she'd created, showing him photos of the other locations that the coffee shop occupied. "It's doubled its revenue within the last year, and my bet is the CEO will be looking to acquire more real estate." She pulled up the slide with the financials she could find online.

A flicker of interest showed in Jimbo's eyes.

"Also on the list is Top Mountain Supply Co., an outdoor clothing company, specializing in boating and outdoor living, based in Florida. They've just opened a second store in Tampa and are now looking to expand." She opened the next document. "At the end of the dock, I'd like to see Rocket Pizza, a new all-organic chain just getting a foothold and looking to open fifteen more stores across the South." She brought up an article about how the company was looking for rural areas in Tennessee, Virginia, and the Carolinas. "And at the other end of the dock, I propose that we get in touch with Samantha Perkins of The Attic Light, a rapidly growing independent bookshop that has locations in three other Tennessee towns." She showed him.

"And your work would be no charge to me?" he clarified once more.

"None whatsoever."

"How can I say no then?"

She shut her laptop, feeling on top of the world. "Exactly."

"As I said, I've got six months, so you've got four." He opened the door and walked out.

"Yes sir," she called after him, giddy with the thrill of doing what she loved most. Now she just had to make it happen.

Elvis ran over to Leigh when she walked around back after dropping off her things inside. The party was still going. Someone had turned music on, and the fire pit was roaring. As she walked down the hill toward the water, she spotted Meredith in her swimsuit, floating on an inner tube in the water with a beer dangling from her fingers, somehow not completely freezing, while everyone else mingled in the yard.

"How was work?" Colton said in a slightly clipped tone, coming up behind her.

She turned around. "Good."

"Did you get whatever it was done?"

"I got it started," she said, squashing the fizzle of excitement she had at seeing him. "Did Meredith know I was gone?"

"Nah," he said. "But that's not the point, is it?" He walked over to the hammock and fell into it, kicking back, putting his bottle of beer up to his lips and taking a swig.

Leigh followed him, and he rolled his eyes at her, clearly irritated.

"Don't judge me," she said, feeling defensive. He had no idea what she was going through and how low she felt right now. "You don't even know me anymore," she said. It was a low blow but his dismissiveness of her situation had flustered her.

"Clearly not." He took another drag of his bottle.

"What I mean is, I'm not the girl who left you here that summer."

He sat up, his eyes flashing. He tossed his empty bottle into the trashcan that only came out for parties, causing Elvis's ears to go up. With a sigh, the dog lay back down in the shade of the tree. "You didn't *leave* anyone here. I stayed of my own accord. Not all of us want the life you lead."

"How do you even know? You don't have a clue what life I lead."

"I can take one look at you in that fancy outfit and guess," he said, getting back up off the hammock.

She squared her shoulders and looked up at him. "What do you mean by that?"

"I mean that you're so buttoned up, it's pretty obvious that you need to live a little."

She ran her hands down her linen trousers. "Just because I care about my appearance doesn't mean that I don't... *live*. I had to work today!" she said, her voice rising, aggravated. She looked around to be sure no one else had heard that and, to her relief, everyone was still chatting away happily.

"I need another beer." Colton marched down to the ice bin by the water, Elvis following, and grabbed a sweating bottle, using the keychain in his pocket to pop the top. He tipped it back, draining a third of it, and then walked down the pier, looking out at the water as it ebbed and flowed.

Meredith waved to him from her float before spinning in the water, the tide pulling her toward shore. Leigh followed him down. She didn't know what she wanted to say to him, but she wasn't going to let him off easy.

"Get in!" Meredith called to Colton, paddling back out with her hands. "Really, because I want your beer," she teased, wriggling her empty bottle in the air. "None left! And the water is glorious tonight!"

"You'll have to come out and get it," he called back. "I'm in my jeans."

"Come on," Meredith whined. "Who cares?"

"Yeah, *live a little*," Leigh chided.

Slowly, Colton set his beer down by his feet on the dock and turned to Leigh, defiant. "You're one to talk," he said.

She peered up the hill at the other partygoers but no one seemed to notice them down there. "What's wrong? Scared?" she pressed, enjoying this new leverage she'd found.

"Definitely not." He crossed his arms.

Meredith had gone quiet, staring at the two of them, but Leigh ignored the audience of one. She was too busy making a point.

"Then what's stopping you?"

He looked out over the water again, nodding as if he'd decided something. Then, he turned to her. "Nothing," he said, suddenly scooping her up.

The next thing she knew, they'd left the dock and she was sailing toward the lake in her cardigan and linen trousers, her two-hundred-dollar wedge slides already off her feet, dropping into the lake underneath her. With a splash, she and Colton plunged beneath the frigid surface, taking her breath away, the gasps and buzz of the crowd from above muffled under the water.

Elvis barked from the dock.

"What in the world, Colton?" she sputtered through trembling lips upon emerging, pushing her soaking hair off her face as her sister laughed so hard she almost lost balance and fell off her float. Leigh paddled over to her shoes, lifting them from the water—ruined—while Elvis continued to bark.

"It was your idea," he said, swimming over to her with a mischievous grin on his face. "You suggested we live a little."

"Not at the expense of my Stuart Weitzmans!" She tossed the shoes back into the water right in front of him, splashing him in the face, making him laugh when she'd been trying to get him back.

"They're just shoes," he said.

"They're really expensive shoes." She pouted, stripping off her water-heavy cardigan and swimming until her feet touched the soft floor of the lake.

"That's why you don't buy expensive shoes," Meredith chimed in, giggling.

"Her priorities are a little bit different from ours," Colton said to Meredith, setting Leigh's waterlogged wedges onto the dock.

They were just teasing her the way they always had, but right now, while she swam in the lake in her ruined linen suit with the entire party looking on, she felt the swell of frustration in her throat and the prick of tears in her eyes. Leaving the two of them, she swam in until she reached the shore, lumping her soaking cardigan in a chair, and walked up through the gawking partygoers to the porch, finally letting herself inside where she stood, dripping, as she broke down into tears.

Pulling a towel from the hall closet, she went into the bathroom and stripped off her wet clothes, turning on the hot shower, her skin like ice, wondering why she'd let them affect her like they had. When she was younger, she'd have dunked him and let him chase her around the lake, but now, it wasn't funny. Not at all. She stepped into the stream of water and let the warmth soak down to her bones, the tears falling silently as she washed herself clean.

There was a knock at the door and then Mama's voice. "Honey, are you okay?"

"Yes," she answered, a catch of sadness in her voice.

"I think Colton was only kidding. But I know you're probably sensitive right now…"

"I'll be fine, Mama, thanks."

As she ran the soap over her face and down her neck, she considered the fact that the reason she was so upset was because deep down, she thought Colton might be right about her.

With the party still going on outside, Leigh sat in her bedroom, still trying to muster the energy to get back out there. She'd pinned her hair back to get it off her face, and she'd also put on a little powder and lip-gloss before slipping on one of her sundresses and wrapping another sweater over her shoulders. She was completely ready to go back out to the party, but she just couldn't. She'd talked it up, reminding herself that this was for Meredith. Her sister had done something amazing and it was worth celebrating. She promised to pour herself another glass of champagne, laugh it all off. But every time she went to stand up, the tears would come.

She went into the living room and pulled out the letter from Nan, her gaze running along the line: *No matter what, you'll be okay.* She needed to hear that.

The back door opened and she shoved the letter into the desk drawer.

"Hey," Colton said from the doorway.

She turned around. "Hi." He'd changed his T-shirt to a faded-green one with some brand name she didn't recognize on the front, the hem of it darker from brushing up against his wet jeans. "New shirt?"

"Had it in the truck." He walked into the room, the yellow slant of evening sunlight sliding in through the window behind him. "You coming back out?"

"I was trying to," she said, taking in a steadying breath.

"If you're worried about having to see people, mostly everyone's gone now or leaving, and your mom convinced Meredith to go with her to take Thomas and Rosemary home by boat, so it's really just me and Elvis." He held the door open. "Wanna come out?"

She followed him through the porch to the patio below, under the lights. They went over to the hammock, and he sat down perpendicular to it, steadying the swing with his feet firmly planted on the ground and patted the ropey space beside him. Leigh sunk into it and he released his hold, the two of them swinging back and forth. Elvis settled by the tree where he'd been earlier.

"Sorry if I upset you today," he said. "I was just messing around. I didn't mean to make you cry."

She hadn't cried in front of anyone. She'd been in the cabin alone when she'd fallen apart. "How did you know I was crying?"

The fondness that she used to see in his eyes rushed back in.

"Your chin does that little twitch just before you lose it. I saw it when you were on your way inside."

She swallowed, her heart thumping. "It's fine. I'm just sensitive right now."

"Wanna tell me why?"

She'd never seen him this serious.

"Just work, and being back at the cabin without Nan. And Mama has something she needs to tell us that she won't." She turned her head to look at him, those dark eyes on her, his golden strands of hair falling across his forehead, and for an instant it felt as if they were seventeen again.

Without warning, a butterfly flew in, settling on the edge of the hammock, flapping its yellow wings. "Oh, look at that," she said, pointing to it. "I wonder what kind that is."

Colton shrugged, his attention moving over to it.

"You know, I saw a butterfly on the way here too."

He turned back toward her, disturbing the insect. The yellow butterfly fluttered off.

"It was right before I stopped into Leon's to get directions."

He grinned at her.

"What?"

"Maybe it's your nan."

She rolled onto her side, jiggling the hammock, supporting her head with her arm. "That's a wonderful thought. You know, she used to draw butterflies in this leather journal of hers, but I haven't seen it. I wonder where it is…" She rearranged herself, attempting to climb out of the hammock. "We should try to find it."

"Right now?"

"Yes." She grabbed his wrist and pulled, causing him to rise.

When Colton stood up, Elvis jumped to his feet, the three of them going back inside the cabin.

"Maybe she has a message for me," Leigh said, rooting through the other drawers that lined the side of the desk. They held a few old paper phone books, some stationery, and a couple knickknacks that looked as though Nan may have stashed them in there with no other place to put them.

She lifted up a few file folders and then shut the drawer she was searching, moving on to Nan's magazine rack that was kept on the floor by the sofa. She thumbed through the magazines, but there was nothing there.

"What does it look like?" Colton asked, scanning the bookshelf.

"It's thin, about the size of a record album, and it's brown with a leather tie." She opened the hall closet and lifted the folded sheets and towels, not seeing it. "Maybe it's in her art room."

They walked down the hallway together, and she stopped at the door of Nan's workshop. She hadn't allowed herself to go in since she'd gotten there. That room had been entirely Nan's. Meredith would stop in to paint with their grandmother every now and again, but Leigh had stayed away from this room most of the time, never feeling like she fit in it.

"When I paint, my soul takes over my body and shows me what it's capable of," Nan had said once when Leigh had been about fifteen. "Sometimes I'm not even conscious of what I'm doing until I step back and take a look at it when I'm done. It surprises me every time."

This room was her soul's space, the place where her nan would be if by some miracle she could be tied to the cabin. One would have thought that Leigh would have gone running for that room first without thinking, but it had been the exact opposite. She'd felt unworthy to enter, unable to match the grandeur of Nan's soul without her physical body to even them out.

Tentatively, Leigh grabbed hold of the doorknob and twisted, the hinges creaking as she pushed it open. She stood in the doorway, with Colton behind her.

Nan's canvases were still on their easels. One of them had an unfinished landscape painting of mountains, the other two blank as if waiting to feel the soft caress of her grandmother's brushstrokes. Nan's paintbrushes still sat in an empty cup with a line from the murky water circling the inside, her shriveled aluminum tubes of paint askew on the table next to the painting. Everything was just as she'd left it the day she'd called and told Leigh's mother that she thought she should go to the hospital to get her cough checked. The room was waiting as if she might be back to pick up where she'd left off.

That was the thing with life: it never seemed finished when people left it. They just disappeared, leaving their lives where they'd been. She'd probably had big plans for that mountain painting—perhaps it would hang in someone's home or overlook an office full of productivity. That painting had no idea it had no future, that its destiny was to sit, incomplete.

"I know where Meredith gets her talent for landscapes," Colton said, stepping up beside Leigh and walking into the room to stand in front of the painting.

With shallow breaths, Leigh followed. The river snaking around the mountains seemed almost fluid, like she could dip her finger in it.

"Yes," she said, finally responding to Colton's comment, her thoughts heavy.

"They weren't that close—Meredith and your nan—were they?"

"No," she replied, "they had tons in common, but Meredith was hardly ever here. She never spent time in the cabin with Nan."

"She's a traveler," he said. "It's just who she is."

"You're making excuses for her," Leigh said. "At the end of the day, she wasn't here for any of us and we felt it."

"You're unbelievable." Meredith's voice came from the doorway, surprising Leigh.

She turned around to face her sister. "How so?"

"Poor you, feeling left out. Well, I felt left out my whole life."

"I should let you all have a minute," Colton said, taking a step to leave.

"No." Meredith stopped him, blocking the door. "We don't need a minute because I'm getting out of here."

"Typical," Leigh said under her breath. Leave it to Meredith to make this conversation a whole dramatic thing when really it should be solved in a calm manner, together. That had been the problem all their lives. Communication was nonexistent. Before Leigh could stop her, Meredith was already down the hall, the smack of the screen door telling them she'd left the cabin.

"What in the world is going on?" Mama said, pacing down the hallway toward Leigh and Colton. She stopped halfway there, clearly not wanting to go any further. Meredith's issues were enough to deal with, without having to face Nan's studio. "Meredith and I just had a lovely boat ride, but we're not home two seconds and she's storming out. What did you say to her, Leigh?"

"Nothing she doesn't already know, but she refuses to act like an adult about anything."

Mama rolled her head on her shoulders, blowing a puff of breath through her lips, that edge to her beginning to show like a crack in a porcelain cup; one wrong move would shatter it. "Meredith is right: we won't be on the same page. I'm going to have to tell you both the news whether we all like it or not. When Meredith has cooled off, we need to all sit down together and talk."

It hadn't escaped Leigh that Mama had agreed with Meredith. What was happening?

"I'm going to the back porch to clear my head," Mama said.

"I didn't mean to ruin anything," Leigh said, "but truthfully, Meredith is prickly about everything when this could've all been avoided."

"It's just never easy," Mama said in surrender. "Let me have some time, okay? I've got a lot on my mind."

"Okay." Leigh let her mother go, wishing she could turn back time a few minutes and take her comment back. Their problems wouldn't change, but the night would've ended very differently.

Chapter Eleven

"The butterfly book isn't here anywhere," Leigh said to Colton, who'd reluctantly stayed after their little blowup when she'd asked him to. Her hands trembling with anxiety and frustration, she closed the bottom drawer of Nan's art stand in her studio.

When Meredith had stormed out and Mama had retreated to the porch to cool off, Leigh resumed looking for the book, and she and Colton had turned the house upside down. It was as if it had vanished, just like Nan. She needed something to console her in all this, but it seemed like even that was a struggle.

"Wanna get outta here?" Colton suddenly asked, as if reading her distress.

She righted herself and faced him. "And go where?"

"My house. I need to change my soaking jeans, but it might also be nice to get away for a second."

Elvis, who'd curled up on a wadded tarp in the corner of the room, stood up and walked over to Colton, whining as if he'd understood.

"What if Meredith comes back?" Leigh asked.

"We won't be gone long. But if she does come back soon, she certainly won't be in any mood to talk with you and your mom—you know how she is. She'll need at least twenty-four hours to come around."

"You know her better than I do," Leigh said, the whole idea baffling. She'd lived with her sister her whole childhood and barely knew her. They were like two ships passing in the night. "All right," she relented. Maybe shifting her attention to something outside the family would recharge her.

Colton nodded toward the hallway. "Go on," he told the dog. "Lead the way and we'll head home."

Elvis's tail wagged furiously and he started walking while spinning in circles of excitement, directing them to the kitchen. Colton tossed Leigh the keys. "Can you let Elvis into the truck? I'll go out to the porch to tell your mama we're leaving."

"Okay. Tell her to text me if she needs me." She patted her leg. "Come on, Elvis. Your daddy wants us to get into the truck."

Leigh and the dog went outside, Elvis running around by her feet as she opened the heavy door to the old Ford. Elvis jumped in, sitting on the passenger side of the bench seat with his chest out and his ears on alert. Leigh went around and slipped the keys into the ignition, starting the engine, the truck revving to life with a growl. Elvis kept one eye on the door, waiting for his master.

"He's coming," she assured the dog, scooting over to leave the driver's seat open for Colton.

Elvis seemed content with that and settled down, curling up beside her on the tattered bench seat. She stroked his fur until she saw Colton in the sideview mirror, jogging over.

"All good," he said, climbing in. He could always keep everyone from losing their minds. He put the truck in drive and headed out to the dirt road, going west.

The clean, earthy air pushed its way inside through the open windows of the truck, the aromatic scent of vegetation unavoidable as they bumped along the gravel path away from Nan's cabin. The setting sun offered up snippets of pink and blaze orange through the canopy of trees. If she closed her eyes, it would take Leigh right back to the days of her youth when she and Colton would take long drives in his jeep with no destination. The drive *was* the destination.

How had she kept herself from this for so many years? It was such a departure from the fluorescent lighting and durable slate-gray indoor-outdoor carpeting of her office. She'd been so busy ensuring the success of her future that she'd completely neglected her past.

Colton looked over at her and smiled a few times, as if he could read her mind.

They finally turned off the dirt road onto a tire-track drive that wound its way through an endless expanse of empty fields.

"You can't see it now," Colton said, "but under all that dirt there are cotton seeds, and after I finish plowing the rest, the whole farm will be full of white flowers in a matter of weeks."

"That's amazing," she said, looking out at the vast fields and imagining the rows of blooms.

He maneuvered around a turn that took them past a huge free-standing garage toward a massive, yet charming, brand-new farmhouse. It had a historic-inspired look to it with white clapboard and twin stone chimneys on either side of the tin roof, but it was clear by the colossal sleek windows and double-front door under an oversized porch with whirring paddle fans and lantern lights nestled stylishly beneath the overhang that it was a new construction.

"This is your house?" she asked.

He pulled the truck to a stop and got out. "Yep."

"Something tells me that Jax Wrigley didn't live here..." she said, after Colton had opened her door. She stepped down onto the aggregate circular drive, the truck out of place against its backdrop.

"He did. But Smash owns his own construction company now and he gave it a facelift." He walked her up the wide steps to the porch and let her in through the front door.

Rugged hardwoods stretched out through the open-concept space to the kitchen, where she was met with stainless-steel appliances and lustrous drop-lighting that illuminated the bright white-and-gray marbled quartz counters. A leather sofa sat at the other end, flanked by two trendy recliners, all facing an enormous stone fireplace and a flat-screen TV.

"This is incredible," she said.

"I'm glad you like it."

Elvis sauntered over to his bowl and began munching on kibble.

All of a sudden, Colton's cell phone rang in his pocket. With an apologetic glance, he took it out and peered down at the caller, his kind look fading. His eyes narrowed at the screen, and he dismissed the call, slipping it back into his pocket.

"Everything okay?" she asked.

He took in a deep breath as if inhaling the sight of her, and a genuine smile returned. "Yes," he said. "All fine." He waved a hand in the air. "Have a look around. Elvis—"

Elvis stopped eating and looked up.

"Keep an eye on this one, okay?" Colton threw a thumb over to Leigh, and the dog peered up at her. With a grin, he said, "Be right back in a dry pair of jeans."

Leigh went over to the living-room area, lowering herself on the sofa. A sophisticated coffee table with thin iron legs and a high-gloss wooden top held a stack of men's fashion magazines and a tobacco-scented candle. She flipped through one of the magazines, stopping on the brand name she'd seen on Colton's T-shirt: "Down South" in curly script with the word "Athletics" in boxy print underneath. She ogled at the price, her mouth falling open. All those years he'd teased her about her "uppity lifestyle" and there he was, in his massive house with his tobacco candle, wearing $250 T-shirts? He probably only drove that truck for show and had a stash of sports cars hidden in that garage of his.

"All dry," he said, coming back into the room with a new pair of jeans on. He noticed the magazine open on the table and came over to her. "Ah, I see you've found some light reading."

"Yes." She tapped the T-shirt. "Investing in high-end clothing lines?"

He gave her a questioning look.

"You're wearing one of these shirts."

"Ah, yes. Guilty," he said, holding up his hands.

"Wasn't it you who claimed that because I chose to wear high-end clothing my priorities were *a little different?*"

"Not because you chose to wear it, but because you chose to spend so much of your money on it."

"You're one to talk! Look at you—" She jabbed a finger at the logo on his chest. "Wasn't the one you had on at the party also that brand? You've got a stockpile of two-hundred-fifty-dollar T-shirts. How is that any different?"

Elvis perked up, walking over to them. He sat down next to Colton as if taking his side.

"I didn't pay two hundred fifty dollars for them. I got mine for twelve dollars."

She crossed her arms, skeptical. "How?"

"Because I bought them at cost."

"So do you spend late nights finding online clothing discounters?"

He laughed. "Definitely not." He reached down and picked up the magazine, flipping to an article and holding it out to her. As she honed in on the glossy headshot of him, he said, "I own Down South Athletics."

"You started your own clothing brand?" She looked up from the magazine, stunned.

He shrugged. "I had all this cotton and nothing to do with it…"

Leigh clapped a hand over her mouth. He'd completely surprised her. She took the magazine from his hands, seeing the brand with new eyes. The color scheme was traditional southern: barn red, John Deere green, white, khaki, washed-out denim blue… The script was reminiscent of the old Coke signs, and the style was simple. *Genius.* "You designed all these?"

"Mm-hm."

"I never knew you were artistic."

"Neither did I. I mean, I have a team to help me, but I provided the original design." He walked over to the kitchen. "Want a drink? I've got a bottle of white wine in the fridge."

Leigh closed the magazine, putting it back on the coffee table. "When did you start drinking white wine?" she asked, shuffling behind him as he led the way over to the bar separating the living and kitchen areas.

"When I had to entertain the people from New York who launched my brand. I drank white wine for six months straight while we planned the launch of Down South Athletics. I started to develop a taste for it."

She grinned.

"Don't get me wrong. I'd choose a Bud Light during football season any day, but a nice unoaked Chardonnay isn't a bad summer drink."

Leigh let out a loud laugh. "I never thought I'd hear Colton Harris say 'unoaked' anything." She laughed again.

"Well, you haven't been around for a while." He reached into the fridge and pulled out the bottle, uncorking it and pouring two glasses, handing her one.

"Thank you," she said, seeing him differently now. "You surprised me tonight."

He held up his glass. "To surprises."

"To surprises." She clinked hers to his.

"We never found that butterfly book of your grandmother's," Colton said, as Leigh sat on a barstool at his kitchen island, her fingers around the bottom of her half-empty wine glass, the view out the window now a dark purple as the sun made its final exit. Colton had topped off their wine a few times now, and she was feeling the low buzz of it, relaxing her shoulders, and warming her cheeks.

"I know. I wonder where it is." She toyed with the stem of her glass, thinking. "You know, I used to do the same thing with birds that Nan did with butterflies. I just couldn't draw them." She took a sip of the fruity, crisp wine. "While she and I were very different in terms of talent, we shared our love of the outdoors. Being back has made me realize how much I miss it."

Something crossed Colton's face and he got up. "Want to see something cool?"

"Of course."

"Bring your glass."

Leigh followed Colton through the large expanse of the living room, down a wide hallway, past a handful of immaculately decorated bedrooms to the back of the house, where he led her into a great room with a pool table, an entire wet bar for hosting parties, and a full-sized basketball hoop. She tried not to gawk as she looked up at it.

"Not much to do in winter," he said. "But this isn't what I wanted to show you."

Colton went over to the back wall that was made entirely of glass and unlatched a bolt in the middle. The entire thing folded up like an enormous, transparent accordion, opening the whole back of the house to the huge deck with glass walls as railings, a stone fireplace at one end, and the sweeping view outside. As far as she could see were rolling hills of cotton fields and a private section of the lake. The only structure visible was an old bungalow on the edge of the shore. It was quiet tonight, with the exception of the cicadas' chirp and the crickets.

"Holy cow," she said, stepping onto the deck, the cool spring breeze blowing her hair back.

"It's incredible out here in the mornings." He pointed to a small table and chairs set at the end of the deck. "Sometimes, I sit with my coffee and a book, and lose track of the time because it's so peaceful. It's just me with all the wildlife."

"I can imagine what it must be like," she said, sipping her wine and basking in the glow of the moonlight and the twinkling stars that had started to emerge.

Colton kept his eyes on the horizon. "I'll bet it's different from New York…"

"Yes. Definitely." She took in the extensive view in front of her—the hills in varying shades of purple against the ever-deepening sapphire-blue sky—and thought about her one-room apartment back home. How hard she'd had to work for that little bit of space.

He took a drink of his wine and faced her. "You always had this unsettled need to prove yourself that I never had. I never left, but I never wanted to either. And success sort of found *me*. But you know what? I think it found me because I was meant for this." He waved an arm across the view. "I couldn't live without it."

"You say success found you, but you built Down South Athletics, right? That was from your creative mind—you found it, not the other way around. You just didn't have to go anywhere to get it."

He nodded. "How about you—have you found your thing? Are you happy?"

She tried to put on a brave face, but the tilt in his head told her that he could see right through it. "Of course," she lied anyway.

He stared at her as if willing her to spill the beans.

"Sometimes I wonder why I stayed away so long," she said, hoping the half-truth would satisfy him.

"You used to count down the days until you could come to the cabin and see your nan."

She nodded, the years away feeling like lost time. "I'd forgotten how great it was for a little while, and how comforting the cabin is for me, but I won't do that again."

"I'm glad to hear that," he said, stepping up next to her, the two of them side by side under the stars. "I hope you visit a lot."

His admission filled her with joy. "Yes," she said, unsure of how to do that once she was back in New York, under the pressure of a new job, but she was certain that she'd figure it out.

When Colton dropped Leigh home, the house was dark and all the bedroom doors were shut. After her night with Colton, Leigh was energized, and she felt slightly at peace, despite the lingering tension with her family. Whatever her mother had to tell her, she could get through it if she just channeled the peace of this place. While Nan wasn't there physically, she was still all around, and Leigh could finally feel her.

Clicking on the lamp in the living room, she went to sit down on the old sofa and curl up under one of Nan's quilts that always hung on the arm, but then she spied the old trunk where Meredith had kept her things. Had Nan left her sister a note too? The buzz of the wine gave her the courage to take a look for herself. With a glance at the shut doors down the hallway, she quietly paced over and unlatched the trunk, lifting the lid.

Inside were old canvases with a few of Meredith's elementary paintings on them from when they were little girls. There were coloring books, a couple of the dolls she used to keep there to sleep with, and a pair of Meredith's swimming goggles. But the thing right on the top was what made Leigh's skin prickle. It was the leather butterfly book with an envelope paperclipped to the cover. And on the envelope was Meredith's name in Nan's writing.

Meredith probably hadn't thought once about this book since she'd arrived, and yet Nan was giving it to *her*? Leigh had been the one with the interest in nature like Nan; Leigh had studied birds the way Nan had studied butterflies; Meredith hadn't spent a single moment with Nan, talking about anything. Nan had left Leigh nothing but a note. So why in the world would her grandmother give that precious book to Leigh's sister? She had to know why. Quietly, she slid the envelope from under the paperclip and slipped it into her pocket, closed the lid of the trunk, and took the note to her room.

With the door closed and locked, Leigh stared at her sister's name on the envelope, wishing it had been her note that had been attached to the butterfly book. She pulled out the single sheet of paper, gasping when she saw how long the letter was, when hers had been short. Her curiosity piqued, she dove in and started reading.

Meredith, my sweet child,

You and I never spent more than a few minutes at a time together— you were always in motion, like your heart, following the moment's desires. Even though I wasn't by your side a lot of the time, I watched you come and go, knowing that the movement was essential to who you are. But I also understand that a restless soul doesn't have it easy most of the time.

Once, on a tree down by the lake, I stopped in my tracks at the sight of a butterfly emerging from its chrysalis. I watched it struggle every single day for about a week and a half. It was working so hard and it seemed like no one was noticing its incredible struggle. I couldn't bear it, so I grabbed my tweezers and started to help it get out. When I finally freed it, it fell to the ground and it never got back up. The next day, when I went to check on it, the butterfly had died. I was devastated.

Convinced I'd let it struggle too long, I started to research butterflies, jotting down my findings in this journal, feeling just terrible. But what I found surprised me even more. You see, by helping it out, I'd killed it. When leaving its cocoon, a butterfly needs the struggle to push the fluid from its body into its wings. So essentially, without the struggle, it never flies.

*My hope for you is that, by the constant struggle within you
and what you've had to endure, you've found your wings. And if
I'm allowed from the big paradise upstairs, I'll be watching you fly.*

All my love,
Nan

Slowly, Leigh folded the letter and placed it back into the envelope,
her mind whirring, tears filling her eyes. All this time, Leigh had
thought that it had been she who'd worked the hardest, studying long
hours and pushing herself to the limit to climb the corporate ladder;
she'd thought it was she who'd struggled the most, leaving everything
she knew behind and building a life in a brand-new place. But Nan
had thought differently.

Nan's words *always in motion* and *restless soul* floated back into her
mind. Her skin burned with the realization that the reason Meredith
wasn't close with her was because Leigh had never understood her sister.
She'd seen her restlessness as avoidance and her laid-back attitude as
laziness. Had she gotten it all wrong? Was Meredith really the stronger
of the two of them? After all, it did seem that she'd found her wings,
while Leigh was flapping around on the ground, trying to survive.

She slid the letter back into its envelope and took it back to the
living room, where she returned it to the place where Nan had left it
for Meredith. As she stood in the silence of the cabin, suddenly nothing
about her life felt clear to her anymore.

Chapter Twelve

Leigh tentatively sat next to Mama outside at the fire pit, watching the sun rise and trying to gauge her disposition this morning.

"Mornin'," Mama said, tipping her head up to view a sparrow that flew overhead. "What are your plans today?" she asked.

"I'm going to start calling different companies to see if I can get a meeting with them for the Greystone property." If she was ever going to feel better about herself, she needed to get a move on and figure out what to do with her life. "I want the emails in their inboxes Monday morning."

Mama nodded, rearranging a log on the fire pit with the stoker. "Did Meredith come back last night?" She stabbed a log, the sweet charcoal scent of it reminding Leigh of summer.

"Yeah," Meredith answered from the doorway of the porch, tucking a runaway strand of curls into the tangled, messy knot on top of her head. With a huff, she walked down and sat across from Leigh, pulling at her baggy jogging pants to keep them up.

"It's chilly out here. Should we go inside?" Mama asked.

"Yes," Meredith answered in almost a hiss of desperation.

Before last night, Leigh would've interpreted Meredith's response as her not wanting to be there, but after reading Nan's letter, she wondered if sitting outside with two people who totally didn't get her was more difficult for her than she let on. Was that what Colton had understood about Meredith that Leigh had not?

Mama got up and went inside. Leigh and Meredith followed behind her. Without warning, their mother turned around and said, "I think it's time I say what I've brought you two here to tell you. We'll let the chips fall where they may…"

The three of them sat together at the kitchen table where they'd shared so many meals, where they'd laughed until they'd cried while Nan told them stories, where they'd made big breakfasts and covered the surface with flour to bake cookies, the place they had gathered—they were there, ready to hear whatever it was that Nan had to tell them from the grave.

"Your grandmother gave me a letter just before she died. It was addressed to me, and I didn't have the strength to open it right then, so I tucked it away in the back of a drawer. It was all too much for so long… I couldn't bear to read her words to me, knowing she was no longer there to say them. Then, years later, when I finally felt like I could read it without crumbling, I opened it."

Leigh hung on her mother's every word. So far, Nan's letters had been quite surprising, so she couldn't wait to hear what was in this one.

"When I read it, I literally couldn't believe it." Mama's eyes filled with tears. "I had to come back here to try to make sense of it."

Meredith folded her arms on the table. "What did it say?"

Mama sucked in a long breath, looking both of them in the eye, one of her daughters at a time, her distress clear. "She didn't leave the cabin to me."

Leigh's eyes widened. "What? Why?"

Mama sniffled, and Leigh reached over and grabbed a tissue off the counter, handing it to her.

"She told me in the letter that she knew I'd be all right and this would all make sense in the end." Mama wiped her tears and took in a jagged breath. "She wants one of *you* to have the cabin."

The hair stood up on Leigh's arms. This was why Nan's letter to her had been so short. This would be the perfect gift from beyond the grave. Nan knew that Leigh would include her mother in taking care of the house, which was why Nan had skipped over her mom in the inheritance. And Nan also understood that this was *Leigh's* place, where nothing could go wrong… She silently thanked Nan for this incredibly generous gift, her whole future changing before her eyes.

Mama put her unsteady hands on the table, leaning in toward them both. "Meredith, she wants you to have it."

"What?" The word burst from Leigh's lips in a defiant, angry snap. She realized in the silence that followed that she was standing now, her limbs trembling, the rejection from Nan stinging her like a swarm of bees. "Meredith doesn't even like this place!" she managed, tears beginning to spill from her eyes, her chin wobbling. "She's never settled anywhere in her life. What would make Nan want to give it to *her*?"

What Leigh wasn't saying was that the cabin had been the place she and her mother had felt most safe. So many of their memories were there. And now, when Leigh's world felt like it was turning upside down, it was the cabin that had grounded her. The butterflies she'd seen—the one that had flown into her car, the one on the hammock—she'd thought they'd meant something. Suddenly, it all meant nothing. Just as she'd been so sure about the job that Rebecca had pulled right from under her, now her sanctuary of love and memories was being ripped away from her and her mother as well. The worst part about it all was that Nan had seemed to have this deep understanding of Meredith and what made her tick, but hadn't noticed how much *Leigh and Mama* had loved that place.

She lowered herself back down, trying to calm the hurt that was scratching at her insides. "You're going to give it to me, right?" she asked Meredith, desperate to save it. "I mean, it only makes sense since you were barely ever here. It's my favorite place…"

Meredith pursed her lips. "Your favorite place that you haven't bothered to visit for the last eight years."

"And you have?" Leigh asked, hearing the mix of anguish and frustration in her voice.

"We'll figure it out," Mama said, trying to soothe her.

Meredith stood up and faced the window, leaning on the sink. "I'm not sure there's anything to figure out," she said with her back to them. "Nan wants me to have the cabin. I'm sorry if the two of you find that tough to swallow."

"She said she's left you both notes here," Mama said, her voice small. "I haven't seen them."

Meredith looked around, pensive, before she walked over to the doorway. "I'll bet I know where to get mine." She walked into the living room, leaving Leigh stunned, still shaking, at the kitchen table. She returned with the butterfly book and the letter. "Found it. Leigh, yours is probably in your desk drawer." Then she left them alone once more.

"I was hoping I could get the three of us on good terms before I dropped the news," her mother said in a whisper. "The last thing I want is for Meredith to be so upset with us that she alienates us and doesn't let us into the cabin." Mama's eyes glistened with more tears, one of them escaping down her cheek. She blotted it with her balled tissue.

Mama's words were going in but not connecting. All Leigh could think about was her nan's betrayal and the letter that Meredith was probably reading right now. Completely disheartened, she stood up from the table. "May I have some time alone?" she asked gently, wiping the tears that were now streaming down her cheeks.

Mama nodded. As Leigh took a step, Mama reached for her arm. "I'm so sorry, Leigh," she said.

The pain in her mother's eyes only served to make Leigh feel worse. Leigh stared at her, speechless, the rims of her eyes burning with her pain.

"But Leigh, there *is* something else to it..."

There wasn't anything else her mother could say to make it better. "I need a minute," she said to her mom, ignoring the comment. She didn't want to hear anything more about it right now.

Leigh went into the living room, opened the desk drawer, and took out her letter. Then she walked quietly back to her room and shut the door. Falling onto the bed, she opened the envelope and reread Nan's cryptic message.

I know you and your sister are very different people, and sometimes you can't always see eye to eye, but she's family. Remember that. Embrace her. And no matter what, you'll be okay.

Nan had clearly known how Leigh would take this news, yet she'd done it anyway. And no matter how hard she tried to understand Nan's motives, Leigh had no idea why.

Leigh sat at a coffee shop about twenty minutes from the lake in the small Tennessee town of Goodlettsville. The morning rush had subsided, leaving a half-empty dining area of a few people on their laptops and one woman in the corner reading a book. Leigh had needed to get away to try to collect herself and make some progress on the Greystone project, but it was nearly impossible to have her entire head in the game when the issues with Nan and the cabin plagued her every thought.

She'd settled at a tiny bistro table with no view and free Wi-Fi, scooted the small vase with a single red carnation to the side, and opened her laptop, attempting to direct her attention to the task at hand. While she tried not to feel sorry for herself, she couldn't help the niggling idea that no one seemed to understand her—not her boss or Nan, or even Colton at times.

Until last Thursday, she'd felt invincible, and now all she could do was question her every move. As she tried to construct an email to Green Hat Coffee Roasters' corporate office, the words she'd typed rambled on in front of her, her confidence shot.

Maybe Nan had thought Meredith would need a place to live, while Leigh had already started her life elsewhere… Or it was possible that Nan felt the cabin might be better for an artist… But none of those answers felt right. Family was everything to Nan—why would she tear them apart like this?

Leigh squeezed her eyes shut and then opened them, forcing her focus back to the email, her untouched double-shot caramel latte sitting on the table next to her. With a deep breath, she told herself that the only way to dig out of this hole was to do what she did best and climb back up that ladder one rung at a time. She rolled her shoulders to alleviate the pinch and started typing.

…I'd like to introduce you to 24,100 potential customers. Meet the residents of Old Hickory, Tennessee, a neighboring town of

metropolitan Nashville. With over 1,200 homes on the national historic register, it holds a vibrant past, and, lucky for you, a completely untapped market for Green Hat Coffee...

Forcing herself to get the initial introductions done, she took a draw of her latte, the sweet caramel and bite of the coffee helping to direct her. She continued, firing off emails to Top Mountain Supply Co., Rocket Pizza, and The Attic Light bookshop, with her contact information at the bottom of each one. She felt a little better after finishing, so she gathered her things, and just before she walked out of the coffee shop, she tossed her cup into the trashcan, sinking it in one shot, a tiny wave of who she'd been a few days ago washing over her.

Chapter Thirteen

The next day, after compiling more statistics for her pitches to the companies she was courting for Greystone, Leigh found Meredith and her mother sitting at the kitchen table.

"We were just talking about you," Mama said when Leigh set her laptop on the table.

The two of them talking without her gave her a twinge of unease.

Meredith patted the seat vinyl beside her. "Take a load off."

Leigh wasn't sure what it would solve, but the truth was that she didn't have anywhere else to be, so she sat down. The windows were open, letting in a fresh breeze despite the thick heaviness between them. Mama scooted a plate of fresh cinnamon rolls Leigh's way, the sweet spice of them dancing into the air under her nose, but she didn't take one.

"You said you were talking about me?" she asked, folding her hands and trying to look casual when she wasn't comfortable in the slightest.

"I know our relationship is… strained," Meredith said. "But it's important to remember that Nan left the house to me. I didn't seek it out."

"That's just it: you *didn't* seek it out. Do you even care to have it at all?" Leigh asked.

Meredith leaned over her cinnamon roll. "You think this makes any sense to me?"

Leigh shook her head, knowing the argument was the wrong one. Even if Leigh could convince Meredith that she was the one who deserved the cabin, it still didn't change the fact that Nan had chosen Meredith. Leigh would have to live with that forever, and if Leigh resided in the cabin, she'd always feel like an outsider now. Tears suddenly swam in her eyes, and she swallowed hard while trying to blink them away.

"I know this is so difficult for you," Mama said, reaching out and placing a gentle hand on Leigh's arm. "It's hard for all of us…"

"I'm sorry," Leigh said, rising too quickly and knocking the table, the plate of cinnamon rolls shimmying on the surface. "I need to be alone."

She rushed back to her room, closed the door, fell onto the bed, and sobbed into her pillow. She couldn't stop the question of why Nan had done this to her. It rushed through her mind like a hurricane. She felt betrayed, belittled, like she was less than what she thought she'd been in Nan's eyes. And with the loss of her job and the fact that she only had a few months of savings to make rent on her apartment in New York, she felt as if she were breaking. If she were completely honest with herself, there wasn't anything left for her in New York. It was the worst pain she'd ever felt, and all those thoughts just kept spiraling around in her mind.

She prayed for some sign to make this all okay. "Nan, if you can hear me, tell me what I've done wrong so I can fix it. Whatever it is, I didn't mean it," she whispered into her pillow, her voice breaking with another sob. With no answer in sight, she rolled over and stared at the ceiling, the cloudy beaded light fixture blurring through her tears. Leigh stared at it until the numbness took over, her tears subsiding, her breathing lethargic and steady.

As her sadness and confusion settled upon her, she turned her head to the side and took in the view of the lake through her window. Unexpectedly, she wanted to take a walk, to breathe in the clean air and put her feet in the water. With resolve, she dragged her fingers under her eyes, grabbed her cell phone, and slid on her flip-flops. Then she headed outside through the back porch door, slipping past her mother and sister in the kitchen.

As she made her way across the yard and down to the soft sand of the lake shore, the morning sun casting its white light over the rippling water, she already felt more peaceful. The water lapped onto the sand as if beckoning her in. She slipped off her flip-flops and dipped her toes into the cold water, striding through the small waves. The breeze blew through her cotton shirt and then the trees, their rustling like quiet applause for her small success yesterday.

Her phone pinged with an email in her back pocket. She took it out and had a look at the notification, surprised. Rocket Pizza had come back to her already and wanted to have a call… She stared at it, wishing she could be elated by it. But, as she stood in the calming pulse of the water, it occurred to her that while everything else seemed to be going wrong, this new job was the only thing that was very slowly, little by little, going right. And it was the most positive thing in her life right now, so she had to give it the attention it deserved. She opened the screen and fired off a date and time to talk.

"Working while walking now?" Colton's voice sailed over to her.

She turned around, slipping her phone into her back pocket.

"Whoa. You okay?" he asked, immediately noticing the emotion lingering in her stinging eyes and stuffy nose. Elvis came down the hill and headed for the tree line.

She shook her head, not wanting to speak for fear it would come out as a sob.

He stepped up next to her, the water darkening the leather of his boots, but he didn't seem to mind. "Meredith texted me and said you were dealing with some issues and you might want to talk."

She tried to answer, but the words were stuck in her throat.

While she didn't love the idea of Meredith spreading around the fact that she was a head case, she was already glad Colton had come. Having him there was a comforting force in her storm.

He looked at his watch. "It's almost noon. What do you say we go back to my place and I make you lunch? I make a mean coconut curry chicken."

She allowed a little smile at that. "I'd heard you cooked," she managed.

"Wow. You know you've got talent when it becomes a rumor around the lake."

She grinned again and sniffled.

"Ah, that's what I like to see." He called Elvis. "Come on. Let's get a bite to eat."

They drove back to Colton's and before she knew it, Leigh was wrapped in a soft blanket and left on the cozy sofa of the living room, with a view of the lake out the window to her right and the warmth of a fire in the stone fireplace to her left. Elvis curled up beside her while Colton sliced cubes of chicken on the cutting board.

He chopped an onion and a pepper too, tossing them into the pan, the warmth of it causing them to hiss. He then dropped in some garlic and butter, the savory smells making her stomach growl.

"Want to tell me what's going on?" he asked.

She told him about Nan's wishes for the cabin. With every word, she hoped he'd have some sort of epiphany that hadn't occurred to her.

"That's definitely odd," he said, to her disappointment. He added in the chicken and coconut milk along with the spices, setting the pan to simmer, and then came over to her with a tray of cheddar and crackers. Elvis hopped off the sofa and sat at attention by the coffee table, clearly hoping for a bite.

"I just don't understand it," she said, focusing on stacking the cheese onto her cracker to avoid diving down into despair again.

"You know," he said, drawing her attention back to those dark eyes of his, "sometimes the best parts of our lives come out of the things that make us feel the most uncomfortable."

"But look at you," she countered. "You're a success and you look comfortable."

"*Look* is the key word there. We all have battles."

"What are you battling right now?" she asked, curious.

"Nothing I want to worry you with," he said, getting up. "Enjoy the crackers while I make the rice."

Colton finished cooking and plated the dishes, taking them to the repurposed farmhouse dining table made of old planks of wood that had been highly lacquered and attached to sleek iron legs. He pulled out a chair for her. "For drinks, I've got lemonade and sweet tea. What tickles your fancy?"

"I'd love a lemonade," she said, tucking into her seat.

Colton filled two glasses and brought them over, sitting down across from Leigh. "So, what are you going to do about the cabin? Are you going to try to get Meredith to give it you?" he asked, resuming the conversation from before.

"I can't go against Nan's wishes," she said, stabbing a bite of chicken and popping it into her mouth. The aromatic curry mixed with the cream of the coconut was to die for.

Colton scooped the curry onto his fork, the bite hovering over his plate as he asked, "What do you think Meredith's going to do with it?"

"I don't know. She's never around to enjoy it."

"You don't think she'd sell it, do you?"

Her last bite settled like a cinder block in her stomach. "She'd better not," she said, fear creeping in. "Mama would never speak to her again." She took a bite and then had a sip of lemonade to wash it down. "I guess it'll just sit there empty."

"She might want to live in it," he suggested. "She said to me the other day that she doesn't have a house right now."

"I have no idea," she said. "But let's not dwell on it." She really couldn't stand to think about it anymore. "Thank you for coming to get me and cooking me lunch. It's delicious."

"Of course." She noted fondness in his eyes when he said it. "I have been holding out on you, though."

"What do you mean?"

He leaned forward dramatically. "I have key lime pie in the refrigerator."

She gasped, his excitement nearly erasing her thoughts about Nan and the cabin. "You know that's my favorite."

"Still?" he asked with a laugh, but she could tell by the adoring look in his eyes that he knew that.

Colton seemed pleased that he'd been able to make her happy. And she suddenly wondered: the chicken curry, the pie—had he thought of her when he'd bought it all? She dared not even consider it, given the state of her life right now. Plus, Rose Thompson had said he threw dinner parties. Perhaps he was always prepared...

After lunch, Colton gathered their plates and set them in the sink. "What's the verdict? Pie or no pie?"

"I'm gonna be really sorry I said this later," she said, partly because she'd miss out on the pie but mostly because she wished they could spend more time together, "but I'm just too full to have any. The chicken curry was so good that I cleaned my plate."

"I see," he said, nodding toward the empty dish in the sink. "Another time then," he said, giving her stomach a lurch of excitement at the thought of spending more time with him. "I want to show you something," he said with a sparkle in his eye. "I just put it up this morning. It'll be perfect for relaxing with all this curry in our bellies."

He led her out to the back deck with Elvis on their heels. Along the side of the deck with the stone fireplace, he'd hung a massive two-person hammock from posts on either end of the decking.

"Oh wow," she said, running her hand along the thick rope of it.

"You first." He motioned for her to hop on.

Leigh climbed onto the hammock as he held it still. Then he went over to the fireplace, grabbed a pack of matches off the mantle, and lit the logs, a flicker starting at the bottom and swelling upward. When he'd gotten onto the hammock beside her, he clasped his fingers and put them behind his head, his body so close that she could've curled herself around him if she'd wanted to.

"Know why I put this here?" he asked as they lay under an electric-blue sky.

"Why?" she obliged.

He nodded toward the view. "For that."

Leigh turned her attention past the glass on the edge of the deck. She could see all the way to the lake, the sun sparkling off its surface like diamonds.

"You can literally lie here looking at that until you fall asleep."

"Mmm," she said, her troubles almost melting away.

He turned his head to make eye contact, his dark eyes finding hers. "I wondered about you over the years," he admitted.

She tried not to acknowledge the flutter in her chest at his confession.

He peered out at the view. "Can I confess something?"

"Of course."

"I had grand plans for us that last summer before we turned eighteen."

She twisted toward him, the hammock ropes creaking. "You did?"

"Yep." He smiled a knowing smile. "I was gonna make a move and kiss you."

Happiness bubbled up. "You *did* kiss me."

"Out of desperation! You dropped the bomb that you were leaving. I figured I'd better do it right then or chance wondering for the rest of my life what your kiss felt like."

"How was it?" she teased.

"Freaking amazing. I mean, better than Mary-Jo Sanders and Sharon Easton—the other two girls I'd kissed by then."

Leigh laughed. She'd missed his wit and lighthearted banter. "I'm sorry," she said. "I really am."

But then he sobered. "I remember holding in my sadness that last day with you—I thought I'd never meet another girl like you."

"Ah, I'll bet you did."

He smiled but didn't answer, leaving her to wonder. As much of a disaster as she felt she was at this moment, and as different as the two of them were, she wanted to hear his response. "May I ask you something—seriously?"

"Absolutely."

"What was it about me that *fit* you back then?"

His brows pulled together as he constructed an answer to her question. "You were always thinking, always one step ahead. It's in your blood."

How did that make her a good fit for him? "What do you mean?"

"Your sister Meredith needs physical movement, but you need mental exercise to be happy. And I rose to the challenge of keeping you excited. I'd never read books before I met you—that was all for you. But when I would lie beside you, reading, I felt what it was like to be in your world, and I loved it. You challenged my everyday thoughts. You taught me to look at things differently, see bigger outcomes. Having your perspective made me feel like a whole person."

He flipped onto his side, shifting backward so the hammock didn't make them roll into each other.

"So, you enjoyed learning, like I did," she said.

"Yes, but that wasn't all. You just see things differently than I do. The world is this giant place that you can experience—you're not afraid of any of it. Deep down, as a kid, I was terrified of what was out there, scared the world wouldn't understand me. You taught me that there was nothing to fear, that my world was only as small as I made it."

He stared at her, vulnerable, the two of them looking into each other's eyes, their arms supporting their heads and his fingertips tickling hers. If she pushed her head forward, she could press her lips to his. She considered it, but then thought better of it. She had a lot to learn about the older Colton. The untamed child had been replaced by this refined southern man.

But their eyes met just before he rolled onto his back again, and she had to force herself to breathe. "That's not to say you didn't drive me crazy too—in lots of ways," he said.

"How so?" she asked, still trying to regain her composure.

"Well, besides putting me in the friend zone for all of our teenage years, no matter how hard I tried to make you see me as more, you wouldn't see it."

"I did," she said. "But I didn't want to ruin things."

"That's what I mean by saying you're always thinking. Your worry that you were going to ruin something kept you from ever experiencing it."

She lay there, her eyes on the black outline of a bird as it flew between her and the sun, as she considered this.

"It's the same with Meredith. You avoid her."

She sat up, the hammock wobbling underneath them. "I do not try to avoid my sister. I've been there with her the whole time! It's her who's always leaving."

He gently reached up and took her hand, pulling her back down, but her shoulders were now tense and she wasn't comfortable anymore.

"I've been there with the both of you. You don't talk to her. You don't ask her about her life."

"I did! The other day," she said, defensive, remembering their conversation on the porch. "I asked her what she did for a living because I didn't even know."

"That's a start," he said, still holding her hand. "But Leigh, you didn't even know what your own sister did for a living. Why did it take you so long to ask?"

"You don't understand, Colton. She's different with you."

"Because I ask her things. And I listen to her. That's why she's different."

"She's never wanted to be around any of us—ever. When I left for college, she didn't even bother to come out of the house to tell me goodbye."

"And did you ask her why?"

She lay there on the hammock, silently frustrated. Should she have to extend an olive branch when she'd done nothing in the world to warrant Meredith's behavior?

"Nobody hears her," he said, his voice serious. "And that's all she wants."

That was ridiculous. "If you're so great at reading people, what do *I* want?"

He grinned, the corners of his eyes crinkling adorably. "You want to have purpose. You're a doer, a worker. And you want to be able to show off what you can do because it's spectacular."

The hairs on her arms stood up, his compliment warming her. He'd hit the nail right on the head. "What about you?" she asked quietly. "What do *you* want?"

"I wanna fish off the side of my boat and watch football out on my porch in the evenings. I wanna go into town and know everybody there."

She smiled at his lighthearted comment, but a flash of heat rose through her, remembering his teenage desires. "So, you still want to do all that?" she asked, curious about the man in front of her, their years together just a tiny piece of who he was now.

"Yes—all those things make me happy—but I forgot one thing. I want to fish and watch football and know everyone in town, but what I only *kind of* knew back then was that I want to do it with my favorite people around me, because none of it means anything without the people you love. I want to make my own enormous family one day, but until then, I'll take my parents and your family if that's okay."

"Ours is a bit of a mess," she said, warmed by his candor.

"Only if you let it be. Talk to Meredith."

"Maybe I will," Leigh said, wondering if he was right.

Chapter Fourteen

When Colton dropped Leigh off, she got straight out of his truck and walked over to her rental car to take a drive. She wasn't able to face her family at the cabin quite yet.

"You gonna be okay?" Colton asked, with his elbow hanging out of the open window of the Ford.

"I'm going to try," she said, as she opened the door of her rental, still feeling uncertain about everything.

"Call me if you need me," he said with a gaze that told her he, too, saw someone in front of him who was no longer exactly the person he'd known.

She nodded and then closed the driver's side door of her Honda, cranking the engine. Colton headed out down the road toward his place.

With the windows down, she meandered along the winding lanes, under the crisp coolness of the shade from the canopy of deciduous trees, their new growth a bright green. The idea that an aerial view of those roads would look like wilderness to an outsider made her feel protected, as if she were in her own little cocoon where no one could touch her—not Phillip, not her family, not Jimbo and his unfriendliness...

As she drove, with only the sound of the cool spring wind in her ears, she kept coming back to the idea that her entire adult life had been wrapped up in her job. She didn't even have a houseplant in her apartment because she wasn't present enough to water it. Her nose was always in her computer, searching, studying, scarfing down the latest facts to propel her through her next meeting like a rocket. She'd wrapped her entire self-worth in it.

But now, in this moment, she forced herself to pay attention to the rustle of the trees, the snippets of sun through their branches, the way the car ground on the dirt road and hugged the curves as she took them, following alongside the edge of the sparkling lake. She took it all in, thinking how these things were what Nan held dear, and she wanted so badly to have her guidance.

"You picked a terrible time to not be here," she said out loud, hoping Nan could hear her. "That's not like you."

She'd intentionally pointed fingers at Nan, hoping to fire her grandmother up enough to come rushing back into the car to tell her she had no say in the matter. Leigh's senses sharpened, hoping to catch "I'm still here," whispered on the wind, but there was nothing.

It would be so easy to spiral down into her sadness that the cabin wasn't nearly the same vibrant place without Nan, that every minute Leigh struggled right now made the shiny memories of her youth seem more and more like a fantasy. But it wasn't in Leigh's nature to wallow—she'd already done enough of that. Like Colton said, she was a doer. She wanted to work, to think, to figure out how to change what wasn't right.

Her phone went off with an email alert and her doer instincts kicked right in. She slowed to a stop, pulling two tires onto the soft wild grass of the shoulder, and grabbed it from the passenger seat. Green Hat Coffee Roasters wanted to talk. There, on the side of the road, she did what she did best and scheduled a time to have a phone call. Her pitches were spot on—she'd had two of the four clients return her unsolicited emails in less than twenty-four hours. In her world, that was unheard of.

With a satisfied sigh and a swell of hope, she decided it was time to go back to face her sister.

"Meredith," Leigh called when she opened the door to the cabin.

"I'm on the porch out back," her sister replied.

Armed with Colton's words, she headed to the screened-in porch where Meredith and her mother were sitting, and lowered herself on the sofa next to her sister. "Can I ask you something that I've always wondered?"

Meredith eyed her, closing the art magazine she'd been reading, holding her place with her finger. "Sure."

Mama looked on, clearly wondering what all this was about.

"Why didn't you come out in the driveway to see me off when I left for Northwestern?"

The skin between Meredith's eyes wrinkled and she looked at Leigh like she was crazy.

"I've always wondered what I'd done to make you so upset with me." Leigh felt a release, saying the words that she'd held in for so many years, as if she were uncaging a flock of doves and watching them lift into the air.

Meredith set her magazine onto the coffee table, and leaned her forearms on her knees. Her attention moved from Leigh to her mother and back again, that look of confusion sliding into one of heaviness, as if she, too, had been holding on to something for all those years.

"Leigh, when you went off to college, Mom and Dad threw you a huge party—remember, Mom?"

Mama nodded, her reading glasses now off and her book in her lap, interested as if she, too, had been wondering this same thing.

"But two days before, when I'd told you that I was finishing my classes early to waitress in Florida until I could bartend, I got a lecture on selling myself short by taking the easier diploma. Instead of a party, you and Dad gave me a packed lunch for the trip and a wad of cash so that I could get home if I ever 'got stuck.'"

Leigh could recall, with perfect clarity, the unique mixture of irritation and hurt in Meredith's eyes that day. Meredith had run in as excited as if she'd won the lottery, a folded piece of paper in her hand.

"I finished," Meredith said. "Four years of high school done in three!" She shoved the printout into their faces.

"What's this?" their father asked, trying to make sense of the information on the sheet of paper.

"I have enough classes that I can get out a year early with a general education degree." Meredith had always viewed high school as a jail sentence that she would one day break free from. And in that moment, she finally had.

"But honey," their father said—if he'd been the type to shake his head and say, Bless your heart, *this would've been the perfect time. "How will you get into college with this?" He waved the paper as if it held some sort of plague.*

"I don't need a college degree," Meredith said, to her father's horror.

The thing they'd been trying to avoid her whole life crashed down on him. Neither of their parents understood what to do with someone who wasn't an academic like they were.

"You don't know a trade," he said. "You have no path laid out in front of you. What in the world are you planning to do with your life?"

"Well, right now, I'm going down to Highway 30A and waitressing by the beach," she'd said, defiant.

"But Meredith," Mama said now from her chair on the porch, bringing Leigh back to the present, "we threw the party for Leigh because getting into Northwestern took a hell of a lot of effort over many, many years. We were celebrating all her work."

"That's the problem though," Meredith said. "What about celebrating each other? I was just as happy going off to waitress on the Gulf Coast as Leigh was about going to Northwestern, but you all always put work ahead of happiness. Some of us *work* differently. I'm a wild success in my field, and what in the hell did I take in high school to prepare me for that?" She folded her arms, still hurt. She turned to Leigh. "I wasn't angry with you that day," she said. "I was angry with the fact that no one understood me or lifted me up."

Colton's assessment floated back into Leigh's mind: *Nobody hears her, and that's all she wants.*

"Is that why you didn't invite us to your gallery opening?" Mama asked. "We'd have liked to have been there."

"You never supported me growing up, so it didn't occur to me that you would support me now."

Meredith's comment clearly hit Mama hard; she folded in on herself and tears swelled at the rims of her eyes. Leigh could only imagine the weight that was on her mother's shoulders as she realized that she and her father had gotten it wrong with Meredith. All those years with tutors could've been art classes… Meredith wasn't always just running; she was running from *them*.

"I'm sorry to have upset you, Mama," Meredith said.

Mama waved it away and peered out at the lake, her lip wobbling. In that moment, Leigh wondered if Mama was looking to the gentle waters to give her calm in her own storm.

After hours of silence between the three following Meredith's confession, Meredith was who knew where and Mama had gone to bed, so Leigh had been checking her email. The sight of one particular message completely changed her mood. Samantha Perkins of The Attic Light had responded with questions after Leigh had sent a follow-up email, and Leigh'd offered to do a video call on location. She'd called Jimbo to let him know she'd need access to the space, and, while he hadn't answered her call, he'd texted that one of his guys would let her in at nine sharp the next morning.

She couldn't wait to land this. It was all going a little too easily… But that was just fine, because it reminded her that she could do the job. If she could get them all on board, she'd arrange to meet them personally in the upcoming weeks. Surely Meredith would let her use the cabin when the time came. But there wasn't any use in asking until she had this project in the bag.

With a renewed sense of purpose, Leigh opened her laptop and searched the most recent job postings, scrolling down to a new one in New York City, about three blocks from McGregor at a company called Rycroft Enterprises. It was an advertising agency looking for a lead in project management. She read on to see the qualifications:

knowledge of public relations, team player, successful experience managing a large team preferred...

Leigh opened an email, attached her résumé, and added that she was heading up acquisitions for Greystone Properties. It wasn't a lie, and she felt as though saying it to someone outside of her head would actually make it happen. Then, she hit send. She found a couple more promising leads and applied for those as well. With every email she sent out, Leigh felt more confident. While it didn't fix all her problems, it was one light at the end of a long tunnel.

Chapter Fifteen

"We could outfit this entire wall with bookcases," Leigh said, walking the white tiles of the Greystone retail space the next morning, holding out her phone for Samantha Perkins, head of retail expansion for The Attic Light bookstore. She hadn't checked with Jimbo to see if they could build bookcases, and he wasn't exactly available to ask, so she'd taken the liberty of suggesting it herself. It would be the least he could do if she filled the vacancies in this development. "You're looking at around 2,500 square feet of retail space here, with all the upgrades."

"Is a remodeling package included should we have any further changes?"

"Anything's negotiable."

"I'd like to fly out to see it," Samantha said.

Leigh produced a smile to cover up the fact that she wanted to run around the room whooping and fist pumping. "Excellent. How does next week work for you? Say 9 a.m., Tuesday?"

"That would be perfect."

Leigh finished her video chat and then called Jimbo, leaving him another message, letting him know her progress. She thought about sharing this news with her mother and maybe even letting Meredith in on the situation, but something about it felt like it was her victory and her victory only. She'd tell them soon enough, but for now, she wanted to keep this little joy within her to light her way. With a pep in her step, she headed home, feeling like nothing could shake her in that moment.

In the doorway to Nan's art studio, Leigh found Meredith, barefoot, holding a paintbrush, windows open, country music playing. The easels had been moved around, Nan's things jostled. Her sister had opened Nan's paints and squeezed an array of colors onto Nan's palette, dragging a streak of blue across one of the canvases.

Leigh opened her mouth to protest but stopped, instead hanging back in the doorway to watch. Leigh's initial outrage that her sister would dare disturb Nan's paints gave way to curiosity the more Meredith painted.

Her sister had a unique method, consisting of three paint strokes, stepping back to look, and then three more. Her movements were almost mathematical, yet in a way, it was also like a dance between her and her art. It was similar to how Nan painted, but Meredith had taught herself her own moves. Her feet shifted effortlessly, as if she were weightless, her brush taking over the canvas, the strokes beginning to take shape into a wide wing. Then Leigh noticed the butterfly book, open on the floor beside the easel.

"That's stunning," Leigh said over the music, walking all the way into the room.

"Thanks," her sister replied, her gaze fluttering over to Leigh tentatively. She continued with her process, the brush moving—swipe, swipe, swipe, then look. She scratched her head in concentration with the back of her paintbrush, nearly swiping a couple of curls with the blue paint, as she peered down at Nan's butterfly drawings. "Nan gave me this book with my letter, and I'm trying to figure out why."

Leigh went over to the radio and turned it down just enough that they could have a conversation. "It is interesting that she gave it to you, isn't it?" A pang in Leigh's chest swelled as she looked over at the book that she would've loved to have.

Meredith set the brush in the tray of the easel and dipped a fresh one in gray paint, adding shadows to the wing. "I keep thinking how butterflies symbolize change, metamorphosis," her sister said. "And in my letter, Nan talked about struggle and how the butterfly has to struggle to find its wings."

"Mm," Leigh said, still trying to make sense of it.

"I get it that my childhood was a struggle, but I feel like I've already found my wings, you know?"

"But Nan wasn't aware of that," Leigh countered.

Meredith leaned into the canvas, painting in the tiniest detail on the edge of the wing. "It's like a mystery, though, what she wanted for me. She wanted change and she wanted me to find my way, but she also somehow thought the cabin was part of that plan. I thought maybe if I paint here, the answer would come to me."

"Maybe she just wanted you to have a safe place to live in case you ever needed it."

"That doesn't sound like Nan, though. Her ideas were always grander than that."

"True." Her sister did have a point. "It could be that she wanted you to put down roots somewhere."

"Could be, but she said she'd be watching me fly from the big paradise upstairs, and she knew how I don't like to be tied down. The movement itself is what inspires me, and she completely understood that." She picked up another brush, dipping it in a vibrant yellow.

While Meredith continued to bring her butterfly to life, Leigh pretended to ponder the situation, but she had her own mystery to solve. Why had Nan left all Leigh's favorite things to Meredith and nothing at all to Leigh? While she didn't feel entitled, the gesture rocked her self-confidence and tore at what tiny shred of family closeness she'd had. Nan had been her rock, the one person who had seemed like she could do no wrong. And while Leigh knew that Nan had her reasons, she couldn't help but feel abandoned by her.

"Well, let me know if you figure it out," she said, forcing a smile that Meredith never saw, her sister's focus remaining on the painting.

That evening, she saw her mother through the window, still in her work clothes from the bank, sitting in one of the Adirondack chairs by the blazing fire pit, facing the lake. She'd rushed in to work to fill in for someone, the instinct to keep herself busy to avoid her thoughts kicking in again. Leigh let herself out through the back door and went over to see her.

"How are you?" Leigh asked, noticing the red rings under her mother's eyes.

Mama's lips wobbled as she shook her head, indicating that she wasn't okay.

Leigh sat down in the chair next to Mama, the two of them facing the water in front of them. The boat bobbed next to the old dock, pulling against the ties that bound it as if reminding them that it was being neglected.

"How was work?" she asked, trying to stick to an easy subject.

Mama shrugged.

"Busy?"

Mama shook her head, wiping a tear from her cheek.

The evening air was getting cooler, but Leigh didn't suggest they go inside. It was clear by the fact that Mama's purse was next to her and her car keys were on the armrest of the chair where she sat that, if she'd wanted to go inside, she would've.

"How could I have gotten it so wrong?" Mama finally said.

"What? Meredith?"

"Everything," she said, her eyes glistening. "Your dad and I didn't understand our own daughter, and she's right: we didn't celebrate you two as people. We only praised your accomplishments—and even still, only the accomplishments that met our narrow criteria of success." She squeezed her eyes shut and then opened them, wiping a tear that had escaped down her cheek. "She's a lot like your nan, the most amazing person in our lives," Mama said. "And I never saw it. Not like I should have. I pushed her into a path that wasn't hers to take."

"You could only do what you thought was right," Leigh said, trying to set her mother's mind at ease.

"I should've been able to see it," Mama said as she shook her head, that distant look that Leigh had seen in her mother's eyes after their father had died returning. She was turning in on herself, clearly submerged by her pain and overbearing thoughts.

Leigh reached over for her hand but her mother barely noticed. That was when Leigh knew that, just like her mother had for Nan and then again for their father, she needed to mourn the loss of the relationship she never had with her younger daughter.

"It's okay, Mom," Meredith said, coming down the steps toward them.

Leigh looked up at her sister.

"I heard you through the window."

Mama tipped her head up to address Meredith as she maneuvered around their chairs and sat in a third, draping her paint-spotted hands on the arms, her eyes on Mama.

"I understood my whole life that you couldn't see it."

Mama bowed her head, defeated, more tears surfacing. "I shouldn't have made you feel less than the gifted and brilliant person God created you to be," she said. "I also keep thinking that your nan could see it all, yet she never told me to lighten up. Not once. I wonder why."

"She was a big believer in letting us all do our thing," Meredith said. "She was allowing you to be a mother, I think. Who was she to tell you differently?"

"But I got it *wrong*," she said, distraught.

Meredith teared up, and for someone else—Leigh had never seen it happen before. As her sister looked at their mother, tears glistened in her eyes in front of the thoughts that swam across her face. It was clear that she felt for Mama.

"Maybe our paths weren't meant to be straight," she said. "Maybe life is supposed to be messy because it isn't up to you to find me. It's up to me to find myself."

Meredith's words seemed to lift a layer of heaviness from Mama's brokenness, and she took in a deep breath, letting it out. "I could've made it a little easier, not subjecting you to all that school tutoring when you could've been painting," she said.

"Well, I have to do payroll for two people, so the extra math was helpful." She grinned at Mama.

Mama chuckled through her tears and Leigh was glad for Meredith's compassion. Then their mother sobered. "I'm so sorry," she said. "I won't ever let it happen again."

Meredith wrapped her arms around their mother, their little family finally together, side by side and still, the cabin watching over them.

As the sun sank in the sky, Leigh sat on the dock with her bare feet hanging over it just like she had as a girl, the new perspective she had of her family swirling around in her mind. Growing up, she'd thought her mother had had all the answers. She'd listened to every single thing Mama had directed her to do. So today, after seeing her mom's vulnerability, and realizing that she was only doing the best she could at raising them, Leigh questioned her own life.

Leigh had happened to be good at school, so she'd easily been able to fulfill her parents' wishes, and she liked pleasing them. But now, she wasn't so sure if she'd done the right thing. She'd put everything she had into her job—her whole life. Even now, she was clinging to what little success she found at Greystone Properties, literally scraping up work in an attempt to find her life's fulfillment.

But what if she was looking for happiness in the wrong place?

Leigh dipped her toes in the cold water, the trees shushing her as if to settle her racing mind. The lake seemed vast today, like one of Meredith's canvases, waiting for something from her. She suddenly felt the absence of little feet that could've pattered along the path behind her, the husband who might have wrapped his arms around her at the end of this dock—none of it a part of her reality. The truth was, she loved doing what she did, and she felt real joy in being a success in the office. But maybe her destiny was bigger than that.

"You've been awfully quiet, Nan," she whispered under her breath. "Wanna help me out here? What are you doing all this for?"

The wind blew her hair behind her shoulders and she strained, just hoping to hear her grandmother. But, as always, there was only silence. Then she applied Meredith's words to her situation: maybe life was supposed to be messy because it wasn't up to anyone else to find us. It was up to us to find ourselves. She was looking to Nan to guide her because her whole life people had guided her. But perhaps, just like Meredith had, it was time for Leigh to find her own way.

Chapter Sixteen

The next morning, Leigh woke with a new perspective. She lifted the shades in her bedroom and opened the windows. The spring temperatures were glorious today, topping out at seventy-one degrees, with sunshine and not a cloud in the sky. Once she was ready for the day, Leigh slipped on her sundress, layering a cardigan on top, and headed into the kitchen.

"Mornin'," Mama said, while packing her lunch for work, filling in again for a colleague, working more hours than she usually did. She was in her bathrobe, her graying hair tucked behind her ears.

"Morning," Leigh returned happily.

Mama slid two halves of a sandwich into a plastic bag and placed it in her lunchbox, then took a seat at the table to eat her breakfast. "You're chipper today."

Leigh pulled a mug down from the cabinet and filled it with coffee from the half-full carafe still warming on the burner, adding cream and sugar before bringing it to the table. She sat down across from Mama and a dish full of breakfast casserole, a spatula leaning against it. "I might go to the farmer's market this morning."

"Sounds nice." Mama got up and grabbed a plate from the counter before handing it to Leigh and sliding the sausage and egg casserole toward her.

Leigh scooped a square of casserole, lumping it onto the plate. She sliced a bite of it with the side of her fork. "Do you know if they still sell those handmade soaps that I used to use when I was in high school? It would be nice to get some."

"I think they do," Mama replied.

"Need anything? I could get you something."

"Thanks, but I don't need anything." It was obvious that Mama was still pensive about the conversation with Meredith.

Leigh sunk her fork through the eggs and into the flaky crust at the bottom of the casserole and scooped it up. "Maybe after you get home from work, the three of us could do something today—you, me, and Meredith." She popped the bite into her mouth, savoring the buttery taste of it.

"I'd love that."

"Me too," she said, and she meant it.

The farmer's market was a mass of brightly decorated stalls and tents, the sellers advertising their wares with A-frame chalkboards in colored lettering and adorably decorated banners. Rows of farm-to-table vegetables and mason jars full of preserves sat on blue-and-white tablecloth-covered tables; bakers waved to customers from behind stacked boxes of pecan pies and peach cobblers.

Rosemary Peabody's stall was still the first one, her table full of handmade necklaces and earrings that sparkled in the sunshine. Her husband Thomas was at his cooler nearby, handing out popsicles to a group of kids who'd gathered. The whole place was festive with the buzz of early morning shoppers. Leigh took in a deep breath, as if she could breathe in the down-home feel of it all and save it for later. She grabbed a basket, waved to Rosemary who was busy tending her stand, and began making her way down the first aisle, her plan to snake along through each one so as not to miss a single thing.

Stopping at a table full of jugs of elderberry elixir, she picked up a bottle to read the back while the owner of the stall chatted with a customer. "You be you!" was printed above the directions. She smiled, setting it back down, and carried on to the next stall of hand-poured beeswax candles, the lavender one catching her attention. She closed her eyes and leaned down, inhaling the flowery scent.

"Whatcha doin'?" sailed softly into her ear, raising the hairs on her right arm and making her smile. She turned around to find Colton with a basket of vegetables and a peach cobbler.

"Hi," she said, unable to hide her happiness at seeing him. "I'm considering this candle," she said. "It smells divine." She lifted the jar to his nose and he took a whiff of it.

"Nice. You should get it."

"I think I will." She flagged down the merchant and paid for it, dropping it into her basket. "I'm glad I ran into you." She walked to the next stall and fiddled with a hand-embroidered towel and dishrag set. "You were totally right about Meredith."

"You talked to her?" he asked, his dark eyes sparkling.

"Mm-hm. And it made all the difference. So, thank you."

"I didn't do anything. I just mentioned it."

"But had you not said anything, I wouldn't have known how to approach her."

He smiled, the gesture reaching his eyes.

"I think the three of us might do something together later today, but I have no idea what," she said, hoping to bait him into joining them. She'd love nothing more than to spend the day with him.

But before she could rope him in, he'd turned at a female voice calling his name.

"Hold that thought. I'll be right back," he said, leaving Leigh and jogging over to the same blonde Leigh had seen at Harvey's Marina.

The woman said something to him, leaning in and putting her hand on his bicep. Leigh turned away, focusing on a jar of preserves, feeling intrusive for staring. She was glad for the diversion because it had helped her to realize that she was relying on her childhood connection with Colton a little too much. If she were being honest with herself, she didn't know him anymore. He'd had a whole life without her, just as she'd had without him. It was a little too easy to fall back on the memories.

Trying not to catch sight of him, Leigh meandered down the next aisle, slowly perusing the tables. She fiddled with a pair of beaded earrings.

"Sorry about that," Colton said, coming up to her again.

"Totally fine," she said with a polite smile, keeping her focus on the jewelry as she walked along the extensive table.

Then he stopped walking, causing her to follow suit. "You said you, your mother, and Meredith were going to do something together, right?"

She finally made eye contact. "Yes."

"Why don't the three of you come fishing with *me* out on my boat today? Maybe you can throw me off the side for payback or something."

Leigh laughed, the lighthearted remark like music for her soul.

"I'd planned on catching dinner and grilling out tonight."

She considered the idea that having Colton among her family might ease the tension a little. "You could ask your parents over too," she suggested, wanting to put as many people between her and Colton as she could so she wouldn't get caught up in her old feelings for him. That wasn't doing either of them any good.

His eyes widened. "We'd better get started sooner rather than later if we want to catch enough fish for six," he teased. "When does your mom get home?"

"She said by noon," she replied. "Let me text both Mom and Meredith right now."

"Excellent." His phone rang, pulling him toward the call. "That's my designer," he said. "We've got a slight issue with the manufacturer and I need to get this."

He left her typing madly on her phone, as someone else pulled him away with a warm hello, his eyebrows rising in greeting, his phone to his ear. With the prospect of spending a day not thinking about the fate of the cabin or her job search, it was shaping up to be a great one.

That afternoon, when Leigh had finished slipping on her jeans to get ready for the boat ride with Colton, her phone pinged with an email. She checked it, surprised to see that she'd already gotten a response from Rycroft Enterprises, the job she'd applied for. She opened it and read the message asking her to respond with a time when she could come in for an interview.

Her pulse quickened as she read that they were interested in her. But then, as she held her phone, standing still in the middle of the room, she considered all the things she'd been thinking about lately. Should she respond? Was this job what she really wanted?

At the end of the day, she had to make a living. If she got this particular job, her life could go along as it always had. Literally *nothing* would change, apart from not having to deal with Phillip and Rebecca. With two more clients to hear back from for Greystone, and the other two doing in-person visits next week, she'd have to think about when she could get back to New York for an interview. She opened the email, pondering her options.

Just then, the rev of a boat motor sailed through her bedroom window and Elvis's bark drew her attention to it. She laughed to herself when she saw the dog barking relentlessly at Meredith as she neared the boat, while Colton tried to quiet him. Leigh clicked off her phone. She'd better get to the boat to help soothe Elvis so her mother and sister could board.

Slipping on her hoodie and flip-flops, she left the cabin and jogged down the grassy hill to the dock, Elvis abandoning his protective stance, jumping off the boat, and running to her.

"Hey, boy," she said, bending down to give him a quick cuddle as she eyed Colton. "You ready to take a ride with me?"

Colton flashed a smile at her before jumping off the boat to help them on.

The dog panted, wide-eyed and happy, his tail wagging furiously as he followed Leigh back to the boat. Colton reached out for Leigh's hand, his firm but gentle grip and the smile lingering on his lips giving her a flutter. While Leigh distracted Elvis, he helped Mama and Meredith on.

Mama sat on the cushioned bench at the back of the boat, wearing her large sun hat and dark glasses, her cotton shirt rippling in the soft breeze off the lake. Meredith lowered herself down beside Mama, her curls knotted up in a bun at the back of her head. Elvis paced between them as if guarding their every move while Colton untied the boat and pushed off the dock, steering away from it until he could hit full throttle on the open lake.

Normally, they always went left from the dock toward his parents' house, but this time Colton took them right, upriver. "I found an excellent cove with tons of fish over here the other day. Here's hoping we'll have the same luck today," he said. He was wearing a tattered ball cap and jeans, looking deliciously casual.

Leigh held her long blonde hair back with her hand, the boat speeding toward its destination, cutting through the water and leaving a foamy trail in its wake.

The boat bucked gently as it fought against the choppy current caused by a passing vessel, the buzz of the motor in Leigh's ears. Elvis was positioned between Colton's feet, but Leigh hadn't braced herself, so when they hit a swell, Colton jolted and reached around her to keep her steady. It had only been a second—an instinct—and then his hands were back on the wheel, but she had to remind herself to breathe. As she took in the open water, her mind was busy. She couldn't deny the fact that she and Colton were tumbling effortlessly back into their old ways, those same flirty, affectionate moments falling upon them as easily as the air they were breathing. But unlike her youth, they were adults now, and once-a-year flings weren't what she wanted anymore.

The boat slowed to a stop, and Elvis, who had finally ventured out from between Colton's feet and had been sitting in the corner of the boat, got up and peered over the edge as if assessing his surroundings. Colton dropped anchor and set a bucket of bait on the stern before pulling four rods from their holders in the center of the boat.

"There's a bunch of bluegill and white bass that swim through here," he said as he loaded one of the hooks with a minnow. "I caught four last week, so fingers crossed." He handed the rod to Leigh and asked, "Remember how to cast it?"

She fumbled with the reel. "It's been a while…"

Colton reached around her and flipped the lever, releasing the spool, his large hands covering hers. Then he tipped the rod back and cast it out, the spool unraveling, the hook and bait sinking into the water until the bobber floated on the surface. "Like that," he said into her ear.

Her heart pounded like a snare drum. Before she could recover, he was helping Mama cast her line down the boat.

Meredith grabbed her rod herself, worked with the reel and figured it out, casting hers smoothly.

When everyone had their bait in the water, Colton loaded his rod and cast it out on the other side of the boat. Elvis sat by Leigh's leg as she kept an eye on the bobber, waiting for a tug on her line.

"You've made a forever friend, it seems," Mama said, pointing to the dog.

Leigh smiled, switching her rod to her other hand briefly to give Elvis a pat. She was starting to love that dog. "He's so sweet," she said.

Meredith turned and wrinkled her nose at Elvis, waving at him and sending him into a barking frenzy.

Leigh threw her head back and laughed. "Why are you so mean to her?" she asked Elvis, who turned his head to the side as if he were trying to understand. He seemed to, because he looked back over at Meredith suspiciously, only making Leigh laugh harder. But then her attention turned quickly to her rod as it bent down toward the water. "I've got something," she said. "Colton, help. I can't hold it."

Colton quickly set down his rod in one of the holders on the side of the boat and ran over to her, his arms around her once more as he helped her reel in the fish on the end of her line. His spicy scent assaulted her when he tightened his grip around her, his fingers working over hers to get the fish reeled in.

"Dang, Leigh's got a fish that'll feed all of us," Meredith joked. "We can all go home now."

Her excitement mounting, Leigh pulled with all her might to keep the rod steady while Colton reeled in the catch. When it finally lifted above the water, it was a massive striped bass that felt to be about fifteen pounds.

Colton took it off the hook and held it up. "Almost, Meredith. This alone could feed about three or four of us," he said, dropping it into the live well on the boat. "Nice job." He loaded her hook with another minnow and she cast it in.

The bright-blue sky overhead and the swish-swashing of the boat in the water were so relaxing that she actually noticed the fall in her shoulders and the release of the tension that usually banded across her brows. Miles away from the hustle and bustle of the city, the honking of the traffic, and the smell of diesel fumes, she understood what Colton had been saying all those years ago when he'd told her that he'd rather just fish than put up with all that.

The sound of a cell phone ringing caught them all off guard.

"It's mine," Colton said, heading over to the wheel and picking up his phone. "Oh, I need to take this. Give me just a second. If you catch another big one, yell." Then he put the phone to his ear and walked to the bow of the boat.

"Tell him that I'll be there first thing the minute he gets back. There's no way I'm letting him do this…" Colton paced the front of the boat. "I don't care what he says. I want to be there... All right. Talk to you later."

He hung up the phone and put it back on the dash by the wheel. "Sorry about that."

"Everything good?" Meredith called.

"Yep, all good." But he took in a breath that made Leigh wonder if he was being truthful or not. Whatever it was, he didn't want to elaborate.

They'd caught five fish—two striped bass and three bluegills—and Colton had taken them back home to clean them for dinner, so Leigh had retreated to the screened-in porch of the cabin with Mama, soaking in the beautiful spring breeze. Cicadas chirped in the trees, their sound like a distant hymn of impending summer as the water rippled onto the sandy shore.

Meredith came out with three lemonades, handing one each to Mama and Leigh before she dropped onto the outside sofa. "I've been thinking about what I want to do with the cabin."

"Oh?" Mama said, leaning forward in her chair, holding her lemonade in both hands.

"I think I might renovate it and turn it into an Airbnb."

Leigh waited for the laugh, the indication that her sister was only kidding. Meredith knew better than to even mention such a thing. But when she stared at them, her face serious, an icy chill snaked through Leigh's veins.

"You want to rent it out to people?"

Meredith crisscrossed her legs on the sofa like a child and took a sip of her lemonade. "Yeah. I was thinking about reasons Nan would've given me the cabin, and it occurred to me that I need to travel to be creative, so I could make this an artist's retreat, put it on the Airbnb site, and rent it to others who needed a new space to create." She waved her hand at the yard. "I'd flatten all this, take out the fire pit, and maybe pour cement there so we can set up our easels outside more easily. Maybe even have some cool quote about art in the cement. And inside," she continued, "I'd like to completely renovate the place: high ceilings, bigger windows, sheetrock over those wooden walls so it's bright in there. I'd gut the place and give it an open floorplan."

With every word Meredith uttered, Leigh felt sicker. "You want to get rid of all that Nan did," she said. "The flower beds and the little vegetable garden outside by the fire pit—she planted those herself; the cabin was completely designed by her…" She stopped talking, fighting the lump in her throat. This was *their* place. No one else's.

"But she's not here anymore," Meredith said, bristling as if conditioned for confrontation when it came to expressing herself. "She's given it to *me*. Shouldn't I use it for my own purposes now? Wouldn't that be what she'd want?"

"Why don't you make it your *own* artist's retreat?" Mama suggested, not hiding the fear in her eyes very well as she tiptoed around the idea.

"I know you two don't understand this, but staying here for any length of time would drive me crazy. It would suck the life right out of me. I need fresh perspectives, movement, the energy of new places and people."

"Then leave the cabin to us," Leigh said. While it wasn't what Nan had wished, it was far better than the alternative.

"If Nan had wanted that, she'd have left it to *you*," Meredith rebutted. "But she didn't."

Meredith's words stung, driving home the one thing that tortured Leigh most.

"We can stay in the Airbnb for free, whenever we want," Meredith offered, but it wasn't enough.

Why would Leigh want to stay in a place that Meredith was going to make completely unrecognizable? "You're missing the point."

Meredith set her lemonade on the table and twisted around to face her sister. "Which is?"

"We were a terrible excuse for a family—let's just admit it," Leigh said. "We never learned how to get along or understand each other. But this place was the one spot where our troubles melted away for a little while. You could go off and do your thing while I stayed back and reset. We all actually ate dinner at the same table at night without arguing. This was the only place that could do that for us. We've just now found it again. Changing it would remove that, and we'll scatter like before, but with nowhere to return to as a family. As bad as we were at being one, this is it, Meredith. Me and Mama are all you've got and you're all we've got."

"We could meet up at Mom's," Meredith said.

"It's a one-bedroom apartment, Meredith," Leigh countered.

Mama looked down at her lap as if she'd failed them, but there was nothing she could've done to save them from this.

Meredith stared at the sweating glass of lemonade that had now made a tiny ring on the outdoor coffee table, not saying anything.

"I have to agree," Mama finally interjected. "This isn't just your nan's home. It's our home too. It's a place we want to come back to."

"You haven't been here in eight years," Meredith said, crossing her arms, followed by a frustrated exhale.

Mama locked eyes with Meredith. "That's because it's such an emotional place to return to. I have a ton of memories here—we all do. Family *is* important, Meredith. So important that I'm letting my mother skipping over me and giving you the cabin fly away because her intentions are what's most important here."

"Are we really a family at all?" Meredith challenged.

It was a low blow, and Mama immediately responded, shrinking in on herself. Mama stared out at the lake, her lip trembling, before pushing her emotion out of view and looking back at her daughter.

"I think that you're the only one who doesn't believe we're a family... Even Elvis agrees."

Meredith and Leigh turned their attention to her, both of them taken completely off guard by her insight.

"He was a stray, right? And he barks at you every time he sees you. I think it's because he appreciates family, and he can sense it."

"Sense what?" Meredith asked, clearly annoyed that she was giving in to this absurdity.

"Elvis had no family and I think he senses that you won't let any of us in," Mama said. "He can feel your hostility."

"That's ridiculous." Meredith let out an incredulous laugh.

"Is it?" Mama asked. "It seems to make sense to me."

"Me too," Leigh said, jumping in on her mother's side. "It is odd how he barks at you. He doesn't bark at Mama as much as he barks at you. Dogs are very intuitive."

Meredith shook her head. "I'm going to take advice on what to do with the cabin from two people who believe a canine is aware of our family dynamic." She rolled her eyes.

"One thing I can say for certain," Leigh cut in, "is if you do rent this cabin out, we may never be a family. We were just getting started."

Mama stood up, taking her lemonade to the edge of the porch, and looked out. Leigh followed her lead and peered over at the place they'd taken family boat rides, both Meredith and Leigh holding on for dear life while they went tubing behind the boat, and the dock where they'd run after the car ride there, stripped off their cover-ups, and jumped in, signaling the start of summer.

"We all know that it won't be the same if this is gone. Nothing will," Mama said.

"Well, at the end of the day, it's my choice. Nan gave me the cabin, and I want to use it for something that represents me and also reaches out to others. How can that be a bad thing? And I've already started calling contractors." Without another word, that wall that they'd worked so hard this week to pull down slid back into position. Meredith got up and went inside.

In that moment, Leigh knew her mother had hit on something: nothing would ever be the same.

Chapter Seventeen

With the fate of the cabin in Meredith's hands, and no clue as to what the state of the place would be in the upcoming weeks and months, Leigh felt she needed to secure the Greystone Properties leases sooner rather than later. She'd need to get her work finished so she could focus entirely on changing her sister's mind. Leigh fired off an email to Top Mountain Supply Co., checking in to see if they had any questions for her. Then, she looked at her calendar to reply to the interview offer from Rycroft Enterprises, giving them a few dates and times when she could come in.

But with no more tasks to complete, all she could think about was losing the cabin. She lay back on the bed, her head nestled in the pillow, and exhaled. "What in the world, Nan?" she whispered at the ceiling.

Then her phone went off with a text from Colton: *Want to take a ride?*

She stared at it, considering. She wanted to focus on her family and try to repair what little relationship they had. She also needed to check on Mama and make sure she was okay—she hadn't seemed so after Meredith had dropped the bomb about the cabin. But there was also a part of her that just wanted to get away from her problems. It would all still be there when she got back, right?

She texted: *A ride sounds amazing.*

Colton returned: *Good, because I'm already in your driveway.*

With a grin, she got back up, ran her fingers through her hair, and headed outside, relieved for the immediate distraction.

But when she got outside, what was waiting for her wasn't Colton's usual Ford.

"What's this?" she asked Colton through the open window of the shiny black Silverado that was idling in the drive.

"It's my other truck. You don't think I pick up dates in the farm truck, do you?"

She narrowed her eyes at him. "So, you're saying this is a date?" Then she immediately regretted it, realizing he'd meant "dates" in general.

"Not unless you're planning on going out with two guys at once." He leaned back and Elvis popped his head up, giving her a punch of amusement.

She climbed up into the truck, its soft purr quite different from the old farm vehicle he'd been driving. He pulled off, the Silverado gliding over the gravel as if it were a sheet of ice.

"My mom and dad are back at my house cooking for tonight," he said. "Mom's got at least three casseroles going. She's so excited to finally get to spend some quality time with all of us."

Leigh grinned, charmed. "I needed your energy," she said. "You showed up *right* when I needed you. How did you know?"

He raised his eyebrows, looking happy with himself. "It's my superpower."

She wasn't going to argue with the fact that it probably was.

"Why, what's wrong?" he asked, his concentration bouncing from her to the lane in front of them.

She groaned and rubbed the pinch that had been forming in her shoulder since Meredith's announcement. "My sister."

"What now? I thought things were good."

"Nan gave *her* the cabin. Just *gave* it to her without consulting any of us. And now she wants to completely change it and rent it out to vacationers." Elvis put his head on her lap as if consoling her, so she stroked his head.

"Did she say why she wants to do that?" He rounded a turn and headed toward the cotton farm.

"She thinks it'll help other artists. But what about *us*? We're her family; we're all she has."

He pursed his lips the way she remembered him doing whenever he was thinking. "I'm not sure renting it would be the best idea. We don't have a lot of tourists on this part of the lake. It's kind of what makes it so great."

"Tell *her* that."

"I might." He pulled into the farm, the vast fields stretching out in front of them all the way to the shore. "I'm serious. That's the very last thing I'd want."

"Maybe she'll listen to you," Leigh said. "She won't listen to Mama or me."

"Okay, I'll pull her aside at dinner."

Then the truck came to a stop in the middle of the dirt road.

"What are we doing?"

"I promised you a ride," he said, hopping out of the truck. Elvis followed, jumping down onto the dirt path. Colton went around and opened her door, taking her hand to help her out.

"How will we take a ride outside of the truck?"

He pointed to an enormous tractor with a large plow on the back of it that stretched halfway across the field. "We're riding in the cultivator. I need to weed the fields so they don't get overgrown." He peered down at her flip-flops. "Piggyback?"

"You want to give me a piggyback ride across the field?"

"Unless you'd rather have Elvis do it."

Elvis stopped sniffing the ground and peered up at them.

Colton leaned over and waved her toward him. "Gotta protect those pink toes of yours."

"You really want to give me a ride in that thing?" She shook her head. "Aren't your parents in the house? Don't they need help with the casseroles?"

"Definitely not." He waved her onto his back again. When she didn't move, he righted himself. "We do have dinner to get to tonight," he said, tapping his watch. "I need to get it done today. I've got two staff meetings tomorrow, and this field won't plow itself."

Against her better judgment, she jumped onto Colton's back and he grabbed hold of her thighs, her feet dangling on either side of him. Elvis followed along as Colton stepped across the rows of planted cotton seeds, headed for the tractor. Her hands clasped around his broad shoulders, the stubble on his chin grazing her skin as she bumped through the immense fields. Never would she have thought she'd be doing this a week ago.

When they reached the enormous tractor, he let her down and climbed the ladder to open the door. Elvis, apparently an old pro, hopped into the cab while Colton gestured for Leigh to climb up and get in. She complied, sliding onto the cool vinyl.

Colton started the engine, the massive machine lurching with a jolt and then, as if decidedly content, it began to roll quietly while Colton turned the wheel to line it up with the fields.

It felt as if she were flying, soaring through the air above the farm, a panoramic view of her entire childhood playground in front of her all the way out to the lake. "This is gorgeous," she said over the soft growl of the blades behind them, which were dutifully tilling the ground.

"That's why I thought you'd like it," he said. "There's nothing but unspoiled land as far as we can see. It's what I love about living here."

"I'd forgotten," she admitted. "I stayed away so long that the memory of this life had become almost like an old dream. Thank you for reminding me."

He grinned at her. "That's what I'm here for."

They drove along in silence for a while, back and forth across the cotton fields with nothing but water, rows of dirt, and blue sky as far as they could see.

"I'm glad you're here," Colton said as he steered them toward the lake. "I had you pegged wrong. I didn't think you'd ever come back."

"Why?" Leigh asked, taking in the square of his jaw and the way the little lines that formed around his eyes when he smiled lightened with his serious expression.

"I thought once you had a taste of city life, you'd never want to come back."

"I do love it in New York," she admitted. "But I'd like to find a way to merge my two lives."

"That's a big job," he said. "I'm not sure you can bring the big city here."

He had a point. It was as if she were divided into two distinct parts, and trying to fit them together wasn't an easy task.

When Colton and Leigh entered the house, Ruby's hands were under the stream of water at the sink, the savory smells of sage and butter filling the air. His mother grabbed a towel and dried her fingers, coming around the massive island to greet them.

Paul threw his hand up from the sofa, the Braves versus Cardinals baseball game on the large screen above the stone fireplace. "Hey, y'all."

"Would you two like some sweet tea?" Ruby asked. "I just made a jug." Leigh hadn't answered, but Ruby was already over at Colton's cabinets, pulling down two glasses.

Colton followed his mother to the other side of the island, giving her a kiss on the cheek before retrieving a dish of the cleaned fish from the refrigerator.

"Let's take a look at that new grill," Paul said, standing up and addressing his son. "Grab the butter and the salt and pepper, would ya?"

Ruby shook her head as Colton and his father went outside. "Colton is such a good boy," she said, as if he were still twelve. "He listens to his dad, even though Colton knows good and well he can cook better than any of us." She slid a glass of tea toward Leigh.

Pulling up a barstool, Leigh settled in across from Ruby. "I didn't know he could cook. Where did he learn?"

"Well, it started with cooking classes that he took when he was dating a young lady a handful of years ago."

Leigh shouldn't have been as shocked as she was at the mention of another woman. Colton was incredibly attractive, single, and had done quite well for himself. He was the perfect catch, so it made sense that he'd have a healthy dating life. She ignored the twinge of unease the thought had caused as she considered hers.

"He never really knew he enjoyed cooking," Ruby continued, wiping the counter with a dishrag. "But it just fit him. He's so artistic, you know?"

"I never realized how creative he was growing up," Leigh admitted. "He never let it show." She wondered now if that was why he'd always understood Meredith, another invisible line now drawn between Leigh and Colton.

Ruby folded the rag and set it next to the sink. "I don't think it occurred to him until later in life."

Everyone seemed to be moving along, gaining these epiphanies about themselves, when she was stuck in the same place she'd been, unable to move forward.

"What's the matter, dear?" Ruby asked.

Had her thoughts shown on her face? "Oh, it's nothing," she said. "I was just thinking."

"Well, I always say that thoughts are just our voice itchin' to get out."

Steering clear of her personal woes, Leigh told Ruby about the cabin and how she and her mother were dealing with Meredith's plan to change it, as well as her mother's distress over it all. "By giving Meredith the cabin, Nan excluded both Mama and me. I know she had to have considered that when she decided to leave the cabin to Meredith."

"You poor thing," Ruby said. "And I can't imagine what your mama's going through. She's lost so much already, with your dad and her mother... And now to have this kind of unrest." She put her palms on her face and shook her head. "I feel awful for her." Then Ruby took Leigh's hands. "Life is a strange thing. Somehow, when you're able to look back on this, you might just be able to see the reason."

"I can't imagine ever understanding the reason for this," Leigh said.

Colton's voice interrupted their conversation. "Fish's done," he said, holding a platter of blackened seafood, the buttery spices sailing over to her.

Insisting on bringing the food to Mama, to give her more time in the cabin, Ruby burst into Nan's kitchen behind Leigh with excited flair. Paul wedged the door a little wider with his foot before Colton caught it, holding it open for him as his father walked in with three of Ruby's casseroles and a tray of grilled fish covered in foil, teetering in a stack in his arms. He gingerly set them one by one onto the counter and then straightened, his tall frame towering over them all.

"I've got a bottle of Chardonnay open," Mama offered, sending Ruby into a frenzy of assistance as she grabbed stemmed glasses and commenced pouring.

"Who wants one?" Colton's mother called, making herself at home and holding up the first glass.

Leigh took it gratefully, the buzz of the evening settling in before the alcohol had even hit her bloodstream. The two families used to get together quite often when Leigh was young, and they fell back into the rhythm of it easily, as if no time had passed at all. But that was how people were on Old Hickory Lake—they were all family, no matter how long they'd been apart.

Meredith hooked her arm through Colton's. "Wanna see something I'm painting?" she asked, grabbing them each a glass of wine from Ruby and then leading him out of the kitchen toward Nan's studio.

Leigh got into the drawer of the hutch where Nan kept her tablecloths and retrieved the blue-and-white checkered one, along with a pair of scissors, taking them out to the porch. She spread the cloth along the dining table at the end and grabbed three candles that sat in silver buckets, placing them in the center of the table. Then, with the scissors in hand, she went out to the tree line past the patio to cut a few magnolia bunches to lay around the candles, like Nan had done. The soft scent of them always lingered in the air deliciously against the warmth of the flames.

As she finished, her phone went off in her pocket. Setting down the last of the greenery, she pulled it out and took a look at the email: Top Mountain Supply Co. Leigh left through the screen door and went down to the hammock, lowering herself onto it and opening the message.

They were interested. And they wanted to talk more next week.

She fired off a response, letting them know she was meeting with others as well next week, but she could certainly find a time to answer their questions, just to make them feel that there may be competition—a tactic she'd used at McGregor on a daily basis.

"Hello." Meredith waved a hand in front of her sister's face. "Want to join the land of the living and get off your phone?"

"Sorry," she said, looking up at Meredith and Colton, hiding her annoyance for the sake of their guests who had now settled on the porch. "I had to do something quickly for work. The table's set and ready to go." She slipped her phone back into her pocket.

"Mama's bringing all the food out now," Meredith said. "Let's eat!"

Leigh got up, Meredith leading the way. When she reached Colton, she questioned him silently, mouthing to him to ask if he'd said anything about having renters to Meredith, but he didn't answer. Colton was a tiny ray of hope in all this. Maybe he could make Meredith see…

With the empty dinner plates still on the table and the candles flickering in the moonlight, Leigh, Meredith, and Colton sat on the dock like they had when they were kids, their parents chatting away on the porch.

Leigh leaned back on her elbows and gazed up at the stars in the inky black sky, the moon a bright crescent above the trio. They'd had a few glasses of wine, the alcohol casting a net of calm on them all.

"I still remember the first summer when y'all didn't show up here," Colton said. "That was when it hit me that I'd lost my best friends."

Leigh's heart squeezed with his confession.

"For a while, I was angry because I wanted it to be the way it used to be, but then I realized that both of you had things you needed to do in life. It made me feel a little better knowing you were busy building the lives you'd always wanted."

"I'm sorry I didn't come back," Meredith said.

Colton nodded, accepting her apology. "Promise you won't leave again without coming back?"

"I promise." Meredith flashed a wide, relaxed smile. "We'll make it up to you," she said, her eyes glassy from the wine.

"I want a Henderson-family party at least twice a year at the cabin," he demanded.

"Okay," Meredith said easily.

"And how will you do that if there are renters in it?" he asked gently.

Meredith squinted as if trying to force sobriety upon herself. Then she scowled at Leigh. "She told you."

Colton faced her. "Mm-hm."

Meredith looked past him at Leigh again, rolling her eyes. "It's just like her to run whining to you when things don't go her way."

"I didn't do any such thing," Leigh said. "I simply mentioned our disagreement. But you're right. I shouldn't have brought Colton into it. I'm sorry."

"I know how you work," Meredith snapped, ignoring her apology. "Nan left the cabin to *me*, and it's up to me to decide what to do with it."

"May I say something?" Colton asked.

Meredith let out a heavy breath and then relented, listening, her bare feet swinging above the water, her arms folded.

"What would your nan want you to do with it if she was still here?" he asked.

Meredith sucked in a breath as if to fire off an answer, but she was stumped. Then, she pulled her feet up and twisted around on the dock, standing up. "If Nan had had a particular opinion about what to do with it, wouldn't she have said in my letter?"

Colton pulled away from Leigh and stood to face Meredith, shaking his head calmly. "Maybe not. Could she have assumed you'd know?"

Visibly flustered, Meredith turned away from them and stormed up the dock and inside, the screen door smacking shut behind her.

Colton sat back down. "Give her time. She'll make the right decision for all of you."

The problem was that Meredith had had a lifetime, and she'd barely come around in the last few days. What would a little more time do?

"You look tense," he said, bringing Leigh back to his gorgeous face.

She shrugged it off, trying to look as if it wasn't all too much for her. The thought of removing any last shred of Nan in the cabin tore at her.

"Wanna get out of here?" He took her by the hands and pulled her up.

"Where are we going?" she asked as he held her hand, leading her along the dock and through the yard.

"You'll see."

They passed Colton's parents and Mama, waving to them.

"Just like old times," Mama teased as they went by.

When they got to the kitchen, Colton grabbed a bottle of wine by the neck and the blanket off the arm of Nan's sofa, taking both with them. He opened the door to the Silverado and she climbed in.

Then, they were off.

Under the stars, the crickets chirped through the open truck windows, the cool spring air giving her a chill as they headed away from the cabin, toward town. She pulled Nan's blanket from between them and wrapped it around her shoulders.

"You don't want to tell me where we're going?" she asked.

"It's a place I always wanted to take you but never did," he replied.

The white light from the moon cast a stripe down his chiseled cheekbones, the rest of his face in shadow. "I was here every summer," she said. "How come you never took me?"

"Maybe I'll tell you later," he said, flashing her an affectionate glance that sent her stomach into a whirlwind. His strong hands held the steering wheel loosely, his toned muscles showing beneath the sleeves of his T-shirt, and his legs now filled out his jeans. He'd become a man in the time they'd been apart, and suddenly the years away seemed like a tragedy.

He pulled to a stop along a dirt road, grabbed the wine, and ran around to open Leigh's door.

Leigh hitched up the blanket and held it together with one hand while she took Colton's with the other. They'd stopped at a park with a playground and a horse ring that she remembered going to a few times with Nan. He led her up a grassy hill. She could barely get to the top of it with her flip-flops on, requiring Colton's firm grip on her hand to keep her steady on the incline. Her breathing increased with her pulse as they hiked the long walk to the very top. Halfway up, she took off the blanket and folded it, draping it over her arm before grabbing Colton's bicep to keep her balance.

"Turn around," he said after they'd reached the summit.

When she did, she gasped. "You can see the whole world from here," she said. The lake stretched out in front of her as far as she could see, the trees meeting the sky in almost an arc, a bowl of black ink and shiny stars above them. Far off in the distance, she could even see the bright lights of Nashville. "This is incredible."

Colton had taken the blanket from her and spread it over the grass. Then he pulled the cork out of the wine. She sat down on the blanket as he offered her the bottle.

Leigh tipped it up to her lips and took a sweet, flowery drink of it, handing it back.

"It's amazing up here, isn't it?" he asked, before taking a swig from the bottle himself.

"I can't believe you never showed me this." She looked back out at the lake, the two of them falling into silence, the view taking center stage in their moment. She lay back on the blanket and peered up at the stars. Colton followed, his head next to hers. When he did, Leigh rolled over to face him, the wine giving her courage.

He did the same, his gaze devouring her as if he had a hundred things to say, but he stayed quiet. He leaned on his elbow and propped his head up with his hand.

Then he inched closer to her, his hand finding her waist, his other moving behind her head to support her. "You asked why I never brought you here," he said, his face so close she could almost taste the bite of the wine on his lips. "Because with nothing else to distract me," he breathed, "I wouldn't have been able to stop myself from kissing you."

Leigh looked into his eyes. Her mind was filled with uncertainty. If she kissed him right now, she would change everything. Could she stay here for him? Indecision swarmed her and pushed out every other possible thought. She reached out and traced the typography on his T-shirt with her finger, the picture on his shirt a symbol of how far they'd both come and how much he'd changed. Then she pushed away from him, rolling onto her back. He didn't protest, and she wondered if the same questions were going through his head. As she lay there with him, she was sure of only one thing: for better or worse, nothing would ever be as it had been between them.

Chapter Eighteen

When Leigh rose from the most magnificent night's sleep, she checked her phone to find an email from Top Mountain Supply Co. They wanted to come out to see the property. That was all four. With Jimbo back this morning, she got ready for the day, had breakfast, and jumped in the car, headed for the Greystone Properties office. When she arrived, she knocked happily on the little trailer door.

"Yeah," Jimbo's muffled voice came from inside.

When Leigh let herself in, Jimbo was on the phone. She smiled, despite his absolutely awful business etiquette.

He stared at her over a pair of readers. "You don't have to fight me on this," he barked into his phone. "The revenue alone will drive up your property value." He rolled his eyes, listening, and finally hung up the phone. "Yeah?" he said on a frustrated exhale.

"All of the retailers have agreed to meet," she said. "I've got them scheduled for next week."

He brightened just a bit when she said that—as much as she'd seen Jimbo brighten. "That's great news," he said. "I need to get those buildings filled sooner rather than later. I've got a fight on my hands with a resident, and maybe getting those businesses open will shut him up. He needs to know that I can get this done with or without a fight."

"Not to intrude, but who's fighting you?" she asked, wondering if she could use her negotiating skills to sway them.

"Just some nobody farmer named Colton Harris. He's a thorn in my side."

She could literally feel the blood run from her face, down her body, and into her feet. "Colton Harris?"

"Yeah." He yanked off his readers and tossed them onto the coffee-stained desk calendar. "He's been against me since the beginning."

"Why?"

"He claims that retail will ruin property values." He blew a heavy breath through his lips and shook his head with disgust on his face.

She could definitely see how Jimbo could rub Colton up the wrong way, and she could only imagine what he must think of a man like Jimbo heading up retail property in the area, but the development would be strong—she was making sure of it. The property was located well away from residential areas and the companies she was courting would be an asset to the locals. "I know him," she said. "Let me talk to him."

Jimbo let out a skeptical laugh. "Good luck."

"While I've got you," she said, pushing Colton's issues aside, "there's the matter of fronting the cost of getting the four businesses here."

"What do you mean?" He stared at her.

"Well, there's sorting out their travel details," she said, "organizing and arranging their flights and accommodations once they land in Nashville. And we'll probably want to send them each an e-gift card to use for their entertainment while they're here, along with a hired car to pick them up at the airport."

"I don't have that kind of money," he barked. "I thought you were doing this pro bono."

"Well, I am. You aren't paying my services, but you still have to front the cost to get them here."

Jimbo rubbed the scruff on his face. "I'm in the red," he said. "I don't have enough to pay for it."

While she didn't love the idea of using some of her savings to pay for everything, maintaining a good reputation by being true to her word with the companies involved and giving Greystone a good name in the industry would be worth it for her career. Especially since she'd already put it on her résumé and she had the interview with Rycroft looming. "I'll pay for it, but once we seal the deal, I'm sending you an invoice."

As she looked at Jimbo's snarling face, she couldn't help the uncertainty that bubbled up within her. She had to make this work.

When she got home from Greystone, she texted Colton that she needed to talk to him. While waiting for a response, she wandered through the cabin, looking to see if anyone was home, finally finding Meredith outside, sunning herself down on the dock. With a sigh, she retreated to the kitchen.

At the table, Leigh spent an hour organizing the potential retailers' visits to the property. She'd corresponded by phone with all four contacts, securing their details and getting them set up for their visits. With every online reservation, her bank account took a hit, and she prayed she was doing the right thing. Working with McGregor's massive budgets, she'd never felt the vulnerability that filled her right now. She didn't have the giant machine of McGregor and its reputation behind her. This was all on her shoulders and the pressure to get it right was mounting.

A knock on the outside door got her up. She opened it to find an arm holding a bundle of red roses. The owner of the arm peeked around from the side of the door with a ridiculous grin on his face.

"I couldn't help myself," Colton said, handing them to her. "I saw them at a road stand and thought you and your family might love them."

She couldn't deny the zinging electricity that shot through her when she took the flowers from him, smelling the aromatic fragrance of the roses. "These are beautiful." She shut the door after he came inside.

"I'm glad you like them." He sat down at the kitchen table and put his hands on his knees, all his attention on her while Leigh pulled a vase from the cabinet and filled it with water, arranging the flowers. "So, what did you want to tell me?"

Leigh placed the vase on the table and sat down across from him. "I wanted to talk about Jimbo."

His eyes suddenly focused on hers, zeroed in like lasers, his breath seeming to linger on his lips. "What about him?" he asked cautiously.

"Look, he's not the easiest to like, I get it."

He stared at her unblinking, his jaw now set.

"But one thing I know how to do is land clients, so I've been working with him…"

Colton's face turned as white as a ghost.

"Listen, I already know what you're going to say, but this isn't necessarily going to draw more tourists to your area. It's a *good* thing. Bringing retail to the lake is genius, actually. If it's done right, development will create revenue for the county and—I think I even heard Jimbo tell you—it'll raise your property value."

His mouth hung open. "You were there when he was on the phone with me?" he asked disbelievingly. "You know what he wants to do and you're actually *working* with him…" His words trailed off to a whisper, his complete surprise etched across his face.

"Yes," she said, the word withering on her lips as she took in the sight of him. He looked like a volcano about to erupt. "It's what I do best," she said, in a feeble attempt to convince him, his demeanor becoming more and more menacing.

"How could you spend all this time with me and not tell me?" But then he drew back in his chair, his gaze moving around her face as if he were assessing her. "You were hoping to convince me, weren't you? Is that the real reason you've been coming around?"

She'd never seen him with a single feather ruffled before. He was visibly furious.

"Well, yes, I would like to convince you, but that isn't the reason—"

He pushed away from the table, the chair protesting in an angry moan. "You are exactly who I thought you were, helping him," he spat, standing up and heading to the door. He twisted the knob and opened it.

"Wait," she said, scrambling to her feet and grabbing his arm to stop him. "What do you mean?"

He kept his gaze on the door. "You don't care about anything but the rush of power you get doing that job of yours. You don't even care about who you hurt…" He trailed off, refusing to look at her, clearly not planning to stay any longer.

"That's not true," she said desperately.

He opened the door and stepped outside without responding.

"Didn't you say yourself that sometimes the best parts of our lives come out of the things that make us feel the most uncomfortable? This is a *good* thing!" she repeated from the doorway. Tears swelled in her eyes at the sight of Colton walking away from her. It all felt so wrong, like she was losing the one thing she'd been looking for her whole life. "Talk to me!" she called to him.

"There is nothing good about this," he said. "And out of everybody, *you* should know that." He turned around, and the relief she felt at meeting his gaze faded with the sight of his raging face.

She clambered onto the porch.

"When you think about the things that I want in my life, you *know* this is all wrong. And you did it anyway," he said through his teeth.

"Can't you just hear me out? I've got some great clients set up! It will all be fine!" Was it really that big of a deal if there was one retail establishment on the lake? A swell of insecurity overtook her the same way it had when Phillip had let her go, and again when her best friend Julie had turned on her. Was she missing something about herself that everyone else was seeing?

"I can't look at you right now." He got into his truck, pulling the door shut loudly behind him, leaving her stunned and completely confused.

"He just walked out?" Mama asked, kicking off her work shoes by the door after Leigh had told her about the bizarre conversation she'd had with Colton.

"Yes," she said as she stood beside Mama by the table, letting her eyes fall on the roses, that moment of sweetness now seeming like a faraway dream. "He was so angry with me for helping Jimbo. It's a well-done development. I don't see what the big deal is."

Mama put her hands on her lower back and stretched. "He likes to keep things the same."

A plume of frustration erupted within Leigh. "I understand that he likes things to stay simple and unspoiled, but this is down the lake, in an area that would be able to support the extra boat traffic. He won't be impacted at all."

"Apparently, he doesn't think so."

"Who doesn't think what?" Meredith asked, coming into the kitchen.

Leigh filled her in on what had happened. "And he said I'm exactly who he thought I was," she told her sister. "What does *that* mean?"

"Easy," Meredith said. "He means you're putting your working life over him, because that's what you've always done."

Leigh's stomach churned at the thought.

Meredith rooted around in the pantry, grabbing a family-size bag of chips and digging in. "You knew he wasn't happy with that level of growth in this area and you did it anyway."

"That's not true," she replied. "I didn't know his thoughts on the matter at all until he told me, but by then I'd already begun securing the clients."

Mama dropped down into a chair at the table, rubbing her foot. "Maybe you should tell him that."

"He said he can't even look at me. How am I supposed to explain things if he won't listen?"

"Stand outside his house and yell it through a window if you have to," Meredith said. "Come on, be creative and let him know that you care about what he thinks."

"But what if I disagree with what he thinks?" Leigh countered.

"Then you hope he'll eventually get over it," Mama replied. "But you can't just let it go."

"The way he looked just now, I don't think he will get over it…" Her heart plummeted in her stomach. Had she ruined everything?

"I'm making spiced cider," Mama said, her face pensive, offering a blanket to Leigh to combat the cool evening air sending a chill through the porch. "Want some?"

Leigh understood the gesture perfectly, her cheeks warming with the unease that she'd only added to Mama's distress and now she was trying to cover it up with cider. She lifted her laptop and draped the blanket over her legs, fearing that if she didn't let her mother busy herself, she'd slip into her thoughts, and worry herself to pieces. "That sounds really good."

Mama went back into the kitchen, leaving Leigh to her emails. She opened the new one from Rycroft Enterprises, asking for an initial phone interview. They loved her experience with Greystone and wanted to talk next week to hear the specifics of the project and which retailers she'd secured.

She should have been thrilled, but all she could think about was the fact that Colton hadn't returned her calls. She'd called him twice, left a message, and texted once.

"Let me have some of the blanket," Meredith said, coming in and plopping down on the sofa with two mugs of cider—probably her way of trying to make amends for the earlier blowup over the Airbnb idea. She handed one of the mugs to Leigh before tugging the blanket over her own legs.

Leigh rearranged herself to fit under the new portion and closed her laptop, setting it on the coffee table.

"You look like you've lost your best friend," Meredith said.

"I kind of *have*," she said, the weight of Colton's anger still sitting on her chest, overwhelming her other problems. She sipped the warm cider, the sweet spice of the cinnamon and cloves doing nothing to console her.

"What's going on, Leigh?"

So much was going on that Leigh wasn't sure of her sister's angle. "What do you mean?"

"You've been different. You're not as sure about things as you used to be. You've sort of drawn into yourself." Meredith seemed genuinely curious about Leigh. Her sister was looking at her, head cocked to the side, concern on her face.

"I lost my job," she blurted, before she could think through whether she wanted Meredith to know it or not.

"Oh, that's all it is? Well, get another one." Meredith took a drink from her mug as if it was the easiest thing in the world to switch jobs.

"It's not that I lost my job," Leigh explained. "I thought I was great at it and I was replaced by someone they thought was better. I've never come in second before."

Meredith pursed her lips as if contemplating this idea. "I believe that we're put places to impact others and when we can no longer impact them, we should get out. It's the universe's way of moving you on to something better. You just have to listen to find what it is that you need to do next. So, if they're going in a different direction, that's your cue to keep going in *your* direction. Someone else needs you."

"You have a point," she said, holding the mug with both hands to keep warm as the breeze blew in off the lake. "I thought I was going in the right direction with the Greystone property. But Colton's really upset about it, which makes me feel like I'm not on the right path when I thought I was. I'm second-guessing myself. I don't usually do that."

"I didn't say your path would be easy," Meredith said. "I have firsthand knowledge that it can be a pain in the ass." She laughed.

"But all you can do is follow your gut because your path is within you, not anyone else."

"So, you're saying that I might have to choose between Colton and my career?"

Mama came in and settled in the chair opposite them with her steaming mug.

"Your whole life, you've worked to get yourself to this career," Meredith continued. "What you have to ask now is: who are you and what do you want?"

Leigh thought about the question. "If I ever moved forward with Colton, should I have to choose?"

Meredith leaned forward to put herself in Leigh's line of view. "Would giving up your job for someone fulfill you?"

That question was even harder. Leigh pulled the blanket up further and thought long and hard about it. She might go crazy if she couldn't do what she'd spent her life working for, but there was a part of her that wanted to wake up every morning beside the person she loved, to have coffee out on a deck somewhere and talk about nothing in particular. "I think I'd go crazy without the thrill of my career," she said. "I feel like I need to make Colton see that it's really all going to be okay."

"I think you've just answered the question," Meredith said.

She couldn't actually have to choose work over Colton. That didn't make any sense.

"Look, my whole life, I wanted my family to be happy about what I chose to do with my life because that's who I am," Meredith said. "If you all aren't happy with who I am, then you can't really love *me*. So, while I wanted the love of my family, I had to leave. It's a lot like what you're facing now."

"But you helped us to understand," Mama said, piping up. "And if you'd let us, we'd love to be your family again."

Meredith stared at her, her thoughts visibly moving inward. Her gaze fell to the blanket, her eyes unstill, as if she were reading some imaginary text, her mind clearly whirring.

"The difference between your situation and this one is communication," Leigh said. "You never explained it to us in terms we could understand. But now you have, and we totally get it." She linked her arm with Meredith's. "We'll have differences—sure. Some of them really big ones, like what to do with this cabin. But in the end, we're sisters."

Mama set her mug on the table and reached for both her daughters' hands. "There's no instruction manual on how to be a parent and I haven't always done the right thing. I'm still learning even now. But one thing I do know after being with you girls this week is that love has to come above it all. We have to follow our hearts and accept the things we can't change."

Meredith set her cider next to Mama's and drew her into a hug. Leigh followed, wrapping her arms around her mother. In that moment, their mother's tears were different, as if they were tears of relief.

Love has to come above it all. Mama's words rolled around in Leigh's head. She needed to find Colton and make him talk to her. And she needed to listen to him. That was what love was about.

Chapter Nineteen

Elvis howled from the other side of Colton's front door as Leigh knocked for the second time. The porch light was on and had been for quite a while—she could tell by the bugs that were circling it—and she could see through the window that there was a light on in the living room, so he must be home, right? She knocked again and then rang the bell, sending Elvis into another fit.

"Colton, it's Leigh. Please answer the door," she called through it, hoping he could hear her. "Please. I want to talk to you."

When he didn't answer, she went around back to find both his trucks in the open garage. "Colton?" she yelled up to the deck, but she was met with silence. With purpose, she marched back around to the front door and rang the bell again. Elvis ran back and forth inside, barking. Why wouldn't he answer? If he was avoiding her, that was ridiculous. They could certainly have a conversation like two grown adults.

She went back down the steps and peered up at the house. An upstairs light was also on and she could've sworn she saw his shadow. When the door still hadn't opened, she ran back up to it and banged on it with her fist. "Colton!" she called out. "You're being incredibly immature!"

Nothing.

Leigh crossed her arms and paced the long front porch, letting out a big sigh. She wouldn't sleep tonight, knowing he was this upset with her. It gnawed at her from the inside out. Leigh considered what she really felt here and, her emotion taking over, she decided that he was like family. She needed to tell him something that she'd always wanted to say. Stomping back over to the door, she rang the bell three times in obnoxious succession. "Colton! I never told you as a kid, but I love you! You're important to me, and I *need* to talk to you about this!"

There was a click. Then the front door opened and a dripping wet Colton stood in a towel, all abs and tight pecs, taking her breath away.

"I was in the shower."

"Oh," she said, shrinking back. "Sorry."

Elvis came onto the porch and greeted her as Colton opened the door wider, gesturing for her to come inside. She stepped over the small puddle that his dripping body had made on the hardwood, and tried not to look at the wet footprints leading across the room and up the stairs for fear she'd imagine him standing in the shower where those footprints had started—she needed to focus on the issue at hand.

"That was a little dramatic, don't you think?" he said, his fondness for her winning out over his anger for a moment.

"Sometimes drama is necessary to get your point across," she replied.

He offered her a seat at the bar in the kitchen and then, still in his towel with a bare chest, he poured her a glass of wine, setting it in front of her. *Mamma mia.*

"I'm going to get dressed and then you can profess your love to me in person," he said over his shoulder as he headed for the stairs, maintaining his poker face.

She swallowed, trying to keep her breathing steady until he was out of view, and then sipped her wine, the fresh citrus notes hitting her like a splash in the pool on a hot summer's day. She willed the alcohol to still her trembling fingers.

As she waited for Colton, her mind raced with how she wanted to approach the issue. She hadn't meant to say what she'd said outside—it had just come out in her desperation to get him to listen to her. But it was true. She couldn't deny it.

Elvis plopped down beside her barstool with a groan.

A few minutes later, Colton jogged down the stairs in a pair of jeans and a T-shirt, his wet hair now combed. Elvis hoisted himself up to greet his master while Leigh fiddled with the stem of her half-empty wine glass.

"What was it you wanted to tell me?" he asked, sitting down beside her, his expression guarded.

She sat up a little straighter. "I'm here to convince you that Jimbo's retail shops are an important development for this area. But first I want to hear you. What's going on to make you so angry about it?"

His expression hardened. "Forgive me, Leigh, but what do you know about this area? You haven't been here in almost a decade."

"I know the market and I know numbers," she said. "This is a good thing. The space is incredible and I have wonderful, national companies involved."

He sucked in a breath before his jaw tightened. "You've filled all the shops?"

"Nearly. I'm meeting with them all next week."

"Jimbo's paying you to do this?" He shook his head, pushing away from the bar before she could answer. "I can't believe him."

"He's not paying me. I'm doing it for free."

Colton wheeled around, causing Elvis to stand. "For free? You're ruining our landscape *for free*? Leigh, do you realize what you're doing?"

"Yes," she said, matter-of-factly. "I do. I'm not ruining the landscape at all. I'm increasing the revenue in Sumner County and providing jobs to area residents. Why is that a bad thing?"

He took her lightly by the wrist and led her out to the back porch, the shimmering lake under the moonlight against the horizon looking like a postcard.

"You want to destroy *this*?" He waved his hand across the fields. "Your work is so important that you'd give this up?"

"I think we can have both," she refuted.

"And that's exactly why I walked out last night." He turned his back to her and spread his arms along the glass railing, his gaze on the water but his thoughts clearly elsewhere.

"I don't understand," she said, coming up behind him. "It's just a couple of shops."

He spun around. "Jimbo couldn't find anyone to rent his place because collectively every local merchant he asked shut him down. They boycotted it and no one would dare fill it."

"Why?" she asked, completely mystified.

"Because if he's successful, his next build will be *here*." Colton jutted a finger into the air, toward the lake in front of them.

"What?"

"I only own to the end of the fields. Jimbo somehow managed to get the land on the other side of them rezoned for mixed-use—residential *and* commercial. He's planning a massive build that would knock down that old house out there and put a giant structure and its parking lot between me and the lake."

Leigh's blood ran cold. "Oh my gosh," she breathed. "I didn't know…"

"Well, it might be best not to meddle in things you know nothing about," he said. "Leave the development to the people who live here."

"I could try to change his mind," she said, grasping for anything she could do to fix this.

A loud laugh burst from Colton's lips, startling her. "You think Jimbo's gonna do anything other than what *he* wants?" He laughed again, a sarcastic frustrated laugh. Then he sobered. "If you weren't so worried about work all the time and spent a little bit of your life with the people in it, you might have avoided this."

"That's not fair," she said, shaking her head, tears brimming in her eyes without warning.

"It's not? How so?"

"I lost my job," she admitted. "I saw an opportunity with Greystone Properties and I took it, hoping to build my résumé. Yes, that's work, but I have to be able to *live*, Colton." She folded her arms in anguish and frustration. "There was no way I could have known what he had planned."

"But see, the difference between you and me is that, when you lost your job, getting another was the number one thing on your mind. Over what your mom had to tell you, over seeing your sister after years away, over coming back to the cabin..." He trailed off, thoughts dancing across his face.

She remembered his words when they were kids: *I wanna fish off the side of my boat and watch football out on my porch in the evenings. I wanna go into town and know everybody there.* Those were his priorities. And she couldn't argue with any of them.

"I'm sorry," she said, looking out at the untainted view, feeling like she'd failed at literally everything. "It's true. I love what I do. And it's incredibly sad that I have to choose between making you happy and having a career when I should be able to achieve both."

"It seems like it isn't possible to have both, so I guess we're at an impasse."

"I guess so," she said, her voice breaking, feeling that between her career and Colton, either of the two was too big to lose.

Still unsettled after talking to Colton, Leigh walked along the lake shore at the cabin, her bare feet digging into the cold sand as she strode through it.

Things aren't good, Nan, she said to herself, trying to channel the one person she needed most right now. *Mama and I are trying to be cordial with Meredith even though we completely disagree with her changing the cabin, I'm nearly sure that the whole town is going to hate me for helping Jimbo, and I've ruined Colton's happiness. I don't know what to do.*

She tipped her face up to let the night breeze blow through her hair. It pushed against her softly, as if it were trying to console her stormy mind.

What would Nan want her to do?

"Look," her mother's voice came from behind her. "A butterfly."

Leigh turned around to find her mother holding out her hand, a bright-green butterfly resting on it.

"That's actually a Luna moth—they come out at night," Leigh said. "I remember Nan telling me about them." She peered down at the beautiful creature. "She used to tell me they represent determination."

The moth lifted off Mama's finger and fluttered into the air, hanging over them a moment before disappearing into the woods. Had Nan sent her a message when she'd needed it most?

"I keep seeing butterflies," she said to her mother.

Mama looked around the sky as if more would come. "I hear that they're a sign your loved one is near."

A prickle of happiness ran over Leigh's skin. "I was just talking to Nan in my mind, and I wondered if it was her."

"Mm." Mama smiled, taking in a breath of the earthy air.

"I've really messed up." She told her mother about Jimbo's plans to build near Colton's.

Mama tucked a loose strand of her gray hair behind her ear. "You couldn't have known."

"But what if I could've done things differently? Colton thinks I put work above everything else."

"We are who we are, Leigh."

Leigh stopped walking and faced her mother. "That's true, but I also think that even though I can't change what's happened, maybe I need to take a long look at my priorities. I asked myself what Nan would want me to do…"

The current washed over their toes as the two of them faced the water.

"The one thing about you that's always been incredibly strong is your drive. What only you can figure out is: what's the end result you want? *That* will direct you as to how to live your life. Even Nan couldn't do that for you. You have to decide that yourself." She looked back at the cabin where Meredith's silhouette could be seen, painting in Nan's studio. "That's something Meredith figured out before all of us."

Leigh contemplated the idea, starting with her feelings about her sister.

"What are you thinking about?" Mama asked.

"Meredith," Leigh replied. "What do I want the end result to be with her?"

"And?"

"I want to know her better. I want Meredith to feel like she can call me and tell me when things are going great. And when they aren't…"

Mama smiled, looking distracted.

"What are *you* thinking about?" Leigh asked.

"There's something I haven't told you, but I don't think I can yet."

"Mom, you have to stop with the cryptic messages or I'm going to lose my mind. Let's get it all out in the open. What is it?"

Mama shook her head. "Nan told me not to say."

Leigh blew air through her lips, unsatisfied. "This is ridiculous. I've got enough going on. Please don't do this. Tell me what it is."

Mama walked a little further into the water, her gaze on the hills on the other side of the lake, clearly deliberating. Finally, she turned around. "There's another letter from Nan," she said. "For you."

Leigh had to close her gaping mouth. She splashed down into the icy water and demanded, "Let me read it."

Mama shook her head. "I can't yet."

"Why in the world not?"

"I almost told you I had the letter earlier but I backed out…"

"Mom," she said. "What's going on?"

Mama turned around, the moon at her back. "Nan said I can't give it to you until you and Meredith agree on what to do with the cabin."

"What?" The word came out in a whisper as the reality of that sunk in. "So, she knew we wouldn't be on the same page about it." Her mind buzzed with this new information. "You mean, I have to get Meredith to agree with me on what to do with the cabin, and her only motivation in doing so is that *I* get another letter from Nan? She'll never agree."

"In order to get Nan's letter, you have to figure out a way to make her. Nan insists, and I love her too much not to follow her wishes."

Leigh stared out at the lapping water, having absolutely no idea how to make that happen.

Chapter Twenty

Leigh rocked on the hammock the next day under a warm quilt and the rustle of the trees, the morning dew shining on the shore, still thinking about her conversation with Mama. What was her end result? She used to say easily that it was a career, but she didn't want a career at the expense of her loved ones. She wasn't even sure that a career was the most important thing anymore. She'd hurt Colton, and if she'd had it to do over again, she would've easily given up the Greystone job to save that view from his house and make him happy. But she also knew that eventually, she'd go crazy without a career.

She also had Meredith and her mother to worry about. They should be the first ones she called when she wanted to share her life. The three of them had spent their lives fractured, spread out across the country when they should've been together. She'd lost time, but it wasn't too late to make a fresh start.

What was at the center of Leigh's life now? If she had to let everything else go, what did she really want most? If she were honest with herself, it wasn't her job. She wanted people around her who cared about her. She wanted family. Even the cabin or whatever Nan had to say in her mystery note didn't compare to that.

She got up off the hammock, wrapped the blanket around her shoulders, and went inside.

"Meredith?" she whispered, climbing into the bed in her sister's room like she'd done when she was a little girl. "Hey," she whispered.

Meredith sucked in a long breath and rolled over, gaining faint consciousness. "Hm?" she croaked.

"I wanted to tell you something," Leigh said quietly, shaking her arm.

Meredith opened one eye. "What time is it?" She yawned.

"It's a little after seven."

"What's wrong with you that you don't sleep?" Meredith pulled the blanket and rolled onto her side, away from Leigh.

Leigh leaned over her sister and said into her ear, "I should've been there to celebrate your gallery opening. And I should've gotten the first dinner you served at the restaurant where you took your first job."

Meredith rubbed her face, turning over. "What?"

"I was clueless growing up. I'm sorry about that."

"You're not gonna get me to give you the cabin if that's what you're after," she said, turning back over. "Especially at seven in the morning."

"I'm not trying to get the cabin. It's yours. I'm trying to tell you that I'm sorry. I really am."

Meredith sat up. "What's all this about?" She yawned again and then stretched her arms over her head.

"Last night, Mama asked me what I wanted at the end of everything. When my life is coming to its final chapter, what do I want in it? I want a sister."

Meredith stared at her, blinking and clearly trying to focus.

"But not just any sister. I want an artist sister who'd rather take boat rides than sit on a porch. I want a sister who drinks beers out of a can and sleeps in the woods just because she likes to."

Meredith looked her over as if she were some new and rare being that had just landed on her bed. "Why would *you* want that kind of sister?" she asked.

"Because she can show me the parts of our world—and of myself— that I'd never see otherwise."

The skin between Meredith's blue eyes wrinkled. "Aren't you worried we'd kill each other if we spent too much time together?"

"Not at all."

"You sure?"

"I've never been surer in my life."

Meredith squinted at her skeptically. "So, you'd let me show you how to sleep in a tent in the woods?"

Leigh chewed her lip, thinking.

Meredith laughed. "*You're* the one who mentioned it."

"I would for you," Leigh said finally.

"Done. Tomorrow night then." Meredith crawled out of bed, evidently calling Leigh's bluff.

"Wait a minute." Leigh scrambled after her. "It's still cold at night. Let's wait until summer."

"Okay, fine. We'll wait until summer. Why don't we start this new togetherness with a cup of coffee instead?" Meredith grabbed Leigh's arm and linked hers through it. "I'll work you up to the camping."

They walked into the kitchen together where Mama was packing her things for work. She looked up from her lunchbox, curiosity consuming her as Meredith dropped Leigh's arm and went over to the coffee maker.

"Morning," Mama said, eyeing them both.

"Morning," Meredith returned.

"If I go camping," Leigh said to Meredith's back, continuing the conversation, "then you have to do something in my world."

"Camping?" Mama asked, zipping up the lunchbox and setting it next to her handbag by the door.

"Yes," Meredith answered over her shoulder. "We're bonding."

Mama gawked at them disbelievingly, a smile playing at her lips.

"So, you okay with doing something I want to do?" Leigh asked again.

"Like?" Meredith reached into the kitchen cabinets for the mugs, getting two down, setting them onto the counter, and filling them with coffee.

"Like shopping."

Meredith's eyes widened in mock horror, making Mama snort with amusement as she sat down to put on her shoes.

"Mani-pedis," Leigh continued, sitting down next to Mama.

Her sister offered a don't-you-dare face.

"Makeovers. With varying shades of eyeshadow."

Meredith clinked a mug of coffee in front of her sister. "You're just being mean now."

Leigh laughed, and it felt so good. Better than anything she'd felt in a long time.

Trying to get Jimbo on the phone was no small feat. Leigh had called twice and nothing. It was nearly five o'clock on a Friday, and he was probably about to go home for the night, so she thought she'd try to head him off. She pulled the rental car to a stop in front of the trailer and got out just as he was locking up.

"Hey," she said, walking across the dusty gravel drive. "I tried to call."

"Sorry," he said, unaffected. "Busy day."

"I need to talk to you." She took a step to put herself in his path.

His lips curved into a frown and he looked down at her from under his old ball cap.

"I need you to not build on the land in front of Colton Harris's property."

He moved to the side to get around her, but she jumped in his way. "I'm serious."

"I knew you wouldn't be able to convince him, but I'm surprised he was able to get you to sympathize with him. That property isn't his."

"I know," she said, darting around him once more as he kept walking. "But there are other factors at play that will either tear down or build up the Greystone Properties name. You have to consider the people around you. It's good business."

"You keep doing what you're doing and let me worry about the expansion, okay?"

She stepped in front of him, leaning against his truck door, in his way. Time to play hardball. "You build on that land and I'll get every single one of the retailers that I've lined up to pull out."

"And how will you do that? I can easily take over from here."

"Not if I take away all the money I'm putting into it—*my* money. You're out of money—I read the articles. I'm wining and dining these people. You gonna fly them all here, hire their cars, give them meal allowances?"

"Once I have the renters in my development, I'll have the revenue I'll need to get started. And I'll sell my house if I have to," he pushed back. "This is actually happening, thanks to you, and I'm grabbing the opportunity and running with it."

"You'll face the same issue with local boycotts on the new location," she said, her heart hammering at the idea that he wouldn't back down.

"Wasn't it you who taught me to think bigger than that? I don't need those local businesses. I'll go national. Especially once I have four major players at the first development."

Leigh's shoulders slumped in defeat. "Look, you can't build there. It would ruin the landscape, and despite what you might think, *drop* area property values of the surrounding homes. You have to think about other people."

"I have to think about putting food on my table," he said. "No one is there to do that but me. And one lone farmer isn't going to stand in my way. Now, if you would please move, I'm trying to get to my dinner." He brushed past her, making her move out of his way, got in his truck and left, leaving Leigh standing alone in the gravel drive.

When Leigh got home, she sat down at the kitchen table and stared at the roses Colton had gotten them, wishing she could go back in time and change what she'd done for Greystone Properties. She pulled out her phone and dialed Colton's number, with no clue of what she wanted to say. The phone pulsed in her ear and then finally went to voicemail. Discouraged, she hung up without leaving a message. Probably for the best that she hadn't reached him.

"You look awful," Meredith said, coming in and plopping down in a chair, her hand in a bag of chips. "What's wrong?"

Leigh told Meredith about what she'd said to Jimbo and how he'd reacted—everything.

Meredith sucked in a breath and blew it out through her lips like a motorboat. "This is why I paint for a living. No harm, no foul." She offered the open bag of chips to Leigh, but Leigh declined, her stomach in knots. "What did Colton think?"

"I haven't been able to tell him what Jimbo said just now, but he's upset, as you can imagine." Leigh put her head in her hands. "I don't know what to do." She looked up at her sister, completely disheartened. "Trying to talk to Jimbo is pointless. He's such a jerk." She reached into the bag and took a chip after all, absentmindedly taking a bite. The starchy salt of it did nothing to distract her thoughts.

"And I might have also told Colton that I loved him yesterday."

Meredith smacked her forehead. "You have got to be the most confusing person on the planet. You ruin the man's life by putting a shopping mall in his backyard and then, in the same visit, you tell him you love him? I couldn't make this stuff up. What, did you think that would soften the blow or something?"

"It just came out." Leigh toyed with one of the roses, a petal coming off in her hand. She rubbed the soft surface of it between her fingers. "I don't know why I said it. I have an interview for a job back in New York next week." She was already feeling torn just uttering those words out loud. "There's absolutely no reason for me to have said it."

"It makes sense that you'd go back to New York," Meredith said. "He knows that, I'm sure. You two just have a long history together, that's all."

Indecision swam around inside her like a hurricane. "Should I go back?"

"Of course you should."

"Why?" Leigh asked, surprised by her sister's certainty.

"What else would you do? You'd be bored stiff here with nothing to keep you busy. I'll either be in San Diego or traveling. Mama will be back at her apartment and working. And there's nothing here at the cabin anymore. It'll be rented out. So, it just makes sense that you go back to New York. It's who you are."

"Is it? Because I don't know anymore."

"I think you're having some sort of breakdown or something." Meredith put her hand to Leigh's forehead. "Are you sick?"

"Stop it," she said, waving Meredith's hand away. "I'm serious."

"So am I." Meredith rolled the chip bag over and moved it out of the way, leaning forward, her face in Leigh's personal space. "Before we got here, you were on your game, I'm sure. I'm also pretty sure that your job was everything to you."

"It was," she said, taking in that fact and rolling it around for size.

"And then you lost it. You don't know who you are without your work, so you're clinging to the old life you had here to try to figure it out. But you're Leigh Henderson, commercial agent extraordinaire. You were the top pick in the hiring pool—I remember hearing from Mama that your boss told you that. You're awesome at it. You just forgot for a second."

"You could be right..." she said, still unconvinced. She set down the petal and stared at the bouquet of flowers. Maybe all that family talk was wishful thinking. The reality was that she had rent due and a job to get. But something still didn't feel right about it. It was like trying on a shirt she was dying to buy and having it be just a smidge too small. She was tugging at her life experiences, trying to stretch them over who she was, and they just didn't fit anymore.

She needed to stay there for a while and figure it all out because she felt really strongly that this was a turning point, a time in her life when the wrong move could change her future beyond repair. The cabin was the neutral party in all this, the one place with no questions, the spot where she felt completely at ease.

"Are you really going to renovate this place and rent it out?" she asked Meredith.

Meredith exhaled loudly and leaned her chin on her hands as if she didn't have the energy to hold her head up after that question. "You act like change is a bad thing."

"Sometimes it can be."

Her sister righted herself. "The world is about change. Nothing stays the same. Our lives are fluid, like the lake outside. Keeping a shrine of Nan isn't going to bring her back. I want to breathe new life into her home instead. It needs new energy passing through it so that the feeling when we come in is *life*, not death."

"But what about celebrating Nan? Shouldn't we honor her?" Leigh offered.

"We are, by giving it a new life."

Leigh let it go. The two of them seemed like they were on completely different pages, and she wasn't sure she'd ever change her sister's mind. She thought back to the letter Mama had from Nan. From the looks of things, it might never be opened.

Chapter Twenty-One

Leigh hadn't slept well at all, tossing and turning, her mind not releasing her. Her eyes stinging from the lack of sleep, she needed the fresh spring air to clear her mind and wake her up, so she picked up the keys to her rental car, ready to put the windows down and take a morning drive through the countryside.

"Where are you going this early?" Meredith said, winding her curls into a ponytail, coming into the kitchen with Mama.

"I'm just taking a drive," Leigh replied. "Wanna go?"

"It's too early for me," Mama said with a yawn. "I'm gonna go to the back porch and have my coffee. Then, when I'm awake enough, I'm going to make my famous blueberry crumble cream pie for later."

Leigh and Meredith gave one another a wide-eyed glance. Mama's blueberry crumble cream pie was the one unifying force in their household during their teenage years. Was Mama trying to get them to see eye to eye?

It seemed to be working, because Meredith said, "I'll go with you... Beats sitting in the house."

"I was hoping the two of you would help bake," Mama said, while Meredith made a cup of coffee for the road and slipped on her flip-flops.

"We will," Leigh promised.

In a matter of minutes, Leigh and Meredith were in the car and headed down the road. As the rolling hills stretched out in front of them in a blanket of bright green, the sun in a clear blue sky shining above, Leigh let the wind coming in calm her. Meredith hadn't asked to put on the radio, which she always had in the past, and the two of them had been quiet on the ride so far. Leigh was glad for the silence. It gave her time to clear her head.

Meredith had her arm out the window, her hand bobbing up and down on the wind. Leigh wound through the curving lanes, hugging the hills, and going in and out of the trees, lost in the maze of country back roads, until they came to a stop at a dead end. Only then did she realize that her path had led to the side of the old bungalow on the lake in front of Colton's house. The building seemed unoccupied, so she and Meredith got out and walked over to it, peering into the dark windows. The dusty wood floors were bare.

"32 Emerald Lane," Leigh said aloud, reading the house number.

"It's beautiful inside," Meredith said, cupping her hands against the wavy glass. "A little rundown, but incredibly well built."

It had rounded doorways and wide moldings, as well as high ceilings for its time.

"Look at that little chandelier," Leigh said, tapping on the window at the stunning antique fixture, dripping with crystal.

"Incredible," Meredith replied, before turning around and running her hand along the wide porch post.

The house had an enormous front porch, and Leigh could almost imagine pairs of rocking chairs and pots of bright flowers flanking the front door. She walked around to the side of the house, putting her hand to her forehead to shield her eyes from the sun so she could view Colton's massive residence with the extensive deck and wood-framed dormers. Meredith followed.

A heavy sense of dread fell upon Leigh, and she turned back to the bungalow. "I can't believe that Jimbo is gonna knock this down and build another strip mall."

Meredith tipped her head up to view the house. "This place could be so gorgeous if someone stepped in to fix it up."

The two of them walked down to the sandy beach, the tide slow and steady as it pawed at the shore.

"I never even knew this house was here," Meredith said.

"I didn't either, but when did we ever go down to this end of Jax Wrigley's cotton farm?"

"True." Then a big smile broke out on Meredith's face. "Except one time when I was hiding from Officer Minton."

"You had to hide from the police?"

"Yeah," she said, laughing. "He was after me for eating a watermelon out of someone's field across town. He chased me, Theo, and Sheila all the way to the Wrigley farm where we hid behind the one patch of corn he'd grown that year."

"I wonder where Theo and Sheila are now?" Leigh asked.

"No idea. Colton might know."

"I've really messed things up with him," Leigh said. "I've tried to talk to him but I can't blame him for being upset. I wish I could fix it."

"I'll bet this land is a chunk of change," Meredith said, looking around. She chewed on a fingernail in thought, gazing back toward the house.

The weight of the situation made it difficult for Leigh to catch her breath. "We should probably get back to help Mama with the pie," she said.

"Yeah."

The two of them walked to the car together, and Leigh took one last look over her shoulder at the adorable little house before she drove away.

When Leigh and Meredith arrived back at the cabin, Leigh stopped in her tracks at the sight of Mama wearing Nan's denim apron. She hadn't realized until that moment how much her mother was beginning to look like Nan. Suddenly, the idea of her mother not carrying the torch and continuing on in Nan's place seemed like such a loss.

Meredith went off to her room to get something and Leigh stayed, washing her hands.

"Just in time," Mama said.

Leigh took in the movement in Mama's fingers as she pressed the pie dough into its pan, pricking the dough so it stayed flat when it baked. Her mannerisms were almost exactly like Nan's, instantly taking Leigh back to those days so long ago.

Mama slid the pie crust into the oven. "You and Meredith can help me make the filling," she said. "Can you melt some butter for me?"

"Yep," Leigh said, reaching into the fridge to get a stick of butter. They'd made this pie so many times that all of them could bake it with their eyes closed, but this time was different. This could be the last time they made anything there.

A phone camera click pulled Leigh's attention toward it. Meredith had taken a picture of the two of them. She directed the phone toward Mama and snapped another.

"These will be amazing pictures to blow up and frame after the remodel," she said, peering down at her screen and widening the view with her two fingers. "I saw Mama in that apron and I knew I had to have a shot of it. You look like Nan, Mom."

Mama turned around and smiled uneasily. "When you're done, wash your hands so you can help." She pulled a large bowl down from the cabinet and filled it with sugar, flour, and sour cream, stirring the ingredients with a wooden spoon, the bowl pressed against her bosom just like Nan had done. Meredith took a few more shots, smiling down at her phone screen.

After the butter was melted, Leigh added it to a bowl of dry ingredients on the counter and stirred them for the crumble while Mama folded in fresh blueberries from the market into the mixture. The more Leigh worked the mixture, the calmer it made her.

When the timer went off, Meredith had washed her hands and was ready to pull the pie crust from the oven. The warm, buttery smell of it filled the air. With mitted hands, Meredith set the pie crust on the trivet and Mama poured the blueberry mixture into it, sending a whiff of vanilla under Leigh's nose as she topped it with the crumble mixture of butter, brown sugar, flour, and oats.

"It looks divine," Mama said.

Leigh leaned over it and breathed in the sugary smells. "Yes, it certainly does."

"Let's pop it in the oven." Mama wiped her hands on the kitchen towel, and Leigh couldn't help but think about all the holidays and summers they wouldn't have here once Meredith renovated. Just when Leigh was starting to feel like she couldn't live without it.

The water washed up onto the sand, the birds chirping in the trees. While Mama took a slice of pie next door to Luella Wilson, Leigh sat outside on the sofa, wondering if she'd get the chance to find out what was in Nan's letter. She'd been thinking about Nan ever since she'd seen her mother baking that pie. What she'd realized was that there was a bit of Nan in all of them. Leigh's letter had been so brief that she'd felt shortchanged until hearing about the second one, but now she had no idea how to reach an agreement with Meredith, so it looked like she may never know what Nan had to say.

"Whatcha doing?" Meredith asked, holding two of Nan's willow plates with steaming slices of blueberry crumble cream pie on top and a silver fork on the side. She handed one to Leigh.

"Thinking," Leigh said, taking the pie.

"What about?" Meredith lowered herself next to Leigh and sank her fork into her slice of pie.

"Nan left me a second letter that I can't have until you and I agree on what to do with the cabin."

"Yeah… Mama told me," her sister said, before taking a bite.

"That means that Nan not only wants us to be in agreement, but she thinks we will be."

"If she'd have wanted us to be in agreement on it, wouldn't Nan have told me that in *my* letter?"

"Meredith, she knew we'd talk about this."

"Then she could've said, 'Meredith, ask your sister what to do with the cabin,' but she didn't. And now, because I want to do something with it that you don't like, I have to hear about it every second until you wear me down and make me do something else. Well, I'm not going round and round with this. I'm stopping it right here."

"But don't you wonder what's in Nan's letter?" Leigh set her uneaten pie down on the table. "*I* do. And I don't have any control over whether I get to read it or not."

"Yes, you do," Meredith said, taking a bite of her pie.

"How do you figure?"

"Because all you have to do is agree with me that we should make this an Airbnb, and then you can read your letter."

Leigh stared at her sister, wondering if she had a point. Was it really Leigh who was in charge of whether she got to read the letter or not? All she had to do was be okay with strangers staying in the cabin...

"But that's not what I came out to talk about. I came out to tell you that I'm flying home tomorrow."

Leigh snapped out of her contemplations. "What?"

"Well, I've been here way longer than I'd expected and I've been totally absent from the gallery the entire time. Joss, the girl I've got covering for me, has only worked there for three weeks, so she keeps putting things to the side for me to deal with when I get back. It's all piling up. I've also got the trip to Paris planned in a few weeks that I haven't finished preparing for."

A smile spread across Leigh's face, despite herself.

"What's that look?" Meredith asked.

"You sound like me." She wrinkled her nose at her sister. "Maybe being driven isn't so bad after all."

"Maybe," Meredith said, surrendering with a grin.

"Do you *have* to go?"

"Yeah. It's crazy. We only just opened, and I've got so many things to iron out still."

"Okay," Leigh relented. She felt as if she'd only just scratched the surface with her sister. She decided to put their issue of the cabin aside and focus on family. That was what she'd told herself was the most important thing. "Hey, why don't we camp outside tonight—you, me, and Mama? Let's not wait until summer."

"Are you serious?" Meredith asked with a laugh.

"Yes. I'm going to run over to the clerk's office to check on the status of the land by Colton's house, but then, let's camp. It'll be our last night together."

"All right," Meredith said, dragging her fork along her plate balancing in her lap and scraping up a bite of pie. "Why don't I go with you to the clerk's office?"

Her gesture was a tiny olive branch in their relationship, and the fact that she'd asked meant more to Leigh than anything in the world. She smiled at her sister. "That would be nice."

Chapter Twenty-Two

Leigh and Meredith walked out of the county clerk's office, down the tree-lined Main Street toward Leigh's rental car, which was parked in front of a white church with a steeple that reached up above the town of Gallatin. She breathed a sigh of relief for the moment. The rezoned section of shoreline behind Colton's farm was still for sale.

"Now, we just have to figure out if there's anyone that would want to buy it *and* keep the main structure and aesthetic of the little country cottage, along with the landscape," Meredith said. "That's your wheelhouse, right?"

"Not really, but close. Let's think." As she got into her car, she racked her brain for ideas. "I guess it's like finding the clients for Greystone. I'd just have to convince them that they want an old house to restore, and to use my skillset, it would have to be retailers."

Meredith walked around to her side of the car and they both got in. "What kind of retailers would do that?"

Leigh started the engine. "Off the top of my head: antique shops, clothing boutiques, hair salons... The only problem is that none of the establishments are enticing enough that people would board their boats and dock there for one shop, and, if it was something like a hairdresser, it's so far off the beaten path that, by car, no one would be able to find it." She chewed her lip in thought. "Maybe interior decorators?"

"In our area? It's awfully rural…" Meredith rolled down the window and turned her face to the sun.

"We need a real estate agent," Leigh said, thinking aloud as she made the turn off of Main Street, "and finding the right agent *and* selling privately is going to take time. It's a little easier to negotiate aesthetics with a business. A private owner can knock it down and build a castle if they like."

"I don't know if we'll be able to save it," Meredith replied. "Which is a tragedy."

"Yes, it certainly is."

Leigh closed her laptop and ran her hand along the quilted blanket on her bed. She'd searched for at least an hour and had no leads for anyone who could use the bungalow behind Colton's. She needed a small business to fit the intimate structure, but small businesses weren't as apt to expand into new real estate. She'd crossed off everything on her list of possible occupants except veterinarians, although she'd called three and hadn't found any who were looking to move buildings.

She wanted to call Colton. He'd taken a rundown farm and used his talents to build an empire upon it. She closed her eyes, thinking of the beautiful home he'd built and how much he'd done professionally. It was incredible. He'd worked so hard and she'd come in and ruined it. She couldn't go back to New York on these terms. She wanted to assure him that she was trying to make it better, but his silence was enough to give her pause.

"Guess what," Meredith said, standing beside Mama in Leigh's bedroom doorway.

"What?"

"I've got our camping site ready."

"You do?" Leigh asked, setting her laptop on the dresser and walking over to them. "I could've helped."

"It's okay," Mama said as they made their way to the back porch. "You looked busy, and I was able to lend a hand."

Meredith opened the door. "Setting it up reminded me of the movie nights that we used to do when we were really little. Remember those?"

"I do," Leigh replied fondly, recalling those weekend nights when they'd pile all the pillows on the floor of the living room and watch kids' movies until they couldn't keep their eyes open anymore.

She followed Meredith and Mama out back, where they had erected a huge tent in the grass near the roaring fire pit. As they got closer, she could see two thick air mattresses, which were dressed in pillows and blankets, filled the inside of the tent, and a small tray on legs held a store-bought pizza and cans of beer.

"Don't panic," Meredith said. "I got you this." She reached into the tent and pulled out a sparkly pink wine glass covered in rhinestones.

"Where did you find that?" Leigh asked, with a laugh.

"In the back of Nan's cabinet!" Mama answered, smiling wider than she had in a long time.

Meredith squeezed her eyes shut with amusement, handing it to Leigh. Then she grabbed a beer and popped the top, the *pssst* of the can spouting between them. She poured it into Leigh's pink glass as the fire crackled beside them.

"Hungry?" Mama asked, leaning down and cutting the pizza.

"Actually, yes." Leigh took a seat in the Adirondack chair next to the tent, while Mama divvied out slices of pizza and Meredith got the other two beers.

As the three of them sat together around the fire, the heat danced into the cool air, the orange light casting shadows onto the patio beneath their feet.

"I've had that tent for five years," Meredith said, throwing a thumb over her shoulder before cracking open a beer for herself. "This is the first time I've ever had anyone else stay in it."

"It's about time, then," Mama teased.

"And would you have ever guessed that your first tentmates would be your mother and sister?"

Meredith laughed. "Not in a million years."

Leigh held up her beer. "To family."

"To family," Mama repeated, the three of them clinking their beers together. Then, Mama's smile dropped. "You know, I've been holding on to the guilt of how your dad and I parented you two. We did the best we could…"

Leigh reached over and grabbed Mama's hand protectively, waiting for her to stand up and begin to tidy something, but she didn't this time. "I know you did," Leigh said.

"It's all okay now," Meredith said.

"But no matter what we did right or wrong," Mama continued, "you ended up as two pretty amazing women. Your nan would be so happy if she could see this. She loved her family."

Meredith looked behind her at the cabin. "Y'all might not think it hit me hard when we lost her, but it did. I didn't show it, but I was devastated too." She turned back around. "I miss her every day. But it doesn't weigh me down because I think of the situation differently. She's around us all the time. She's here, sitting with us right now."

"You think so?" Mama asked, tears beginning to glisten in her eyes.

"I feel her when I paint," Meredith admitted.

"How do you feel her?" Leigh asked, this new information hitting her like a ton of bricks. She'd been wanting to feel Nan since the minute she'd come back.

"The happiness that washed over me when she used to laugh really hard—that same feeling surrounds me when my brush hits the canvas."

Leigh tried to hone in on any of the feelings she'd had since arriving, wondering if she'd missed the signs. Her mind went back to the table and chairs in the kitchen, the letters hidden for them, and the feel of her bedspread under her fingers. "I guess her presence is in her things for me because I don't have the connection to her through a paintbrush. *My* connection is in the memories."

Meredith nodded and took a drink of her beer, a faraway, pensive look in her eyes.

"I would give anything to hear her laugh," Mama said.

Meredith came to, distracted from the conversation, and pointed to another Luna moth that had settled on the arm of the empty chair. It flapped its massive wings as if on show for them. "Look. Is that a butterfly?"

Mama wiped a tear as it escaped down her cheek. "Now we've all seen them," she said.

Meredith kept her eyes on the bright-green moth. "Seen what?"

"The butterflies. Maybe Nan *is* here after all."

The moth flapped its lime-green wings one last time and lifted off into the air. In the glow of the firelight, Leigh sensed that the three of them were being transformed right there under the stars that had started to peek out in the sky. They were no longer like passing ships in the night. They were becoming a family.

"Anyone heard from Colton?" Meredith asked once Mama had been caught up to speed on the situation with his land, the three of them nestled inside the warm tent, the empty pizza platter now resting on the tray outside, next to the flickering embers in the fire pit.

"I've tried to get in touch with him a few times, but he wouldn't take my call or return my texts." Leigh lay back on the mattress, sinking down into it as if it were some sort of heavenly pillow. She pulled the blanket up over her, basking in the warmth of her little cocoon. "I wish he knew how sorry I was."

"Maybe you could try to stop by," Mama suggested.

"I've already apologized. I don't know what I'd say that could make it any better," Leigh replied.

Mama kept her gaze above her as she lay on the mattress beside the girls. "I hate to think of him stewing on that big farm all by himself. It just doesn't seem right for him to be alone."

Meredith tucked her arms under the covers. "It's odd that he lives out there by himself. That's a mighty big house to have for one person. It's huge, Mama. Have you seen it?"

Mama shook her head.

Leigh rolled onto her side. "I know. It's weird that he never settled down. I'd always pictured him as a family man."

"He used to tell me he was going to marry *you*," Meredith said.

A wave of regret washed over Leigh, her skin turning ice cold.

Mama propped herself up on her elbow to address Meredith. "He told you that?"

Meredith nodded. "Yep. We'd laugh it off because we were so young, but I could always tell that he kind of meant it."

"A house like that isn't meant for one person. That's why I sold the house in Spring Hill. It was too big for just me. I noticed the emptiness."

Leigh suddenly wanted to go back in time and visit more, stay in her old bedroom, and spend long days on the front porch, talking about nothing in particular.

Meredith had been quiet, lying on her side, listening to the conversation. When Leigh and Mama had settled into a comfortable silence, Meredith spoke up.

"Growing up, I never needed anyone," she said. "And I'm different from the two of you. But I *want* you both in my life. I don't want to go that long again without us all getting together." For the first time in their adult lives, Meredith reached around the two of them and pulled them in for a hug.

Chapter Twenty-Three

The next morning, the light tweeting of the birds caused Leigh to swim out of her sleep. She carefully climbed over her mother and sister and crawled out of the tent, stretching her limbs in the crisp air. The sun was just coming up, casting a pink-and-orange glow over the lake. Barefoot, she tiptoed down the path and up the steps to the porch, going inside the cabin, the heat immediately hitting her and making her shiver after being outside.

She turned on the lamp at the kitchen counter and grabbed her phone to check the time. A text notification was waiting on her screen. A pulse of excitement zinged through her, hoping it was Colton. She swiped it open but was met with something different entirely.

Hi Ms. Henderson. This is Pamela Lyons. James Peterson gave me your number—I hope that's okay. I'd love to speak with you about a possible job opportunity. You can reach me at this number.

What was Jimbo doing giving out her number? And did she even want to meet someone who was involved with *him*? She swiped the text alert away and rubbed her eyes, yawning. She'd get to that later.

She set the phone down and walked past the table with the red roses that were now beginning to droop, heading into the living room. She turned on another lamp and dropped down onto the sofa.

A blue early-morning light filtered in through the windows, and the cold air lingered above the floor like a springtime fog that would lift as the day wore on. Leigh grabbed the blanket from the arm of the sofa and draped it over her, pulling her legs up under it, settling her chill.

The creak of the screen door pulled her attention to the porch.

"Hey," Meredith said, her voice groggy, her hair frizzy from sleep. "Need. Coffee. Want some?" She padded past Leigh into the kitchen, her bare feet hardly making a sound.

"What time's your flight?" Leigh asked quietly, her voice carrying easily through the silence into the next room.

"Eleven," Meredith replied above the clinking of the mug she was getting out of the cabinet. "Want a cup?"

"Sure, thanks," Leigh replied.

The coffee maker protested with a sizzle, and after a lull of silence, Meredith came into the room with two mugs. "I'm gonna see if I can postpone the flight." She sat down next to her sister, handing her one of the coffees, and pulled the edge of the blanket over her feet.

"Really?" Leigh asked. "Why?"

"I've been thinking." She wriggled to get herself comfortable and then stilled as she looked at Leigh. "Last night was the first time in my whole life that I actually understood you and Mama. Like, *really* comprehended where you were coming from. My trip to Paris seems awfully insignificant compared to that. I want to stay."

A wave of happiness washed over Leigh. "That's the best thing I've heard in a long time."

"You okay putting up with me for a few more days?"

"*I* should be asking that question. I've been a bit difficult."

Meredith grinned. "I know. I mean, *someone's* got to help you find your direction and get you on track," she teased, turning the tables from their youth.

Leigh put her arm around her sister, and there in the quiet living room, she felt real hope for the two of them.

As Leigh sat on the porch in the stream of light breaking through the trees, she brought up Colton's number on her phone, her finger hovering over the call button. She ascribed the need to reach him and her optimism that she could make him understand her to the inspiration she'd gotten from her newfound kinship with Meredith, but if she were being honest with herself, it was just because she missed him. She dialed his number and put the phone to her ear, listening to the ringing.

Voicemail.

She hung up, an ache in her chest.

"Hey there, sunshine," Mama said, coming out onto the porch and lowering herself next to Leigh.

"Hey," Leigh returned.

Mama narrowed her eyes. "You're not just enjoying the view, are you?"

She pulled her eyes from her phone and focused on her mother. "Hm?"

"Something's weighing on you. What is it?"

Leigh let out a heavy sigh and pulled the blanket up to her waist. "Colton. I can't get him to pick up. I can't live with him feeling this way about me. It's tearing me apart."

"Do you think you could go over there and try to talk to him again?"

"I don't know… If there's anything he thinks I can do to fix this, I will. I've tried to find other retailers that could occupy the space without altering it too much, but I'm coming up empty."

Her phone pinged with a text, sending her jumping for it.

Mama's eyebrows shot up in anticipation. "Maybe that's him now, reading your mind."

"No," Leigh said with disappointment, scanning the text.

This is Pamela Lyons again. Sorry for so many texts, but I forgot to say that I'll only be in Nashville for two more days, so catching up while I'm here would be most efficient. I'm free this afternoon. Looking forward to hearing from you.

"What is it?" Mama asked.

"This woman got my number from Jimbo and wants to meet me. She says she might have a job opportunity."

"Well, that's encouraging," Mama said brightly.

"Is it? Should I really follow a lead that Jimbo set up? He's ruined everything he's touched so far."

"True, but it's worth hearing her out to find out what it is. You can always turn her down."

Leigh peered out at the old spruce trees, deliberating. "All right. I'll text her back."

"You never know. It could be something incredible."

"With Jimbo's hand in it, I doubt that very seriously," she said with a laugh. She opened the text and responded.

"Is it possible to buy more of your firewood?" Leigh asked Leon. "We're running low." She put a bottle of sweet tea on the counter to get the complimentary two logs.

Leon rang up the tea. "You can just take however many you want."

She eyed the small basket of wood. "Do you have more than that? I don't want to empty you out."

"Got a six-foot stack out back. Choppin' wood's the way I relax after a long day's work, and I don't have anything to do with it all but bring it here."

She smiled. "And buying something to get two is your way of ensuring you make a little extra money."

He nodded, his thin face twisting into a smirk. "People think they're gettin' a deal, but really I'm gettin' rid of my wood *and* makin' a sale." He tapped his temple. "Genius mind right here." He handed her the tea, ripped her receipt from the machine and slid it across the counter.

"Couldn't you also just sell firewood?" she asked.

"Naw."

She laughed. "Why not?"

"Because Rudy sells firewood down at the nursery for five bucks a bundle, so why would anyone buy it from me? But you just spent..." He looked down at the receipt on the counter. "Two twenty-nine on that tea for two logs."

Just as she'd begun to relax into the conversation, her amusement at Leon bubbling up, the bells on the door rang and Colton walked through with Smash.

"Hey, Leigh," Smash said, walking over to her while Colton breezed past them to the back of the store. "Long time no see."

"Hi, Smash," she returned, trying not to let her attention wander to Colton's whereabouts. "How've you been?"

"Can't complain. Got a two-year-old at home, so we've had our hands full. Name's Hunter. And Sheila's due in a month with our second one."

A smile of delight spread across her face. She'd have never guessed those two would end up together; Smash was laid-back and athletic while Sheila was mischievous and full of energy. "You married Sheila Leevey?"

"Sure did," he said proudly.

Just as Leigh was mentally tucking away the reminder to give Meredith the update on Sheila, Colton whizzed past her, tossing a few cellophane-wrapped plastic baits onto the counter. "Wanna grab those for us and I'll wait in the truck?" he asked Smash, heading to the door without saying a word to Leigh.

"Hang on a minute," Leon said, stopping him.

With an irritated inhale, Colton turned slowly to face Leon.

"Leigh's gettin' some firewood, and by the looks of her high-dollar outfit, she's not gonna wanna carry it out to her car. Y'all stay put and I'll bring it up front so we can help her."

"Leon, we're kind of busy," Colton said, fixing his gaze on the wall instead of Leigh, shaking his head.

This was ridiculous. He could at least acknowledge her presence.

"You ain't gonna be busy till I ring up your bait, and I ain't ringin' it up till you help me get that wood in her car."

"We've got it, Colton," Smash said, throwing a ten-dollar bill onto the counter for the bait, scooping up the packets, and slipping them into his pocket.

Leon rang up the bill and put the change from the ten in his tip jar. "I'll be right back."

After Leon had left them up front, Leigh leaned to the right to put herself in Colton's view. "Wanna say hello?"

"Hey," he said as if it pained him.

"Wanna be adults about this?"

"I'll tell you what I wanna do. I wanna get what I came for and head out without anyone ruining anything more than what she's already done."

"You ruinin' things?" Smash asked with a sparkle in his eye, his gaze darting between her and Colton.

"She's just out of touch with *real* life," Colton said.

"That's not true—" she began, but Leon came up the aisle and lumped an armful of logs into Smash's hands, then left again for more.

"Wanna show me where to put these, Miss Leigh?" Smash asked, heading for the front of the store.

Colton pushed the door open for them. Leigh followed Smash, walking past Colton, taking in his spicy scent.

"It doesn't have to be like this," she said, stopping in front of him. "Can't we just talk?"

Leon came up again with more wood and fumbled it into Colton's arms. Without saying anything, Colton nodded for her to exit and then followed her to the rental car where Smash stood. She popped the trunk open and both men dumped the wood into it. Colton turned away, heading for Smash's truck.

"You didn't answer my question," Leigh called after him. "Can we discuss this like two rational people?"

"I don't think so," he said, climbing into the passenger side of Smash's truck and leaning across to address her through the open window. "That would take *two* rational people."

Smash shut the trunk of her car. "See ya, Leigh."

"Bye," she said, looking back at Colton, the set of his jaw clear in his profile as he stared forward, thoughts in his eyes.

Smash got into his truck and started the engine. Then they pulled away. As they did, she could've sworn she'd seen Colton finally look at her once in the sideview mirror, but maybe that was just wishful thinking.

Leigh arranged the Adirondack chair, putting the lake in the background and the fire pit in front of her to take her video call with Pamela Lyons. The sunshine was in full force and a few boats drove by, pushing the water onto the shore in lapping waves, but the air was still cool enough to need the heat from the fire to keep her warm. Leigh straightened her cotton shirt and rubbed her lips together to be sure her lipstick was even, feeling so much like herself as she set up for the call. While her surroundings were different from what she was used to, the act of preparation and the mindset of business etiquette came easily for her.

Her phone went off and she answered the call, the screen showing a brunette woman about her age, sitting alone at a table in what looked to be a coffee shop.

She smiled. "Leigh?"

"Yes," Leigh said. "How are you?"

"I'm well," the woman said. "Pamela. Nice to meet you." The picture wobbled as she scooted her chair where she was sitting.

"So, you know Jimbo?" Leigh asked, putting her hands into her lap and getting right to it.

"Well, not exactly. I ran into an acquaintance of his, who introduced us."

Leigh felt relieved already, her interest now piqued.

"I'm head project manager for my family's construction company and we build retail. In conversation, Jimbo mentioned what you did for him, and it took some work, but I finally got him to hand over your number."

"Oh?"

"I was wondering if you could do the same for a development we have in South Carolina."

With her interview back in New York and her trip coming to an end, Leigh wasn't sure how she could help the woman. She opened her mouth to turn her down when Pamela added, "I need someone to research the market and find us tenants, and then I need a superstar to sell it to them, because we just can't get this one off the ground."

Leigh considered the idea. "I'm not sure about traveling…" She trailed off, not having really given the possibility of being anywhere but New York any thought at all.

"You could work remotely. We have a bit in our budget to offer you a small salary while you're working for us, and if you can fill this location, we might consider using your services for other projects." On the screen, Pamela sipped her coffee, while Leigh thought it over. "I was hoping to find your rates online. I tried to locate your website, but nothing came up when I searched. Do you have one?"

"It's currently under construction," Leigh said, thinking quickly and having no idea at all where that response had come from. "It'll be ready shortly." She suddenly hoped that Meredith could use that artistic ability for web design…

"Excellent." Pamela folded her hands as if she were praying and leaned her chin on them, a smile on her face. "So, what do you think?"

"I'll definitely consider it," Leigh replied, wondering if something like this would be worth her time.

"Well, I can send you the details of the property through email and we'd be happy to have you out to see it firsthand, if you feel that would be helpful. Just let me know."

"Yes, thank you," Leigh said, her mind whirring.

"I hope to hear from you soon."

Suddenly, Leigh had a completely different career option in front of her. But could she do anything with it?

"Meredith, I need your help," Leigh said, rushing into Nan's studio and tugging on Meredith's arm, pulling her toward the door. Her sister set her paintbrush down and they left the butterfly painting that she'd been finishing. "I need to get yours and Mama's opinions on something."

Leigh led Meredith into the kitchen where she'd rounded up her mother, the three of them sitting around the table, and she filled them in on her call with Pamela, and her idea.

"I could definitely help you with a website," Meredith said. "I just made one for my studio. It's super easy to do."

Leigh breathed a sigh of relief. "That's so great, Meredith. I don't even know what I was thinking, saying that I had a website."

"Maybe it was your heart speaking," Mama said. "Have you ever considered doing what you do on a contractual basis?"

Leigh put her hands to her face in bewilderment. "I can't go out on my own," she said. "It just doesn't make sense. And I've got that interview in New York coming up."

"Or it makes perfect sense," Meredith said. "If I can do it, you can do it."

Leigh went through her mental checklist, entertaining the idea. She had plenty of savings once Jimbo paid her back, and she could keep herself afloat while she built her client list. "I'd need money for advertisements, insurance, a retirement plan..." she said out loud, as the enormity of it all began to filter through her mind.

Meredith put her hand on Leigh's arm, pulling her out of her contemplation. "It's way less work than you think. I'll help you."

"We'll both help," Mama said.

"I don't know..." Leigh shook her head, her heart pounding, the idea of going out on her own so sudden. Yet she couldn't help but wonder if her pounding heart was excitement instead of trepidation. Maybe this was what she'd been preparing to do her whole life.

Chapter Twenty-Four

Leigh swayed back and forth on the hammock, the morning after her call with Pamela, incapable of stopping the ideas that had started to filter into her mind again in the wee hours of the morning. The more she thought about it, the more she loved the idea of working for herself and starting up a corporate client management company. If she could work remotely for Pamela, she could do it for other businesses. *And* she'd need an office to handle it all. Maybe a nice little bungalow on the edge of the lake where she could get inspiration while creating her client lists… But did she have enough savings to make it happen?

Unable to manage anymore without talking to Colton, Leigh left him a message as she lay on the hammock, the sun sparkling off the lake. "It's early, so I'm nearly sure you're home," she said into the phone. "I was serious when I said that I love you. And it's killing me not to talk to you. I have this crazy idea and I want to run it by you. Please, Colton. Call me."

She ended the call and stared up at the sky. As she lay there, she couldn't get that little bungalow out of her mind. She turned her head toward the sunshine streaming in through the trees. A flicker of a shadow caught her eye. With a start, she sat up, staring at the bright-blue butterfly to her right. It hovered around the glass, flapping its gorgeous wings, the light shining through them, like some sort of angelic creature that had escaped from paradise.

Without warning, tears filled Leigh's eyes and the hair on her arms stood up. "I see you," she said in a whisper. It lingered a moment more and then took off. As she watched it fly away, she couldn't help but wonder if the reason she couldn't get the bungalow out of her head was because it was *supposed* to be in her mind. She thought back to Meredith's mention of how butterflies symbolize change.

Perhaps it was time to change her life.

She threw the covers off her legs and jumped out of the hammock, running up the hill to find Meredith.

"I can't believe you're doing this," Meredith said excitedly, as the two of them walked out of the real estate agent's office.

"It will use literally all my savings, but it would be the perfect house where I could live and run my business. I had to at least make an offer."

Meredith paced along beside her. "You want to leave New York and live at Old Hickory Lake?"

Leigh took in a breath of fresh, clean air, her mind completely made up. Like a movie reel, the memories of her youth flashed before her: the shake of Nan's chest as she threw her hand to her heart, laughing, before she sunk her fists into a basket of fresh vegetables from the market; the way the trees swayed in a summer storm; the soft caress of the lake on Leigh's skin while she bobbed around on a float all day... "I definitely do."

Her sister's gaze remained in front of them, but by the furrow in her brow, she was digesting this new information. Then a smile spread across Meredith's face, and, with an excited wiggle of her shoulders, she asked, "Are you going to tell Colton?"

Just the mention of Colton's name sent a wave of anticipation through Leigh's chest. She wished she could run to him, throw her arms around him, and hear his delighted whispers in her ear. "I might wait to see if my offer is accepted. Then I'll try to tell him. If he'll *ever* return my calls… I just pray that this fixes things between us."

Meredith stopped right there on the sidewalk in front of the bakery in town, the smell of the warm biscuits wafting toward them. "You aren't doing this just for him, are you?"

"Definitely not. For the first time in my life, I don't know exactly what I want, but I do know that this feels very, very right. Righter than anything else I've done, which is something I couldn't have ever imagined."

"Well, let's tell Mama, and then we need to get to work building your website!"

"Yes," Leigh said, a sense of purpose she'd never felt before filling her. "I'll also have a call with Pamela to tell her I'm interested."

"This is going to be great," Meredith said.

"I couldn't agree more."

Leigh and Meredith sat together at the kitchen table, hunched over Leigh's laptop, working on the new website, Nan's butterfly journal sitting next to them. They'd spent the last few hours buying a domain and choosing the template through the host Meredith had set Leigh up on. They were formatting the contact page when Mama came in to join them.

"That looks gorgeous," she said over their shoulders. "The pastel colors are so warm and inviting." Mama leaned forward to get a better look. "What are you going to call it?" She squinted at the screen.

Leigh thought about Nan, about the butterflies she used to sketch, and about how much had changed here at the cabin in the last couple weeks. "I think I'd like to call it Instar Commercial Management." She opened Nan's journal and tapped her grandmother's writing. "Nan says here that the stages of growth that a caterpillar takes before it goes into its cocoon are called 'instars.'"

Mama offered a content smile. "That's wonderful," she said. "I still can't believe that you're actually doing this. Where are you going to live?"

Leigh looked back at the computer. "If I get the lot behind Colton's, I'm going to renovate the bungalow so that it has a small apartment at one end that can be converted completely into office space later, if I need it."

"I love that idea," Mama said.

Just then, Leigh's phone went off. She scooped it up and put it to her ear. "Hello?" Her heart thumping, she mouthed to her mother and sister, "The agent." Then she turned her focus back to the phone.

"The seller wants to counter," the agent told her. He gave her the price. While it was higher than she'd wanted to pay, given the fact that she still needed a budget for renovations, she could do it—not forever, but at least until she got on her feet and started bringing in revenue.

Pausing for a second, it really hit her that she was literally putting everything on the line for this. It was the craziest thing she'd ever done, but despite what Phillip had said that day, she knew by her success at Greystone that she had the talent, and as she looked at her sister and her mother, she also knew that she'd have the support she needed to make it happen. "I'll accept," she said.

Mama and Meredith cheered with giddy excitement, while she waved them quiet to finish the call, unable to control her absolute elation.

When she hung up, she turned to her family, wide-eyed. "I just bought a piece of property!"

Meredith squealed, throwing her arms around her sister; Mama wrapped them both up in a hug, the three of them bouncing up and down.

Once the finality of her decision had settled upon her, Leigh looked at them both. "I'm going to need your help with ideas for how to make the repairs to the house," she said to them, the weight of what she'd just agreed to becoming very clear. "I've got a lot of work to do and I'm sure the home inspector will find more."

"I can stay a few more days," Meredith said, although Leigh knew that her sister needed to get back.

The gesture warmed her to the core, and she gave Meredith another big squeeze.

"I can stay on and help too," Mama said. "I can keep driving in to work. It's totally doable."

Excitement tickled every nerve in Leigh's body. "I need to call Colton," she said, wanting to share this with him. She dialed his number right then and there, her gaze bouncing between her mother and sister as it rang. But after more than a few pulses, her hopes dropped when she got his voicemail again. She left another message.

"Colton, it's Leigh. I need to tell you something, but most of all, I can't handle not talking to you or seeing you. Please let me speak to you. Nothing else is as important to me as making this right for you." She hung up the phone, Mama and Meredith both smiling at her.

"I always knew there was something special with you and that boy," Mama said.

There, in the kitchen of Nan's cabin, Leigh knew her mother was right. Her life felt full, and she could feel herself standing at the precipice of change, becoming something different, something greater than she was.

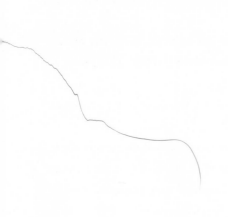

Chapter Twenty-Five

"Knock, knock," Meredith said in Leigh's doorway, holding Nan's butterfly book.

Leigh took one last look in the mirror before facing Meredith, her sister immediately noticing something on Leigh's face.

"What's going on with you?" she asked, looking her up and down.

"I'm in my element, that's all," Leigh replied, running her hand down her best trouser suit, before taking a seat on the edge of her bed to hear whatever it was that Meredith had come in to tell her. "I'm meeting with the retailers this morning, and I have a good feeling about it. It's make-or-break time."

Meredith walked into the room, sitting down beside her on the bed. "Well, you might feel even better when you hear what I have to say. I want to show you something."

Leigh swiveled her legs to the side of the bed to face Meredith as her sister held the book in her lap.

"A lot has changed since I got here," Meredith said, her tone more serious than Leigh had heard it before. "I expected to come in, hear whatever it was that Mama had to say, and then get out of town as quickly as possible. But here I am, eleven days later."

Leigh noticed a kind of tranquility in her sister's eyes that she hadn't seen before.

"I didn't say anything, but while you were on a call with that woman for a job, I saw another butterfly." She looked at Leigh as if they now held some sort of hidden secret.

"You did?"

Meredith nodded. "I'd taken one of Nan's easels out front and I was by myself, painting. It flew over and landed right on my wrist. So, I went in and got Nan's book." She held up the journal and then opened it, pointing to where Nan had jotted down a few lines. "She says here that butterflies only live about a month, so they remind us that we should be in the present rather than the future."

"That's a beautiful thought."

"I feel like she was telling me to focus on what's in front of me."

"Which is?"

"This." She waggled a finger between the two of them. "Being here at the cabin is the first time that you and I have talked in two years."

"I know. It's been nice, hasn't it?"

"Yes. I'd never have thought you, me, and Mama would be able to live under the same roof without going crazy. But it's actually been... fun. And I was so worried that I'd miss it that I put off my trip to Paris until after summer."

Leigh smiled fondly at her sister.

"It got me thinking about the cabin." Meredith twisted around to address Leigh. "I told Mama first and now I'm telling you. I'm not going to rent it out. It belongs to us. The three of us."

Leigh gasped and threw her arms around her sister. "I can't believe you'd do that," she said, her words muffled by Meredith's shoulder as she squeezed her.

"I'll do it for *us*," Meredith said. "We deserve it after all we've been through."

"Yes," Leigh said, laughing with happiness. "We definitely deserve it."

"I was thinking that the three of us could do some renovations to it ourselves—things we want, *together*. We'd only change what would make it ours, leaving lots of Nan here too."

"That sounds amazing," Leigh said. "I'm sure you'll have tons of ideas with your artistic eye."

Meredith grinned, happy, her body uncharacteristically still and calm. "So how will we spend the rest of our lives here?" She waved an arm around the room. "Visits every year?"

"*More* than every year!" Leigh pulled her sister in for a second hug. "Mama could even move here full time if she wanted to."

"Yes," Meredith agreed. "And I'll need somewhere to work while I help you get your business up and running." She winked at Leigh.

"I hate to pull you away from your gallery," Leigh said seriously. "I know how busy you must be."

"I'm used to working on the run, remember?" Meredith assured her. "I can make it work. And I couldn't pass up a chance to spend more time with you and Mama."

Those words were music to Leigh's ears.

"The other three retailers will be visiting after you today," Leigh told Samantha Perkins, the owner of The Attic Light bookstore, as the woman walked around the tiled floor of Greystone Properties, peering up at the display window. "Interest is high."

"Parking looks good," Samantha said, as she toured the space. "What's the total driving time from the highway?"

"It'll run you about twenty minutes, and Nashville's only twenty-five to thirty minutes." Leigh had already sold her on the importance of having a bookstore in the area.

Samantha bent down and opened the cabinets under the counter. Then they walked to the door and Leigh held it open for her, clicking off the lights on the way out. "And the lease contract—is it three or five years?"

"Five," Leigh said, opting for the longest lease to gain as much revenue as possible.

Samantha opened the door to her rental car. "When you get all three of the other leases signed, let me know, and we'll follow suit."

"Delighted to hear that," Leigh said, reaching out for her hand.

Samantha offered a firm shake. "Thank you for meeting me today."

"Of course," Leigh said. "I'll be in touch soon."

Samantha Perkins got into the car and shut the door, waving before she started the engine and drove away.

Leigh checked her watch. One down, three more to go.

Holding a complimentary bag of Green Hat Coffee medium roast that the rep had brought for her, Leigh walked over to the Greystone Properties trailer and opened the door to find Jimbo inside. She lumped the bag of coffee on his desk.

"What's this?" he asked, holding the bag out to read it.

"It's a gift from your tenant. I've signed three of the four contracts with the final one offering a verbal agreement and a promise to sign after the other three." Then she slapped a stack of paper down in front of him. "These are my expenditure receipts for reimbursement."

She couldn't believe it, but she got a smile out of Jimbo, despite the fact that he owed her money.

"Done," he said.

"Perfect. Thank you." She turned around. "Oh, and by the way, you can send payment to 32 Emerald Lane."

The smile fell off his face and two lines formed between his staring eyes. "Why?" he asked with a suspicious tone.

"I own it."

He stared at her, his mouth hanging open. "I didn't want to deal with that farmer anymore anyway. He's all yours."

"I certainly hope so." With that, she walked out, pride swelling inside.

"I can definitively say that this has been the best two weeks of my life," Leigh said from beside Mama as they sat with Meredith outside by the fire pit under the emerging stars, the melodic buzz of the crickets behind them while the lake softly caressed the sand on the shore. "I wish Nan was here to see it."

"Well, I do have her letter," Mama said, pulling it out of the back pocket of her jeans. "It's high time I give it to ya."

Leigh sucked in a breath.

"After Meredith told me that she was saving the cabin, I've had it with me, waiting for a good time." She reached out, offering Leigh the folded envelope. "Go on," she urged.

Slowly, wanting to stretch the moment as long as possible, Leigh took it, staring at the message in Nan's handwriting on the outside:

Give to Leigh once the girls agree on how to handle the cabin. She'd waited for this moment, and now that it was here, she was afraid to let it pass.

"Open it," Meredith begged.

Leigh ran her hand over the writing. "This is it, right?" she asked Mama. "This is the last letter?"

Mama nodded, her stare urging her to read Nan's words.

Leigh slipped her finger under the flap to loosen it, pulling out the paper. She smoothed the two folds, tears filling her eyes at the length of the note. Nan had a lot to say. She took a deep breath and peered over at Meredith and Mama once more before reading it aloud, trying to see the words through the tears that were welling up with every second that she waited to take in her grandmother's final message.

Dear Leigh,

I'll bet you were nice and angry with me, or, at the very least, completely confused by my decision to give Meredith the cabin. You might have even been thinking I've finally lost it and gone off the deep end.

Leigh laughed through her sniffles.

Meredith deserves the cabin. And I trust her to make the right decision with it. I also couldn't just tell you this right away because I'm praying you learned it on your own: giving you the cabin wouldn't have done anything to move your relationships forward. You and your mother needed to connect on a deeper level with Meredith, and Meredith with you two as well. It's important to me that you all see each other for who you really are. Because all three of you are magnificent.

Leigh wiped a tear, giving her mother and sister a loving glance. Mama urged her to keep reading, so she continued.

So, by not leaving the cabin to your mother and giving Meredith your favorite place in all the world, I prayed it would force you all together. I firmly believe that God sent us all here to find our people. We're not meant to be alone. As I'm writing this and my health slips away from me, all I can think about is how you, your mother, and Meredith barely communicate with each other.

As you know, my loved ones are everything to me. And while you're focused on your career, I know deep down what your heart desires: family. I hope that I've managed to give you one in all this. That is my gift to you. It's the biggest gift I could give you.

All my love,
Nan

Mama sighed and put her hand to her heart. "She always knows, doesn't she?"

As Leigh looked around at her little family, she was certain that Nan did always know. She was so very, very right.

Chapter Twenty-Six

"I want to make the front room with the chandelier my office, so I can see the lake while I work," Leigh said, as she and Meredith sat together in the kitchen in front of her laptop.

The inspection of 32 Emerald Lane was done as a rush early that morning, and repairs had been scheduled with the handyman down the road. Surprisingly, there were no major structural issues found. While Mama was at work, Leigh scrolled through furniture options on her laptop as Meredith looked on.

"I was thinking I could have a desk like this one." Leigh turned the laptop to show Meredith the driftwood-colored desk she'd found for a decent price. "I could have the walls painted a light taupe…"

"That would look perfect with a big blue butterfly painting on the opposite wall," Meredith said with a grin. "I might know where we can get one if you like the idea of it."

"I adore that idea," Leigh said, draping her arm around her sister and giving her a squeeze. "We'll want to get that room set up as soon as possible. Know why?"

"Why's that?"

Leigh clicked onto a different screen and opened her new Instar Commercial Management email inbox, showing her sister three emails from potential clients. "I haven't even advertised yet," she said. "Pamela

Lyons has been spreading the word. I've got one from Salt Lake City, one from Omaha, and one from right here in Nashville."

"That's amazing!" Meredith said.

"Thank you for staying," Leigh told her.

Meredith put her head on Leigh's shoulder. "Of course."

That evening, after laying out all the plans for 32 Emerald Lane, Leigh flopped back on her bed, feeling Nan's presence all around now, just like Meredith had, and she knew that her grandmother was with her. After facing her fears about going out on her own and actually taking the steps to make it happen, a surge of serenity washed over her that had been with her ever since, and she knew it was Nan. She could feel it in her bones.

Then, suddenly, she heard a tap at the window, pulling her from her thoughts, and she sat up, frozen for a second. She hadn't heard that tap since she was a teenager, and she knew exactly who was doing the tapping. *Tap, tap*—two more. Leigh walked over to the window and raised it to find Elvis sitting in front of it, wearing a sign that said, "I miss you. Come outside."

Leigh's heart skipped a beat, and she was unable to hide her complete relief at seeing the dog. "You do?" she asked him.

His head twisted sideways to understand her, his tail wagging in the grass.

She closed the window and rushed out the back door, through the porch, and around to the side of the house where she found Colton standing in the yard, his brooding dark eyes on her in the dim light of sunset. Her breath shallow, her mind on high alert to interpret his expression, she walked up to him.

"Hey," he said. He looked tired, but the fondness in his eyes was undeniable, making her heart patter.

Elvis dragged the sign with him as he walked over and greeted her. She rubbed his fur, slipping the cardboard off of him.

The corner of Colton's mouth turned up into a grin. "Do you know why Elvis likes you so much?"

She gave him a meaningful look and shook her head.

"Because he can sense the way I feel about you."

Her mouth went dry, her breath shallow.

"That first day when you arrived and I saw you, it was all I could do to keep my heart from beating out of my chest at seeing you again. So many days I'd wished you'd walk through the door, and after all that time, I'd come to the conclusion that you probably never would."

She held her breath, restraining herself from throwing her arms around him so she could hear him out.

"I spent two years fighting Jimbo Peterson over the land behind my house, and when you casually came in and turned over everything I'd worked for, I was so upset with you." He took a step toward her, invading her personal space, the two of them standing in the deep shade of the pines, the glistening lake behind them. "The whole thing hit a nerve, because for years I was angry at your work, at your drive. I wanted you to show that kind of passion for *me* instead."

She put her hand over her mouth, shaking her head, tears welling up. "I never meant to put anything above you. You were always like magic in my memory."

"I tried to stay away after I found out about you helping Jimbo. It took everything I had not to run straight to you and scoop you up into my arms when I saw you at Leon's the other day. I told myself

I'd get over it." Gently, he put his hands on her waist and pulled her nearer, her breath catching. "I let you walk away because of your career once—we were too young; I was forced to—but I'm not going to let it happen again. I can live with a parking lot in my backyard if it means I get to see you every day. I won't let you go without doing everything in my power to convince you to stay first."

"You don't have to," she said. "And I *want* to stay. So much so that I bought the lake cottage behind your property."

He pulled back, frowning in confusion. "What?"

"I'm going to start my own commercial management company at 32 Emerald Lane."

His brows pulled together in the most adorable way.

"Looks like you've got a new neighbor." She explained to him how she was planning to help others across the country the way she'd helped Jimbo.

Colton drew her into his arms, spurring Elvis to jump around them, barking. "Are you serious?" he asked, his words coming out in a euphoric laugh. He put his hands on her face and looked into her eyes, that gorgeous smile of his spreading over his face.

"I'm completely serious. With every day that I spent here—with you—it felt more like me than anything else has." She looked up at him, willing him to kiss her, never wanting something so badly.

His lips parted, his breath lightly moving through them as his gaze bored into hers with an intensity she'd never seen. That look had nothing to do with the boy he'd been. It was the gaze a man could only offer after years of maturing. "You know that what I'm about to do will change everything between us."

She nodded, looking up at him, every nerve in her body on high alert.

A thought passed over Colton's face, as if he wanted to take in that moment—that final moment before both their lives would be completely altered.

"I've been gone," she said, "but my heart was always here with you."

His eyes crinkled at the edges with fondness for her. He pulled her in once more and pressed his lips to hers. His strong arms held her tightly, the soft stubble on his face rough under her hands as she reached for him. His kiss was urgent, delicious—years of built-up longing rushing between them. It was as though there were something big between them that seemed to span all of time, as if the universe had lined them up just for this moment. She took in the scent of him, the feel of his masculine hands on her, the movement of his lips, and the perfect way they fit together. And she knew that she'd never want anything more than this.

When he finally pulled back, he looked down at her lovingly. "I never told you this when we were kids, but I think it's important that you know." He squeezed her affectionately. "I'm completely in love with you," he said into her ear, giving her a shiver, "and I *never* want to be without you again."

She pushed herself up onto her tiptoes and leaned in for another kiss.

When the chill of evening had fallen upon them, Colton, Leigh, and Elvis went inside to find that Mama had come home from work. "Well, look what the cat dragged in," Katherine said to Colton with a wrinkle of her nose.

Meredith came in and kissed her mother on the cheek before turning to Colton. "It took you long enough to come around." She gave him a playful punch on the arm. "I hope you're planning to stay and celebrate that your girl here found a job in your backyard. Literally."

Colton grinned. "I've got a six-pack in the truck."

"What's it doing in there?" Meredith teased him. "Go get it."

With a laugh, Colton left them in the kitchen, heading outside.

"Oh no," Meredith said, as, left behind with them, Elvis sauntered over, distracting all three of them. She took a step toward the dog while Leigh braced herself for the backlash, but to her surprise, Elvis walked right up to Meredith and sniffed her hand. Gently, Meredith scratched under his chin.

"See?" Mama said, tipping her head back with a laugh. "I was right. He knows we're all family now."

Meredith rolled her eyes playfully, but she didn't argue.

Colton came back in behind Leigh, kissing her on the cheek, giving her a fizzle of elation. His dark eyes sparkled as he set down a six-pack of beer, opening one and offering it to her. He handed out more bottles before settling into the chair at Nan's kitchen table, tipping his own beer up to his lips, and taking a swig. "Quite a different vibe from the first time I came over a couple weeks ago."

They all laughed quietly under the golden light coming in through the window, the final show before the sun slipped below the horizon. Colton reached over and took Leigh's hand, pulling her to him.

As the sun hovered on the horizon over the lake, her fingers intertwined with Colton's, all of them sitting together in the kitchen where they'd gathered for many celebrations over the years, Leigh knew this was but another festive occasion and one of many, many more. She couldn't imagine anything more wonderful.

Epilogue

"I've got a surprise for you," Leigh told Meredith, dragging her through the house to the baby's room. With a doting smile, she stopped at the closed door of the nursery and put her hand on her protruding belly. "Colton just finished the crib, and I couldn't wait to hang it."

"What is it?" Meredith whined. "The drama is killing me."

Leigh opened the door, revealing the oversized white shag rug that covered the dark hardwoods, the billowing, gauzy curtains framing a view of the lake, as well as a tiny corner of Leigh's renovated office across the cotton fields. But that wasn't what Leigh had come to show her sister. Above the new crib was an enormous blue-butterfly painting that Meredith had just finished. This one had a whole mass of butterflies, all fluttering across the canvas.

"I hope you don't mind, but Mama let me take it out of your studio."

"Mind? I *love* it!"

"I wanted our little girl's Aunt Meredith to have a presence in here."

"The blue is just perfect for a newborn." Meredith draped her arm around Leigh and rested her head affectionately on her shoulder.

"What do you think?" Colton asked, coming up behind them, wearing his gameday jersey and holding a small package in his hand.

"I'm honored," Meredith replied. Then she turned to Colton. "Let me know if you'd rather I paint a pink football to put there. We'll start her early."

Colton laughed, the corner of his mouth turning upward in that adorable way of his. "Well, I *will* be getting her off on the right foot." He pulled a tiny yellow T-shirt with the Down South Athletics logo on the front from the package.

"That's the only brand she's going to wear, you know that, right?" Leigh teased Meredith. "It's all her daddy wears."

"Hey, it might pay for her college," Meredith said.

Leigh gave her sister a wide grin. "Or her art lessons."

Meredith broke into a smile in return.

"I actually came up because your mama has come over from the cabin and she's ready for lunch. The game starts in ten minutes. She's got all the fixin's on the table outside."

Mama had left her apartment when the lease was up and moved into the cabin full time. She was to retire next year, so she wouldn't have to drive into Nashville to work for much longer. Meredith flip-flopped between staying with Mama and in the apartment Leigh had vacated in the Emerald Lane office, where her sister loved to paint because she said the natural light was so good. She tried to visit for all the major holidays and a few other times in between.

And for Leigh and Colton's wedding, in late July of the year before— a big southern affair under the oaks, on an enormous platform in the middle of the cotton fields, her mother and sister at the front in blush silk bridesmaids' dresses with gardenia bouquets—Meredith had stayed for three glorious weeks.

Her sister had also come right away when Leigh had broken the news that she and Colton were expecting their first child.

With the big football game playing on the widescreen that Colton had installed under their new porch beside the outdoor stone fireplace, they all gathered around the table to have the fish they'd caught off the side of their boat yesterday, with vegetables and fresh pie they'd bought from their friends at the local market. Elvis had settled at Meredith's feet.

Leigh stepped out from under the porch onto the deck to soak in the sunshine. When she looked up, through the window she could see the butterflies that Meredith had painted—Nan's talent that had been passed to another generation—and Leigh knew that her grandmother could see it all from up above: her whole family. *Whole.*

A Letter from Jenny

Hi there!

Thank you so much for reading *Butterfly Sisters*. It was my favorite book to write, both sisters born from the two sides of myself. I hope it made you want to run to your family and hold them near.

If you'd like to know when my next book is out, you can **sign up for my monthly newsletter and new release alerts here:**

www.itsjennyhale.com/email-signup

I won't share your information with anyone else, and I'll only email you a quick message once a month with my newsletter and then whenever new books come out. It's the best way to keep tabs on what's going on with my books, and you'll get tons of surprises along the way like giveaways, signed copies, recipes, and more.

If you did enjoy *Butterfly Sisters*, I'd be very grateful if you'd write a review online. Getting feedback from readers helps to persuade others to pick up one of my books for the first time. It's one of the biggest gifts you could give me.

If you enjoyed this story, and would like a few more happy endings, check out my other novels at www.itsjennyhale.com.

Until next time,
Jenny xo

7201437.Jenny_Hale

jennyhaleauthor

@jhaleauthor

jhaleauthor

www.itsjennyhale.com

Acknowledgments

I am forever indebted to Oliver Rhodes for shaping me into the author I am today and setting the bar for my own publishing journey. His example inspired every choice I've made along the way.

I owe a huge thank you to my amazing editors: Holly Ingraham, who shaped this book right up, Claire Gatzen, copyeditor extraordinaire, and my lovely proofreader, Lauren Finger. I couldn't have had a better team to help me get this story ready than these women.

The amazingly talented cover designer Kristen Ingebretson is the best of the best. I'm so very thankful to have her at the creative helm.

And to my husband, Justin, who had to deal with me while I wrote two books at the same time, after promising I wouldn't do it again, built a publishing imprint, acquired new authors, and homeschooled a kiddo: I am blessed to have his support. He handled my crazy with ease and was always in my corner, cheering me on to follow my dreams as far as they'll take me.